"My goal isn

"I love this house, Brad. This is *my* house. *Our* house. This is where all my memories are." As Stacey spoke, emotions swept through her, intensifying every word she said. "This is where we started out together. Where Julie and Jim became tiny people instead of just babies. I love this house," she told him again with feeling.

Stacey searched his face to see if she'd gotten through. But there was no indication that she had.

He shook his head. "Then why change it?"

It wasn't changing, it was improving, but she had a feeling that comparison would be lost on him, too. "Because like everything else, the house needs a face-lift."

He glared at her. "You sure that a quarter of a million will cover everything you want done?"

Stacey had no idea what possessed her to glibly answer, "If not, it'll be a start." But it felt good to say it.

Marie Ferrarella

Marie Ferrarella wrote her very first story at age eleven on an old manual Remington typewriter her mother bought for her for seventeen dollars at a pawn shop. The keys stuck and she had to pound on them in order to produce anything. The instruments of production have changed, but she's been pounding on keys ever since. To date, she's written over 150 novels and there appears to be no end in sight. As long as there are keyboards and readers, she intends to go on writing until the day she meets the Big Editor in the Sky.

Marie Ferrarella
Finding Home

FINDING HOME

copyright © 2006 by Marie Rydzynski-Ferrarella

isbn 0373880952

This edition published by arrangement with Harlequin Books S.A.

® and TM are trademarks of the publisher. Trademarks indicated with
® are registered in the United States Patent and Trademark Office, the
Canadian Trade Marks Office and in other countries.

TheNextNovel.com

 HARLEQUIN®

PRINTED IN U.S.A.

From the Author

Dear Reader,

Welcome to my life.

All right, *Finding Home* is a slightly fictionalized version seeing as how I didn't marry a doctor and my daughter isn't in medical school and my son isn't a musician. But I did live through the horror of having several rooms remodeled and I did have a husband who handed me lists every morning to review with a not-so-happy construction person.

Anyone who's ever had remodeling done and remained married after the contractor and crew have left knows what sort of a triumphant feeling that is. Remodeling is definitely in the same realm as trial by fire. It tests the limits of your patience and your love. When it's all over, you come out the other end stronger, more confident, with a reorganized sense of priorities. Either that, or in a straitjacket.

So, consider carefully before you make that first call to the local contractor. Can your marriage take it? If you're afraid to find out, just move. In the long run, it might be safer. But definitely not more interesting.

Affectionately,

Marie Ferrarella

To Katherine Orr, with many thanks.

CHAPTER 1

She couldn't get the song out of her head.

It haunted her, popping up in the middle of a thought or an activity. Like now, just as she was putting a platter of sugar-dusted French toast in front of her husband.

Stacey Sommers first heard the song, which staunchly refused to untangle itself from her brain cells, years ago. At the time, the lyrics had struck her as unbelievably sad. It was playing on the radio while she was driving home from the supermarket.

The incomparable songstress, Peggy Lee, was asking anyone who would listen, "Is That All There Is?" and Stacey had laughed in response. Back then she was busy up to her eyeballs, juggling the care and feeding of two small kids and a husband who was in his last year of residency at a local hospital, all this while working in order to help pay for said husband's staggering medical school bills, not to mention put food on the table.

At the time, she'd felt like a hamster with her foot caught in the wheel and was far too exhausted to wonder if life had anything else to offer. Moments together with Brad were just that, moments. Stolen ones. And all the more delicious and precious for their scarcity.

Now, twenty years later, the pace had slowed considerably,

although time was still a scarce commodity. Her kids no longer needed her for every single little thing. Half the time, she felt shut out of their lives. And Brad? Brad was an established, well-respected neurosurgeon whose opinion was sought after.

But the moments they had together were even less now than they had been before.

Is that all there is?

At this point in Brad's career and their lives, she would have thought they could finally have those idyllic vacations she used to dream about in order to sustain herself while going ninety miles an hour through her overwhelming life. But somehow, Brad was busier these days than he had been back when he was in medical school and even during those awful intern days.

Worse than that, he seemed so much more remote now than he had been back then. As if medicine had taken him away from her.

Slipping into the chair opposite his, her life-sustaining cup of coffee in her hand, Stacey looked across the breakfast table at her husband of twenty-five years, the only man she had ever loved, or wanted. He had the Monday Health section of the *L.A. Times* on one side of his plate of French toast, the latest copy of the *Journal of the American Medical Association* opened to an article he found engrossing on the other. His attention was unequally divided between the two periodicals. Whatever was left over, and there seemed only to be little more than a scrap, he devoted to his breakfast.

Stacey suppressed a sigh. She didn't seem to fit into his life anymore. Had she ever? Had she ever been more than a means to an end for him, taking care of his kids, his bills, his eternally wrinkled shirts?

Stacey took a long sip of her black coffee, swallowing and feeling the tarlike liquid ooze through her veins like semifrozen molasses over a stack of pancakes.

Damn it, where was all this self-pity coming from? she upbraided herself in disgust. She knew Brad loved her. In his own conservative, quiet fashion. Moreover, she knew with a bone-jarring certainty that her husband had never once been unfaithful to her, even though he'd been presented with more than one opportunity to stray.

Thank God she didn't have to grapple with feelings of betrayal the way Jeannie Roberts did. The woman had been completely devastated, not to mention humiliated, when she'd discovered that her neurologist husband, Ed, had been seeing the daughter of a former patient on the side for more than a year.

The only thing Brad had on the side were more old AMA journals. At times, though, she could swear that those old journals aroused her husband more than she did. At other times, she was fairly certain of it.

This morning the emptiness she sometimes felt gnawed away at her insides to the point that it almost hurt.

Stacey studied Brad over the rim of her mug, the one with the crack on the lip near the handle. The mug she refused to throw away because her son, Jim, had given it to her while he was still Jimmy. Before he'd gotten too old to admit to anyone other than an FBI polygraph technician that he actually loved his mother.

She was still very much in love with her husband, she

thought. The man could still set her heart racing. They had just reached the plateau they had strived for and there was no feeling of fulfillment to greet her. No fanfare signaling that now life could be different. It was just more of the same. Life only got more routine.

Is that all there is?

There's got to be something more, she insisted silently, trying to block the lyric. Squaring her shoulders, she put down the mug.

"Brad, let's get away this weekend," she said.

She didn't tell him why she wanted to get away, or that this weekend, this Friday actually, was their twenty-sixth anniversary. She'd sworn to herself that she was never going to be one of those wives who nagged or felt slighted if an important day slipped by unnoticed.

But, in all honesty, she'd made that vow secure in the knowledge that Brad wouldn't be like those husbands who forgot.

And he hadn't been. Until about two years ago, when the hospital had put him on its board of directors and free time went the way of unicorns and leprechauns into the land of myths.

Her eager suggestion faded away, unnoticed. He hadn't heard her. The sound of her voice, much less her words, apparently hadn't even registered. Brad was frowning over something he was reading in the journal. Funny how she'd always been able to tune in to seventeen sounds at once—the kids, the TV, the telephone—and he couldn't even tune in to one.

Inclining her head slightly, she waved her hand as close to his face as she could reach. "Earth to Brad, Earth to Brad."

Rosie, their seven-year-old Labrador, the dog he hadn't wanted but who had stolen his heart when she adoringly followed him around as his unofficial shadow, chose that moment to come into the kitchen.

As if to show her up in a play for power, Rosie headed straight for Brad and nuzzled his leg.

Brad looked up from what he was reading. A fond smile slipped over his lips as he ran his hand over Rosie's back. "How's my girl?" he murmured.

"A little frazzled, thank you," Stacey replied. "How are you?"

Brad glanced at her, puzzled. And then he smiled that soft, tolerant smile of his. The one that had recently begun to irritate her because it made her feel like a five-year-old. A mentally slow five-year-old.

"I was talking to the dog, Stace."

Stacey did her best to remain cheerful. "Yes, I know, and I'm sure Rosie appreciates the attention, but I was first."

About to resume reading, Brad put the magazine down. "What are you talking about?"

"That's just it, I was talking. To you. Not to the toaster or to the dog, although God knows that she's the only one who listens to me at times, but to you. And you didn't answer."

The shrug was careless, dismissive, as if her complaint was unimportant. "Sorry, I didn't hear you."

A sigh escaped, dragging her hurt feelings out into the open. "You never hear me."

The frown on his handsome, lean face deepened. Not to the point of making lines, but just enough to register his annoyance.

"You're exaggerating again." He glanced at his watch. "And I am running late."

Between his going in early and coming home late, she hardly ever saw him, much less had conversations with him.

It wasn't supposed to be like this. They were supposed to be growing closer together, not further apart.

Stacey nodded at the large, round, silver-faced clock on the wall. "It's only seven-thirty." Which was earlier than he usually left.

"I know." He folded the paper and carefully closed his magazine. This was the same man who left his shoes, socks and shirts wherever he shed them. But his journals were in perfect order, unmarred by crumbs or coffee stains, and their pages never even marginally bent. "I have surgery at eight-thirty at the surgicenter. What kind of a message would I send to the patient if I got there late? That his surgery doesn't merit my attention?"

At times she was convinced he made a better doctor than he did husband. She didn't always feel this way, she thought with a pang.

"The hospital is twenty minutes away," she pointed out. "Fifteen if you don't drive like an old man."

His eyes narrowed. "I drive safely."

"You drive slowly." And sitting next to him drove her crazy at times. He never went through a yellow light. The moment a hint of anything amber arose, he came to a dead stop. Driving since he was sixteen, he hadn't so much as a warning to look back on.

Not like her, she thought ruefully.

"Not all of us were born with a lead foot," he told her matter-of-factly.

He'd have a lead foot, too, if he had to be in a dozen places at once, she thought. But she bit back the retort. Voicing it would only lead to a meaningless argument.

She watched her husband rise to his feet. At forty-eight, Brad Sommers looked young for his age. He had the same build from when she'd fallen in love with him more than thirty years ago. Though his career was demanding, his hours at times grueling, there were no undue lines or wrinkles on his face. The Southern California sun he'd once worshipped had had no chance to do any damage to his skin in the past two decades. The last time they'd been to the beach, she recalled, Julie was five and Jim was three. Other that a few gray strands weaving through Brad's thick, deep-chestnut-brown hair, there were no indications that time was advancing on him, or that it even knew where he lived.

She was the one who'd changed, Stacey thought, not for the first time. She was the one who'd had twenty unwanted pounds stealthily sneak up on her over the past fifteen years. The one who no longer looked as if an agent from *Playboy* magazine might be interested in making her an offer.

It wasn't so much that she'd let herself go. God knew she still tried to look and dress attractively, mostly for a man who no longer noticed. It was more that a silent attacker had set siege to her body. When she was driving home from work, she sometimes thought about going to one of those expensive spas where someone could reknead her body back to its former self again.

As if that was possible, she thought, silently laughing at herself. She hadn't the time. And the spa probably couldn't work miracles, anyway.

"So what do you say?" she asked as she followed Brad to the front door—directly behind Rosie.

Brad glanced at her over his shoulder, perplexed. "To what?"

"To my idea. About getting away this weekend," she added when his expression still remained blank.

For a moment, Brad had her going, had her hopeful that he might actually remember it was their anniversary.

"Sounds good." But then he halted at the door. "But I can't," he recalled. Was that disappointment in his voice, or was she just wishing it into existence? "I've got a conference to attend. A local one," he added. They both knew how much she hated having him go away for a conference.

"Can't you—?"

Stacey never got a chance to finish her question. His cell phone rang, interrupting her. Brad held up his hand to stop her in midsentence as he listened to whoever was on the other end.

He mouthed "Goodbye" to her as he walked out.

And left without kissing her.

Again.

CHAPTER 2

That was happening more and more frequently these days, Stacey thought as she turned away from the closed door. She made her way back to the kitchen, trying to remember the last time Brad had kissed her goodbye without her first having to throw herself directly in the path of his outgoing lips.

That long ago, huh?

Once in the kitchen, which was sunnier than she felt at the moment, Stacey began to clear away Brad's plate with its only half-eaten piece of French toast. She supposed, in her husband's defense, for the most part she'd stopped waiting for him to make the first move, to lean forward and kiss her. Because, in her own defense, she didn't want to take the chance on winding up staring at the back of a closed door, feeling as if she'd just been kicked by a mule.

Feeling hollow. Just like this.

Is that all there is?

Damn it, why couldn't she get that stupid song out of her head?

Stacey felt a sudden, overwhelming urge just to cry.

Hormones.

They always picked the worst time to attack, she thought, fighting to reach equilibrium and some semblance of calm.

Stacey looked down at the dog, who, with Brad gone, had shifted her allegiance as she did every morning and followed her back to the kitchen.

Rosie was now wagging her tail, a hopeful look in her eyes.

"You just want another treat, you furry hussy." She stroked Rosie's head and went to the cupboard where she kept the dog's wide assortment of treats. After taking out something that resembled plastic bacon, she tossed it to the animal. With a semileap, Rosie caught the treat and devoured it in the time it took to close the cupboard doors. "At least he talks to you," Stacey said wistfully. "Someday, you have to tell me your secret."

"Talking to the dog again, Mom?"

Stacey turned, surprised to see Jim enter the kitchen. Now that college was over, unless something out of the ordinary happened or the house was on fire, Jim did not acknowledge that any hours before eleven-thirty even existed. As he stumbled barefoot into the kitchen, wearing the ancient torn gym shorts he slept in, his deep blue eyes were half closed.

Six foot, one inch and still filling out his gangly torso, at twenty-two Jim looked exactly the way Brad had at that age. But carbon-copy looks were where the similarities between her two men ended.

At that age, Brad had been driven to make something of himself and to provide not just for himself and the family they'd hope to have, but for his ailing mother as well. Back then, she'd thought of him as being almost a saint.

Except for the sex.

Her mouth curved as she remembered even despite her efforts not to at the moment. The sex had truly been without equal.

And she missed it like hell.

Their son, as Brad was wont to point out over and over again whenever they *did* have a conversation, was not driven. After much pleading, Jim had attended UCLA, emerging after four rather lackluster years with a degree in fine arts. He'd gotten the degree, they both knew, purely to drive his father crazy.

"Damn it, he's a smart kid, Stace," Brad had complained loudly enough for her to close a window. "We all know that. His SAT scores were almost perfect. Why is he throwing his life away like this?"

Arguments over Jim and the course of their second-born's life were as regular as clockwork. And there was never a resolution. Her only answer to Brad's question was that their son was striving to be the complete antithesis of everything that his father was. She kept it to herself.

"I'm talking to Rosie because she doesn't talk back or give me an argument," Stacey told her son cheerfully. "That's kind of refreshing."

Dragging a hand through his yet-to-be-combed, unruly hair, Jim shrugged off the answer. Taking the half-eaten French toast from her, he straddled the chair his father had vacated and put the plate down in front of him. He didn't bother with a fork.

Somewhere between the first and second bite, his lips dusted with a fine layer of powdered sugar, Jim nodded in the general direction from which he'd just come. "Upstairs sink is clogged again."

Stacey sighed as she placed a fresh piece of French toast on what was now her son's plate. So what else was new? It seemed that something was always going wrong with the sinks and toilets in the house. There were four of the first and three of the second. And that didn't take into account the house's two showers and tub.

And lately, the wiring was giving her trouble. The power would go out on certain lines. A month ago, half the house was down until the electrician came to the rescue. Brad had been furious over the bill. Rescues did not come cheaply.

Stacey dearly loved the house they lived in. She'd fallen in love with it the very first time she saw it, over twenty years ago. But she was the first one to admit that it was at a point in its life where it needed loving care and renovating. A great deal of renovating.

Her problem was, she couldn't seem to convince Brad of that. Practical to a maddening fault, her husband would only nod in response to her entreaties, then, when pressed for a verbal answer, would point out that they could make do by calling in a plumber.

"Which is a hell of a lot cheaper than getting renovations." He'd give her that look that said he knew so much better than she did what was needed. And then he'd laugh, the sound calling an official halt to the discussion. "If I let you, you'd wind up spending your way into the poorhouse."

She knew as well as he did what they had in the bank. What they had in all the different IRA and Keogh funds Brad kept opening or feeding. There was no way renovating the house would send them packing and residing in debtors' prison. Or even strolling by it. But telling him that she had no intentions of using solid-gold fixtures or going overboard made no impression on Brad. Neither did saying that most of their friends had already updated their homes and added on years ago. Some had done it twice.

That kind of an argument held no meaning for Brad. He had no interest in keeping up with anything except for the latest advances in his field.

The only other thing that meant anything to him was making sure his children had the best. He wanted them to have every opportunity to make something of themselves—he being the one who defined what "something" was.

Julie had been canny enough to hit the target square on the head. Ever since she'd first opened her eyes to this world twenty-four years ago, Julie had been the apple of her father's eye. Julie could do no wrong—and she didn't. Their daughter was presently in medical school. Her goal was to become a pediatrician.

Jim, who had taught himself how to read at four because he'd been too impatient to wait for anyone to read to him, had been Brad's genius. He'd begun making plans for their son the second he'd detected that spark in his eyes, been privy to the innate intelligence their son possessed. But rebellion had taken root early in their son, as well. Once he got into college, Jim deliberately slacked off. There'd been a few times he'd been in jeopardy of being "asked" to leave the university. Whenever that happened, he'd study enough to get his grades back up. And then backed off again.

Somehow, he had managed to graduate this June. But he still seemed destined to infuriate his father at every turn and raise his blood pressure by ten points with no effort at all.

The problem was, his inherent aptitude for science notwithstanding, Jim had the soul of a poet. A poet who wanted nothing more—and nothing less—than to make music. Brilliant to a fault, with an IQ that was almost off the charts, he had no use for the academic world. As a matter of fact, he had gotten his degree not to please his father but as a grudging tribute to her. Because she'd begged him to give working in a different field a try, "on the slim chance" that he changed his mind later on in life.

She poured a glass of orange juice for Jim and set it down next to his plate. "I'll call the plumber from work today."

He shook his head, his hair falling into his eyes. He left it hanging there. She resisted the temptation to push back his hair, knowing that would somehow only lead to accusations that she was "inflicting her judgments" on him. Meaning that while her generation liked to see a person's eyes, his didn't see a reason for it.

"Doesn't need a plumber, it needs last rites," he informed her glibly. He raised accusing eyes to her face. "Bathroom's ancient, Mom. Why don't you do what you've been talking about and finally get the damn thing renovated?"

"Don't curse at the table," she told him.

Jim pushed his chair back from the table roughly a foot. "Why don't you get the damn thing renovated?" he repeated.

She sighed, giving up the argument. Someone had told her that all sons went through a phase like this and that he would eventually turn around and be, if not the loving boy she remembered, at least civil.

"Your father—"

The sneer on Jim's lips leaked into his voice. "Right, God says no."

There were times when she could put up with it, and

times like now, when her patience was in short supply, that she could feel her temper threatening to flare. "Jim, a little respect—"

He lowered his eyes to the plate, as if the French toast suddenly had all of his attention. "As little as I can muster, Mom. As little as I can muster."

It was an old familiar dance and she had no time to go through the steps today, or to point out in how many ways Brad had been so much of a better father to him than her own had been to her. It only fell on deaf ears, anyway. Besides, she'd promised to go in to work early today to start implementing the new software program.

Stacey had worked at the Newport Pediatric Medical Group for the past fifteen years as their office manager, beginning as their all-around girl Friday—she really preferred the term "girl" to "woman" as she got older. All seven doctors associated with the group depended on her to keep things running smoothly. That included making sure that the new software package helped rather than hindered.

Still, she couldn't just leave the house on this note. Brad might drive her crazy at times, but that had no bearing on his relationship with his son. "He's your father—"

Jim shrugged as he continued communing with his breakfast. "Not my fault."

"No," she said sharply, "but your attitude certainly is."

Jim raised his head. He smiled at her with Brad's smile, tugging at her heart even as he infuriated her. "Tell him to change his toward you and maybe we'll see."

This, too, was familiar ground. Jim claimed he didn't like the way his father treated her. "Your father's attitude is fine, Jim."

The smile became a sneer. "Yeah, for someone out of the Dark Ages."

"Last time you said he was like someone out of the fifties."

The look he gave her said he knew so much more than she did. "Same thing. This is a partnership, Mom. Seems to me he treats you like a junior apprentice."

Come back after you've been married awhile and then we'll talk. Out loud, she said, "Marriage is more like a work in progress—"

"So," Jim cut in, "where's the progress?"

He made her tired. Arguing with Jim always made her tired. It was like boxing with a shadow and trying to knock it out. "I'll talk to you later."

She was at the back door when he said, "I've got a possible gig."

Stacey swung around. She knew he practiced with a band, had even heard them rehearse a few times. In her opinion, they had potential, even though they weren't playing anything she could remotely hum to. "That's wonderful. Where?"

He gave her a serene smile and offered her back her own words. "We'll talk later," he said before disappearing from the kitchen with the last of the French toast.

CHAPTER 3

Stacey glanced at her watch. Okay, so she was going to be a little late. What was more important, getting to the office or having a few more words with her son?

Jim won, hands down.

It was no contest, even if there was a sliver of guilt attached. But then, she was raised Catholic and the blood of both Italians and Jews flowed through her veins. There was *always* a sliver of guilt attached. To everything.

Crossing to the threshold that led out into the hallway, she called after Jim. "You're going to miss these long, lengthy talks when you move out."

Jim had just gotten to the foot of the stairs and he turned to look at her. He knew what she was really saying, no matter how much humor she laced around her tone. She didn't want him moving out. He'd come home every weekend while attending UCLA. And only gotten more estranged from the rest of the family during those years.

It was time for him to fly the coop for good. Way past time.

"Forget it, Mom." He grinned as he proclaimed, "I'm not staying. The end of the week, I'm gone." And then, because at bottom he didn't like being the source of hurt for her, he added, "There's always the telephone."

She looked at him knowingly. "Which you won't use."

He shrugged. "You never know, maybe I don't have any of Dad in me at all." He stuffed the remainder of the French toast piece into his mouth. Powdered sugar rained from both corners of his lips.

His comment was a not-too-veiled remark about all the times she'd waited in vain for a call from Brad, telling her he was delayed, or had an emergency surgery. All the times dinner got cold and carefully made plans got canceled.

It was all true, but she still didn't like the stance Jim had taken against his father. Despite all his rhetoric explaining his attitude, she still didn't understand, still couldn't reconcile the loving boy she'd known to the cynically combative one she found herself confronting over and over again.

"Jim—"

Jim held up hands that were dusty with sugar, stopping her before she went any further. "I can't stay here. He hates me."

"He doesn't hate you," she insisted with feeling. "He's your father, he loves you."

Standing on the second step of the staircase, he towered over her. And used the image to his advantage as he looked down at her with a masterful sneer. "The two aren't a set."

A part of her wanted to take him by the shoulders and shake him. "In this case, they are. He *does* love you, Jim, he just doesn't understand you." *And neither do I*, she added silently.

The look in Jim's eyes had a hint of contempt in it. "That makes two of us."

She jumped at the first thing that struck her. Because she could vividly remember how unsure of herself, of her choices she'd been when she was only a little younger than he was.

"You don't understand do you? That's only natural at this point in your life."

Jim was quick to set her straight. "Him, Mom, him. I don't understand him. Me, I understand." The affirmation was made so casually and comfortably, Stacey realized that her son actually meant it. "I just want to make music. My music, my way."

His way.

The words echoed in her head. And how often had she heard that, in one form or another? Silent or implied. Brad's mantra. "There's more of your father in you than you think."

She saw the annoyed frown and knew how much he hated being compared to the man he was trying so hard not to be. The man he so often so closely resembled in looks and in spirit. But there were times she just couldn't keep quiet, couldn't refrain from pointing out the obvious. And hope that she could get through to Jim. And he would stop thinking of himself as some sort of an island and realize that he was part of the family.

Stacey glanced at her watch again and winced inwardly. She should have already been behind the wheel of her car, stuck in traffic for the past ten minutes.

"To be continued," she promised.

Jim spread his hands before him, giving her a little bow like the performer he felt destined to be. "I'll be here all week, folks. Till Friday. And then I shall be liberated."

She shook her head. "I have no idea how you managed to survive all this cruelty heaped on your head all these years," she remarked as she hurried back to the kitchen to get her purse.

Jim raised his voice so that it would follow her into the next room. "Me, neither."

* * *

"Well, you certainly don't look like a happy camper. The new software giving you trouble?"

Kathy Conners's new perfume preceded her as she leaned over Stacey's shoulder to glance at a screen that made absolutely no sense to her. Although she was better at it than the doctors she worked for, the computer was definitely not her best friend.

Stacey was.

Ten pounds heavier and two shades lighter blond than she had been in her wedding pictures, Kathy Conners was just half an inch over five feet. It was a fact that had annoyed her no end until Stacey had convinced her that petite was a far better description for her than "runt of the litter," which was the way her older brother used to refer to her. She had known Stacey even longer than Brad had and it was Kathy who had gotten this job for her.

Stacey turned away from the screen. Despite her late start, she'd gotten to the office half an hour before everyone else. Early enough to begin installing the new program without having a gaggle of well-meaning but computer-illiterate doctors hovering over her shoulder, asking questions that only impeded her progress. Once patients began showing up for their appointments, the new software was put on hold.

"The software is being software," Stacey replied. "Resisting having its code cracked at first go-round." She shrugged. Since she'd become office manager, she'd learned a great deal about computers and software, all out of necessity. Trial by fire, so to speak. "But that's nothing new. Shouldn't take long to have everything up and running."

Kathy shed the sweater she'd thrown over her shoulders and held tightly to her cup of coffee. "So why the frown?" She raised a perfectly shaped eyebrow. "Trouble in paradise?"

Stacey laughed softly to herself. "Today, playing the part of paradise will be hell." The second the words were out, a faint, rueful smile gave the slightest curve to her lips. "Actually, that's not fair."

Kathy stopped sipping her giant-size iced coffee. "That's your problem, Stacey, you're always thinking about being fair. Stop that," she chided. "Nobody else is thinking about being fair. Life isn't fair. The world isn't fair," she insisted heatedly. "Why should you be so concerned about always being fair?"

Something was up, Stacey thought, studying her friend. Kathy sounded way too bitter. "It's a dirty job, but someone has to do it. Besides, I'm not nearly as pessimistic as you."

"Don't see why not." Kathy took another long sip through her straw. "You're married, too."

Stacey debated asking what was wrong or waiting until whatever was bothering Kathy came pouring out of her. "Marriage is not the end of the dream, Kathy."

"It certainly isn't the beginning of it."

Stacey turned in her chair, her eyes following Kathy as the latter moved around the office. Were those tears shimmering in her eyes, or just a trick played by the lighting? "You seem unusually bitter this morning."

"Thanks for noticing." After dragging the last bit of coffee down her throat, Kathy crushed her cup before throwing it into the trash with enough force to slam dunk a basketball in a championship game. "Ethan wants a divorce."

Stacey looked at the calendar on the side of her desk. "It's the middle of the month. Doesn't he usually ask for a divorce around now? You get the end of the month, he gets the middle. You both realize you can't live without each other around the first?"

Her words didn't evoke a smile from Kathy the way they usually did. "This time, I think he's serious."

On her feet, Stacey drew closer to her. Her voice was soft, compassionate. "Why?"

Kathy raised her head, shaking it a little like a kewpie doll about to stonewall anyone offering the slightest bit of sympathy. Her eyes were even brighter with tears.

"Because he didn't shout it. He just said it. Quietly. Like he'd been thinking about it and just said it out loud to see how it sounded."

Stacey slipped her arm around the woman's shoulders. "Do you want to divorce him?"

This time, the tears became a reality. "Of course I don't. I'm forty-eight years old," she snapped, pulling away. Wishing she had something to punch that wouldn't hurt her knuckles. Like Ethan's soft midsection. "I don't want to have to start over again with someone else."

"There has to be a better reason to stay in a marriage than that," Stacey told her kindly. This wasn't the first time she'd heard Kathy bandying the word *divorce* about. But before, it was Kathy who was vocal about leaving Ethan.

"Maybe." She brushed the back of her hand against her damp cheek. There was a smudge of mascara across the skin. She murmured a curse. She was going to look like a bat and it was all Ethan's fault. "But that's all I got."

Stacey didn't believe it for a minute. Taking her best friend by the shoulders, she forced Kathy to look at her. "And you don't love him?"

Kathy tossed her head. "What's love got to do with it?"

"Everything, Tina Turner." Stacey laughed. "Everything."

Kathy went on the offensive—or thought she did. "After all this time, you still love Brad."

There wasn't a single moment's hesitation on her part. "Yes."

"Even though living with him is like being stuck in a re-enactment of *Where's Waldo?*"

It was second nature for Stacey to defend her own, no matter what she felt to the contrary. "I see him more often than that."

"This is me you're talking to, Stacey, the woman you've poured your heart out to."

Stacey laughed softly to herself. Served her right for talking. "My bad."

Kathy looked at her, confused. "What?"

She'd forgotten. Kathy and Ethan had three dogs and no children. Popular slang bypassed them all the time. "Something Jim says. It means my mistake. My error."

"The error," Kathy said with feeling, "is that God didn't make disposable men. You know, like disposable cameras. You get what you want out of them, then throw them away." The thought really pleased her as she rolled it around in her head, picturing Ethan in a giant wastepaper basket. "Kind of like the Amazons. Those Amazons, boy, they had the right idea when it came to men. You fool around with them, and then you kill them. Neat, clean. No muss, no fuss."

Stacey smiled. She knew Kathy inside and out. Knew what

was behind this display of anger. Coming up behind her, she whispered in her friend's ear. "He doesn't want a divorce, Kathy."

Kathy gave up the ruse. Turning, she covered her mouth with both hands. "Oh, God, I hope not."

"Why don't you go home early today?" she suggested. Granted, this was Monday, which was always busy, but this was an emergency. She could cover for Kathy as long as no one wanted her to give a shot. Besides, there were two other nurses to take up the slack, provided there was any. "Make something special for dinner, put on something sexy, lower the lights—"

A self-deprecating snort escaped her lips. "The way I cook, I'll have to lower the lights so he doesn't see what he's eating."

"Then bring home takeout and warm it up. The meal isn't the main thing. You are." Stacey squeezed her hand. "It'll be all right."

Kathy raised her chin a little, half hopeful, half pugnacious. "Thanks, Dear Abby." And then her smile softened. "I hope you're right," she all but whispered.

Me, too, Stacey thought. *Me, too.*

"I've got to get back to this before the patients start coming," she said, sitting down at her desk.

The front door opened and a child was heard wailing.

"Too late," Kathy announced.

The words sounded more like a prophesy.

Stacey held back a shiver. *God, I hope not.*

CHAPTER 4

She wasn't going to tell him.

As the weekend inched closer to reality, Stacey swore to herself that this time, she wasn't going to tell Brad that their anniversary was coming up. Wasn't going to spend her time dropping broad hints that even a cerebrally challenged person to whom English was a completely foreign language could pick up on. She'd done that once or twice before, but not this time. This time Brad was on his own when it came to remembering their anniversary.

She was still arguing with herself when Friday finally arrived, settled in and drifted into afternoon. The argument continued as she drove home that evening. She had a lot of time for it. MacArthur Boulevard had turned into a pricey parking lot with cars lodged nose to bumper.

A new element had entered her mental tug-of-war. The very real fear of disappointment. She'd given no hints, left no pictures of brides and grooms or wedding cakes. Left the ball entirely in Brad's court.

Can you stand the disappointment when he doesn't remember?

Given how preoccupied her husband seemed to be these days, there was more than a fifty-fifty chance that he would forget.

Fifty-fifty? Hell, she really was an optimist, wasn't she? The odds were more like five to ninety-five. That he would forget. Because their anniversary no longer meant anything to him. It was just something that came and went, like Arbor Day. A date on the calendar, but not something of any great consequence—except maybe to a nurseryman here and there who wanted to move a few trees and used the day as leverage.

Who remembered Arbor Day, anyway?

That wasn't fair, she argued, jockeying for position in the right-hand lane. Their anniversary meant something to Brad.

When he remembered.

Blowing out an exasperated breath, Stacey shook her head. It was catch-22 reasoning and she was going to wind up going in circles and getting a headache. A bigger one than the one she already had.

The opening in the right-hand lane disappeared. She resigned herself to remaining in her current lane. When the time came to turn off, she hoped she would be able to get over.

A song played on the radio, but it was only so much noise in the background. None of the words penetrated.

Kathy had called in this morning, saying that she and Ethan were taking off on a romantic weekend, thanks to her. A romantic weekend. She would have killed for a romantic weekend.

Why was it that she could give everyone else advice, see the way to solutions for other people, but when it came to her own life, everything became this horrible, tangled mess? It hadn't always been that way. Once upon a time, everything had been crystal clear, spread out before her like the waters beneath a glass-bottom boat. It had come to her almost like an epiphany. She was going to marry Brad, have a couple of kids and be the best damn wife and mother ever created.

Unlike the women around her, she had no burning ambition to leave her mark on the world, to cure some dread disease, write the great American novel, have a rose named after her or break fresh, new ground. She wanted the old ground. She wanted home, hearth, husband, kids to love and to love her back. She'd never been ashamed or embarrassed by the fact that all her goals seemed so old-fashioned, so out of step with today's modern woman. Her mother had wanted more for her, but to her, this *was* more. Brad, Julie and Jim had been everything she'd ever wanted.

But somewhere along the line, she hadn't been allowed to enjoy being a wife and mother. Or rather, hadn't been allowed to enjoy just that part in her life. Because there were mouths to feed and Brad's loans to pay off, and they couldn't get by on what he was earning as a resident. So she'd left the kids with her mother and went back to work for a little while.

A "little while" stretched out until it became her life. Until she could hardly remember when she wasn't working. And when money was no longer of paramount importance— to everyone but Brad—she continued working because she liked the people, liked the contact. Liked having the patients talk to her, asking her for advice. She was, she supposed, a people person. A people person who liked helping others.

So why couldn't she help herself? she silently demanded again as she narrowly managed to get her car over in time to make the turn onto University Drive. Why couldn't she get the people she loved the most in the world to do what she needed them to do?

Her advice to Kathy had certainly gotten the desired results. And her assurances that Ethan really didn't want a divorce turned out to be right on the money as well. Ethan had been feeling a little neglected. The romantic dinner had been exactly the right move on Kathy's part.

Kathy had come into the office half an hour late the next morning, with a very goofy smile on her face and a dreamy look in her eyes. The latter remained in place all day and part of the next. And then she'd announced that they were going away together on a romantic weekend.

Her romantic weekend, Stacey thought with more than a little tinge of envy. A little romance, just a little romance, that was all she wanted. No grand gestures, no protestations of undying love shouted from the top of the Eiffel Tower. He could murmur it from the sewer if he wanted to. Just something to let her know that she still mattered in Brad's world. That he didn't take absolutely everything she did for granted. That he didn't just notice her whenever she did something to irritate or displease him.

That sometimes he noticed her just to notice her.

Was that asking for too much?

Stacey blinked back the tears, calling herself an idiot. She was wasting time, feeling sorry for herself like this. Brad probably had something planned and she was going to feel like a fool for wallowing in self-pity like this.

The road opened up as she took the turn off. Stacey pressed down on the accelerator.

Ten more minutes found her home. In time to watch Jim pack the last of his belongings into the trunk of his car. Stacey suddenly realized that the loneliness that threatened to explode inside of her had only intensified.

Julie was already out on her own, living off campus in student housing that the UCLA Medical School helped subsidize. She didn't want Jim to leave, too. Because that would leave her alone in the house. Alone, waiting for Brad to come home. And even when he would come home, somehow, having the kids gone would just make the growing separation between the two of them that much more prominent.

There was a time when she cherished being alone with Brad. But now, just thinking about that, thinking about coming face-to-face with the fact that they had nothing to say to each other, was filling her with a sense of dread.

Damn, where were all these negative feelings coming from?

She didn't want to be one of those women who had to be medicated with three different colored pills just to face the day. She was made of stronger stuff than that. Stacey couldn't shake the uneasiness. She tried denial. And didn't get very far. Only as far as Jim's car as she helped him carry a box of his things.

"You know, this isn't really practical," she told him, easing the box into the fold-down space he'd created in the rear of his vehicle. "You only have that part-time job of yours." Dusting her hands off, she leaned against the side of the car. "How are you going to manage paying for everything?"

Jim gave her a mysterious look. "I can always sell my body." And when he saw the horror on her face, he ran his hands up and down her arms, as if to reassure her. "I'm kidding, Mom. I'm kidding." He dropped his hands to his sides. "I'm a musician. I'm supposed to starve."

She laughed shortly. "Said the boy who has never lived more than fifty feet away from a fully stocked refrigerator."

He took offense instantly. "Man, Mom. I'm a man."

"Sorry." She held her hands up in mute surrender. "Said the man who has never lived more than fifty feet—"

"I get it, Mom, I get it," he said sharply, cutting her off. He tried again, lowering his voice and doing his best to sound civil. "Look, maybe a little deprivation will be good for me. Make me appreciate you more." As if to drive his point home, Jim paused and kissed the top of her head.

She could feel a lump rising in her throat, but she refused to give in to it. If she cried, Jim would just think she was trying to manipulate him, which she wasn't. She just wanted him to stay. Wanted time to stop moving ahead. To at least freeze in place if it couldn't go back and retrieve the better moments of her life.

Stacey forced a smile to her lips. "You might even get to appreciate your father."

"I might," he agreed, nodding his head slowly. "Right after they outfit penguins with ice skates so they can skate over hell."

Stacey opened her mouth and then shut it again. She wasn't going to get sucked into another argument. Not on her son's last day at home.

She tried again. "So, am I allowed to know where my son's going to be living?" When he said nothing in response, she added, "Or is it a state secret?"

He paused, leaning his lanky body against the side of the vehicle, his eyes on hers. His expression was completely sober. "It's on a need-to-know basis."

She gave him that look that had him confessing pilfering

candy from the supermarket when he was six. It could still put him on the straight and narrow if he let it. "I *need* to know."

He let go of the pretense and laughed. "Just kidding, Mom. I'm going to be in L.A. Pete Michaels's roommate moved out—"

The address brought a chill to her mother's heart. There were places in the middle of a war zone that were safer. "Are you sure he moved out and he's not some chalk outline on the sidewalk?"

Jim frowned, his expression telling her to back off. "This is a safe area, Mom."

"Nothing is safe these days." But she knew that there was no arguing him out of it, unless it were strictly his idea. Sometimes she wished she were versed in post-hypnotic suggestions. "By the way, I had a microchip implanted behind your ear while you were sleeping. It's a tracking device." And then she laughed, banking down the urge to tousle his hair the way she used to. "Don't worry, I'm not that neurotic."

He looked at her knowingly. "We both know that if you could have, you would have. You've got to stop worrying, Mom." Jim made little effort to hide his irritation.

"You show me where it says that in the Mom's Handbook, and I will." She sighed. "Sorry, it's a package deal. You give birth and you worry. Can't have one without the other."

Jim's mouth curved. "I thought Sinatra said that was love and marriage."

"That, too," she agreed. She walked him to the front of the car and watched as he got in behind the steering wheel. "So, no fooling around until after you're married."

His grin was nothing short of wicked. "Too late."

Stacey sighed. "I was afraid of that." He started the car. She fought the urge to pull him out and throw her arms around him. "You'll be careful?"

He nodded. "I won't play in traffic unless I absolutely have to."

"And you'll come for dinner?"

"How about I meet you for lunch every so often?" he countered.

She took what she could get. "Deal—but I'm not giving up on dinners."

He grinned, pulling out of the driveway. "You wouldn't be Mom if you did."

Stacey stood and watched until there was nothing left of the car to see. And then she stood there a little longer.

The walk back into the house was a long one.

CHAPTER 5

Stacey lifted the glass lid from the serving dish filled with the beef stroganoff she'd made earlier. Warmth wafted up, following the curved lid like a vaporous shadow. The condensation inside reminded her of tears. Or maybe it was just her mood.

With a sigh, she replaced the lid. At least something was working right. She'd bought the warming tray years ago in a naive effort to attempt to keep Brad's dinners fresh when he didn't get home in time. Back then, it had been the insane hours he'd kept as a resident that were responsible for his coming in hours after he was supposed to. Once he'd gotten his certification in his chosen field of neurology, she'd assumed that the tray could go into storage.

Really naive, Stace.

Although residency was long in the past, unfortunately, late evenings were not.

She fidgeted, debating whether or not to take off the long, dangling earrings she wore. The ones that went with the little black dress she also had on. Her black high-heeled pumps had come off more than half an hour ago. It seemed that every week, something unexpected would come up. Something that wound up keeping Brad from coming home.

She knew his lateness was legitimate. But legitimate or not, that didn't mean she still couldn't be jealous. And she was. Jealous of his practice. Jealous of the patients who took him away from her during the hours when he should be hers.

Stacey closed her eyes and sighed, wishing that Brad had gotten a nine-to-five job like so many of the people who'd graduated college with them. But then he wouldn't have been Brad. Wouldn't have been the man she'd fallen in love with.

Was he now?

There were times when she caught herself looking at him over the breakfast table, wondering who this man with Brad's face was. Those were the times when she felt he was almost a stranger. A stranger she knew so little about. A stranger who somehow managed to keep her at arm's length, away from his innermost thoughts.

She was making a mountain out of a grain of sand. Brad was dedicated, that's all. Dedicated to a fault. He really enjoyed being a doctor, enjoyed making a difference in the lives of the people who came to him, looking to be helped. A sad smile twisted her lips as she stared at the flame of the candle that was closest to her on the dining room table. Too bad Brad didn't enjoy making a difference in hers.

She glanced over toward the telephone on the hutch. Because Brad always worried about missing a call and misplaced his cell phone like clockwork, there was a phone in every room of the house. Except for someone who'd wanted to clean her rugs, all the phones in the house had conspiratorially remained silent. There'd been no call from Brad, saying he was going to be late. It was rare that he remembered to call about being late these days. Most of the time, he forgot or took it for granted that she would instinctively know that one of his patients needed him.

Took for granted.

There was a lot of that going around, Stacey thought ruefully, pushing back from the table where she'd sat for the past hour, hoping for a miracle. Hoping for her husband to walk through the door, sweep her into his arms and murmur "Happy anniversary."

Stacey bit her lower lip. Damn it, she wasn't going to cry, she wasn't. After twenty-six years, why should this hurt?

Because it did.

She didn't even want a gift. All she wanted from Brad was to have him remember that this day was supposed to be special. To both of them, not just her. And she wanted him to give her a card. Cards meant someone had taken the time to stop the routine of their day and think of her. She would have settled for one created with crayons and construction paper, as long as Brad had been the one creating.

"You're selling yourself cheap again."

The words echoed in her head. Words her late mother had said to her more than once whenever she gave in, or met Brad ninety-five percent of the way.

But her mother didn't know what it was like to love a man with all your heart, love him so much that it ached inside. Her mother and father had had a pleasant-enough marriage, one unmarred by demonstrations of anger. One also unmarred by demonstrations of affection. There were no highs, no lows in her parents' union, just a marriage that flatlined the duration of its life.

She couldn't complain about that. Her mouth curved as

she remembered what it was like when she and Brad had first fallen in love. When they couldn't keep their hands off each other. She'd had highs. Oh, God, she'd had highs. And it was the memory of those highs that had sustained her all these years. Sustained her through the unbearable loneliness that had leaked in now and then.

With a sigh, Stacey rose in her seat and leaned over the table. She blew out first one candle, then the other. And just as she did on her birthday, amid much teasing from Brad and the kids, she made a wish. She made the same wish twice, once for each candle.

But the door didn't open.

Brad eased the door open softly. Then, just as softly, he pushed it back into the doorjamb, taking care not to make noise in case Stacey had gone to bed. He didn't want to take a chance on the door slipping out of his hand and slamming, waking her up.

His wife had been looking a little tired lately. He worried about her, although he hadn't had the occasion to say anything to her. Which was just as well, he supposed. Stacey saw herself as some kind of superwoman. Superwomen didn't like to be reminded that kryptonite existed in the world they inhabited. Stacey took pride in being able to juggle all the balls without dropping a single one.

He didn't know how she did it. Nothing short of pure magic, he mused.

As he crossed to the staircase, he caught a movement out of the corner of his eye. Rosie trotted up to greet him. Probably roused herself from a dead sleep. The dog was getting on in years, and when she wasn't chasing away the visiting neighborhood cat, she dozed.

There was a time when he would go out in the wee hours of the morning and run with her, but a bum knee and lack of time had changed all that. He missed those quiet hours. Missed a lot about his life. Sometimes he felt as if he had no control over anything anymore.

Just the tiredness talking, Brad.

He paused to rub the dog's fur with both hands, savoring the tranquillity of the act.

"How're you doing, girl?" he asked affectionately. "Chase any cats away today?"

"No. And I'm doing better than my mistress," Stacey said as she crossed to him from the living room. She was using the high-pitched voice she always used when she pretended to be the dog answering him.

Surprised, Brad turned around to look at her. He was even more surprised to see that instead of jeans or shorts, she wore a dress. The little black one he always liked on her. It fit a little more snugly than usual and he wondered if he should point that out to her. But she'd only get defensive, so he decided against it.

"Stacey." He stopped petting Rosie. "I thought you'd be in bed."

"It's just nine. Even Cinderella got to stay up past midnight."

"Why are you all dressed up like that?" he asked.

"I thought you were going to come home early."

She didn't even have to say anything else. A certain look came into her eyes, a look that made him feel guilty. And angry with her for making him feel that way. He wasn't up to it tonight. He felt more drained than a tank of gasoline at the end of a NASCAR meet.

"I was," he replied evenly. "But I got a call from the hospital just as I was leaving the office. There was a car accident three miles from the hospital and they were rushing the survivor into emergency surgery."

There was no emotion in her voice as she said, "And they needed you."

Why did she make that sound like a bad thing? She was happy enough to be the wife of a surgeon and to have the lifestyle that came with it. Didn't she realize that it came with a price?

"They wouldn't have called if they didn't," he replied evenly.

She wasn't going to start a fight tonight, she wasn't. So instead, she tried to sound sympathetic. Because she really was. She knew how hard he worked. Did he know how hard she waited? "Wasn't there any other neurosurgeon they could have called?"

His eyes met hers and held for a long moment. "I didn't ask."

She sighed. "No, you wouldn't have." Instead, he'd ridden to the rescue. And she was proud of him, but she just wanted her fair share of him.

Life's not fair, Stacey.

She could hear Kathy's voice in her head, but she just didn't want to believe it. Didn't want to be forced to believe it.

Brad looked at her, puzzled. Concerned. "Stacey, what's wrong? You know that this is what I do—"

She stopped him, wanting to get her two cents in before he got rolling and there was no space for any of her words. Or her.

"I know that you're a doctor. A surgeon. A damn fine

surgeon," she amended. "But I know other doctors, other surgeons, some even almost as good as you—"

"Stacey—"

"And I talk to their wives," she went on, raising her voice to drown out his. "They go on vacations. Together. They have nights out. Together. And some of the time, they even take a break from saving the world. Together."

"Stacey, what's wrong?" he repeated. And then, almost as if his eyes were programmed to take in the sight right at this moment, he glanced toward the dining room. And saw the set table, saw the flower arrangement in the center, saw the fancy tablecloth with the dormant tapered candles.

"Did I forget something?" It was a rhetorical question. She never set the table like that unless it was for a special occasion. "What did I forget?" he asked. Then, because she said nothing, he tried to figure it out on his own. "Not your birthday. Your birthday's in July and this is August." And then his eyes widened as his own words sank in. "This is August." A huge neon sign went off in his head. "I forgot our anniversary, didn't I?"

She pressed her lips together. "Looks like."

Damn it, he'd never forgotten the day before. But then, he thought, she'd always left him enough hints before the day came along. Why hadn't she hinted this year? "Today's our anniversary."

She looked at him impassively. "For another two hours and forty-two minutes."

He took hold of both her arms and drew her into his, folding them around her. "Oh, God, Stacey, I'm sorry."

She closed her eyes and pretended that all the years hadn't

happened. Pretended, just for a second, that they were still living in that one-room furnished apartment where they kept tripping over their own shadows. The Brad she'd loved then would have never forgotten. The Brad who'd lived in that apartment with her had brought her a cupcake because it was all they could afford, stuck a single candle into it and wished her happy anniversary.

"Yes," she murmured, "I know you are."

CHAPTER 6

There was genuine distress on his face. "Look, we could still go out."

Because he felt bad, she forgave him. And put him first the way she always did, especially when her defenses had been dismantled.

"You look exhausted, honey, and this is Friday night. If we go out now, we'll only wind up waiting hours for a table." But it wasn't too late to have a romantic dinner at home. The way she'd originally planned. She caught her lower lip between her teeth, then asked, "How do you feel about cold beef stroganoff?"

"Beef stroganoff?" When his eyes widened like that, he looked almost boyish. God help her, she felt her pulse quicken. He could still excite her the way nothing and no one else could, after all these years. "You made beef stroganoff? That's my favorite."

Affection grew within her. "Yes, Brad, I know. That's why I made it." She led the way through the dining room into the kitchen. "I kept it on the warming tray. I'm afraid it's beginning to resemble congealed butterscotch pudding." Stacey opened the refrigerator where she'd placed the serving dish. After edging it out, she picked the dish up with both hands and set it down on the counter. "I could put it in the microwave," she offered.

He nodded, reminding her of an eager little boy. Of Jim when he'd been little, ready to agree to anything in order to get what he wanted.

"Sounds great."

"It won't taste as good," she warned him. "Nothing out of a microwave except for popcorn ever tastes as good as it's supposed to." She debated her next move. "Maybe I'll heat it up on the stove. It'll take longer, but it'll taste better." He hadn't said anything. "Unless you're starving," she qualified, waiting for him to tip the scales one way or another.

He followed her as she moved toward the stove, his eye on the prize, the dish with his dinner in it.

"I am," he told her, then made the supreme sacrifice. "But I can wait."

All right, she'd give him points. He was trying. Guilt did that to a man sometimes. Made him easier to work with. And right now, she wasn't above using that guilt to her advantage.

Once she moved the serving dish right next to a front burner, she took a pot out of the lower cupboard and spooned in two servings of stroganoff, then added one more for good measure in case Brad was really ravenous. The linguine stood in the bowl where she'd placed it earlier. Stacey dumped that into another pot, poured water over it and set it on the burner beside the stroganoff.

"Five minutes for the linguine, ten for the stroganoff," she announced. Then, taking a chilled bottle of wine out of the refrigerator, she poured some into a long-stemmed glass and handed it to him. "You can have this while you're waiting."

"You're a life saver." He murmured the words to her back as she filled a second glass for herself. Brad took a long sip and let the red liquid pour itself through his veins. For a moment, his eyes had fluttered shut. "God, that feels good."

Stacey felt a slight pinch in the pit of her stomach. There was a time when Brad had said that after they had finished making love.

To her "good" was a paltry word, hardly fit to describe their lovemaking. Though never frequent because of the demands of his work, when they had occurred, the sessions had been nothing short of spectacular. He'd always teased her that it was quality, not quantity that counted, and he'd certainly made a true believer out of her. At least, until the occasions grew fewer and fewer, moving further apart until eventually, it felt as if she was faced with neither quantity nor quality.

Stacey offered him a smile that involved mostly her lips and not her heart. And was then surprised when Brad touched his half-empty glass to her full one.

"To another twenty-five years," he said before taking another sip.

Her heart twisted a little. "Twenty-six," she corrected.

"Twenty-six?" he repeated, furrowing his brow. "Has it been that long?" He tried to think back to the actual year. For a second, nothing came to him. He drew a blank. "Are you sure?"

Did he actually think she didn't remember when they had gotten married? That he'd forgotten cut her to the quick. It was all she could do to keep the hurt from registering on her face.

"I'm sure," she answered with a cheerfulness that rang hollow to her own ear. "Time flies when you're having fun."

He knew her inside and out and he knew that hurt tone. He couldn't fault her, he supposed. But by now, he would have thought that she understood. She shouldn't need the outward trappings, the constant assurances. Shouldn't she just know that he loved her without wanting to be shown, without having him jump through hoops all the time?

Weren't women ever satisfied?

He sought what little patience his day had left him. "Stacey—"

"I'll get dinner," Stacey told him, cutting him off as she turned away. That was his I'm-lecturing-even-though-I-don't-consider-this-a-lecture tone. She didn't want to hear it. The way she felt right now, she wasn't sure if she could hold her tongue, and once things were said, they couldn't be unsaid.

"You know, I think I like stroganoff better after it's been warmed up once," Brad told her a few minutes later as they sat at the dining room table.

Stacey looked at him over the unlit candles. She'd begun to light them once she'd brought his dish to the table, only to have him stop her. There was no reason to light candles, he'd told her. After all, the power hadn't gone out.

But it has, she thought now as she watched him eat. *It's gone out of our marriage, Brad. You just can't see it.*

"Good," he murmured, raising his fork as if in tribute. "After all these years, you haven't lost your touch."

How would you know? she wondered as she nodded in response with a half smile. Try as she might to connect a date, an event, to the last time that they had touched each other, she found that nothing came to mind. It had been so long, she couldn't remember when.

But that was going to change tonight, she promised herself.

* * *

They went to bed shortly after ten, after narrowly avoiding getting into a heated argument about Jim. She'd mentioned that he hadn't said anything about Jim not being around, and he'd responded by saying that he was savoring the quiet. It made her feel that he was happy to be rid of their son. The fact that they were so far apart in their feelings about Jim bothered her to the very depths of her soul.

She would have loved to have resolved something, but that wasn't going to happen. She'd finally tabled the discussion when it looked to be in danger of escalating into a full-blown argument. She desperately didn't want to argue on their anniversary, even though she felt that Brad was just as wrong in his attitude toward Jim as Jim was in his attitude toward his father.

As Brad got into bed, she quickly slipped into the bathroom and put on the sexy black nightgown she'd bought earlier in the week. Running a comb through her hair, she checked over her makeup, opting to leave it on tonight rather than run the risk of looking like someone who'd fallen into the river and been dragged out, pale and ghastly.

When she came out less than five minutes later, Brad already looked on the verge of falling asleep. She purposely jostled the bed as she got in.

His eyes opened. Good.

Curling up beside him, she ran her hand slowly along the ridges of his chest.

"You still have pretty decent pectorals," she commented with a smile. Slowly, she strummed her fingers along the outline of his muscles. Brad was blessed with good genes, she thought, genes that allowed him to retain the physique he'd worked to create more than two decades ago. He still had a membership to the gym, but by his own admission, he had no idea where the card was any longer, or when he'd been to the gym last.

Brad shifted. When she continued running her hand along his chest, he covered it with his own. And then moved it aside.

"Stacey, don't."

Instantly, she could feel herself stiffening inside. But she refused to believe that he was saying what she thought he was saying.

Still, her throat felt tight as she asked, "Don't what?"

He looked at her and frowned reprovingly. By now, she should have known better. Wasn't a wife supposed to be able to read the signs?

"Don't start."

God, but she hated the way he made her feel. Like a lowly supplicant, begging for a crumb of affection. Stacey sat up and looked at him. "Start what?"

Brad seemed more weary than annoyed. "You know what I'm talking about, Stacey. You're starting in and I'm tired tonight."

Starting in. Like making love with her was some kind of a hardship for him that he was forced to endure out of a sense of duty. She couldn't keep the note of bitterness out of her voice, even though she fought it. "Why should tonight be any different?"

He covered his eyes with his hand, like someone gathering what little strength he had left. "Don't do the guilt thing, Stacey. I was on my feet for four hours, trying to save this kid's legs."

"And did you?"

The question surprised him. "I think so."

"Good." And she meant that. Because she was proud of him, proud of the fact that he helped people. But that didn't mean she didn't want something for herself, too. "So how about trying to save our marriage?"

"Our marriage doesn't need saving," he told her with a dismissive air, as if she was babbling nonsense. "And it doesn't depend on sex."

"Thank God for that," she quipped, "because if it did, it would have died a long time ago."

This was old ground. They'd danced over it before. He saw no reason to rehash anything tonight. He had no desire to get into an argument on their anniversary.

"You get it often enough," he assured her. He tugged the sheet up over him, rolling over as he closed his eyes. "I'll owe you," he told her. "I'm good for it."

"You know, if I ever decide to collect on that, you're going to be making love to me for at least six months straight."

"I look forward to it," Brad murmured. He was already drifting off to sleep.

"That makes two of us," Stacey answered.

But she was talking to herself and she knew it. With a sigh, she leaned over, switching off the lamp. And then watched as the darkness swallowed up the room with one bite.

"Here."

Coming up behind her at the kitchen counter the following Monday morning, Brad placed two hundred-dollar bills next to her mug of coffee.

Lost in thought, she hadn't even heard him walk into the room. Stacey turned from the counter, his breakfast—four scrambled egg whites and one slice of wheat toast, no butter—on the plate she was holding. She set it down before him.

"What's this?" she asked.

Brad picked up the newspaper and gave her an amused look. "I know that you like doing everything by credit card or check, but I thought you could still recognize money when you saw it."

Taking her coffee mug and leaving the bills where they were, Stacey sat down opposite her husband. She hated it when Brad got flippant. It always felt as if he was talking down to her.

She supposed that she was being overly sensitive, a holdover from her hurt feelings. Ordinarily, she didn't allow things to fester, but Brad had been gone most of the weekend, attending a local conference. This was supposed to have been their weekend.

It took everything she had to bank down the frown that wanted to possess her lips. "I know it's money, Brad. What was it doing next to my coffee mug?"

Brad moved his broad shoulders in a dismissive half shrug, uncomfortable with having to explain himself. He wasn't a man of words. Didn't she understand that? "I just thought you might want to go buy yourself something."

Stacey stared at him, speechless. Dear God, when had this man gotten rooted in the fifties? Did he suddenly forget they had a joint checking account?

She took a long sip of the black coffee, letting the caffeine jolt through her system before commenting. Very carefully, she set the mug down before her, then curved her hands around it. She had this sudden need to anchor herself to something.

Stacey raised her eyes to his. "If I wanted to go buy myself 'something,' Brad, I would," she informed him evenly. "I have all those credit cards and checks you just referred to a minute ago. *And*—" she underscored the word because it was important to her that she was earning her own way, that he didn't think of her as just so much dead weight he was carrying "—I earn a pretty decent salary, so if I did buy myself 'something,' I wouldn't feel as if I was dipping into 'your' money."

Brad's brow furrowed. He looked at her as if she'd just lapsed into a foreign language, one he was trying desperately to decode.

"Don't be ridiculous." He jabbed at his eggs with his fork as if he expected resistance from that quarter as well. "It's our money."

Right. Until I want to do something with it. This morning, as she turned on the kitchen faucet, she could hear the toilet flush. Since there was no one in the house but the two of them and there was no resident ghost to speak of, that meant the water pressure was weak in the third bathroom. Something else that could be addressed if they renovated the house.

Stacey seized the term he used, cornering him. At least for a second. "If it's 'our' money, why can't I use it to renovate 'our' house."

Finished with his eggs, Brad took a bite of his toast. He'd always been a compartmental eater, Stacey thought as she watched him.

"We've been over this, Stacey," he told her wearily. "It's not a wise move."

She was willing to admit that she was the one who liked to dream, to make plans that weren't always rooted in cold, hard reality and that he grounded her by being the logical one. It was what made them a good team, she'd once thought. But somewhere along the line, it felt as if their team had become a dictatorship, with Brad in the role of Il Duce. She was getting so damn tired of his practicality, his bare-bones approach to things.

It was all she could do not to roll her eyes as she listened to him.

"I don't want to be wise, Brad, I want new cabinets. I want drains that don't stop up and I want bathrooms that don't look as if they were left over from the set of *Leave It to Beaver*."

The toast eaten, Brad pushed back his plate, struggling with annoyance.

"You're exaggerating again, Stacey." Looking past her shoulder, he saw that the money was still lying on the counter. She hadn't put it in her pocket the way he thought she would. "Look, all I wanted to do was make up for forgetting your anniversary." The second the words were out, he realized his mistake and was quick to correct it. "I mean *our* anniversary."

There, he'd said it in a nutshell, she thought. Her anniversary. Like he had phoned in his response to the priest when they'd taken their vows. Like it didn't mean anything to him. The urge to cry was almost overwhelming.

"By throwing money at me?" Her voice cracked at the end of the question.

"I didn't throw it." Irritated, he pointed toward the money. "I placed it on the counter."

She glanced over her shoulder at the two bills. He just didn't get it, did he? Although she knew it was an exercise in futility, tantamount to banging her head against the wall, she tried to explain it to him, anyway.

"Brad, I can buy myself anything I want. That's not the point." When he made no response, she knew that he had no idea what the point was. So she spelled it out for him. "The point is you actually taking the time to buy something for me."

He blew out a breath in disgust. "I'm not any good at that. You're hard to shop for."

Her eyes widened in complete mystification. She'd never made a secret of anything she liked. And she liked a broad spectrum of things. It was hard to find something she *didn't* like.

"Hard to shop for?" Stacey echoed, stunned. "I'd accept anything you bought—as long as you thought I might like it."

"That's just it," he declared as if she'd made his point for him. "I have no idea what you'd like."

Sadness swiped through her like a rusted sword. "You used to." Her mouth curved as a cherished memory whispered to her from across the pages of time. "I still have the trivia book you bought me for no reason that time we were browsing in the used bookstore."

She saw by his expression that he had absolutely no recollection of what she was referring to. She took a stab at rousing his memory. "We'd just started going together. You were looking for used textbooks to buy for your anatomy class and the trivia book was misplaced. You didn't have much money to spare, but you bought it for me. Because you knew I loved trivia." He was nodding. Was that just to put her off or because he finally remembered? "I cried when you gave it to me."

And then the light really did dawn on him. "Oh. Right." He was nodding with feeling now. "I remember you crying." Remembered because it had embarrassed him and he didn't know how to get her to stop. "I thought I did something wrong."

She laughed softly. She supposed in some ways he had always been clueless.

"No, you did something right. Something very right." She searched Brad's face for a sign that she'd managed to get through to him and finally asked, "Do you understand what I'm saying?"

He took a shot at it. "That you want another trivia book?"

Men had to be the most frustrating creatures on the face of the earth. "No, I want you to stop and think. About me. About us."

In a general way, he knew what she was after. And it was foolish. "Stacey, you're not a twenty-year-old girl anymore, you're forty-seven, and I'm not a twenty-one-year-old premed student doing his damnedest to score points with you—"

"Maybe that's the problem," she cut in. "Maybe you should be."

She'd lost him. "Be what? A twenty-one-year-old premed student?"

"No, doing your damnedest to score points with me."

"Why?" he demanded, looking at her as if she'd lost her mind. "We're married." And then he sighed. "That didn't come out right."

"No," she agreed. "It didn't. Did you ever consider that maybe I'd like to feel special? That I still mattered to you?"

"Of course you still matter," he retorted, his temper fraying. "I'm still here, aren't I? Do you have any idea how many of the doctors who I work with have gotten a divorce?"

Was that supposed to make her feel better? That he hadn't divorced her? Why did he always focus on the negative instead of the positive? Was it his profession that made him this way, or had he always been like this? She no longer knew. She just knew that she was unhappy and she didn't want to be.

She shook her head, fighting another wave of sadness. "You wouldn't be able to find the time to get a divorce," she replied quietly.

He gave it one last try. "Stacey, we've been married for twenty-five years."

"Twenty-six," she corrected again, her teeth clenched to keep from shouting. "We've been married twenty-six years."

He huffed impatiently. "Twenty-six, twenty-five, the point is, we've been married for a long time. I'm not about to start pretending that we're still dating. That's juvenile."

It felt as if he'd just slapped her. "I'm being juvenile?"

He neither denied nor verified. He just built on what he'd said. "Maybe that's why you related so well to Jim. He refuses to grow up, too."

The phone rang, the sound wedging its way between them. Stacey ignored it. She was in the middle of an argument and all that mattered to her was getting Brad to understand how much his words, his actions, or lack thereof, hurt her. "Don't drag Jim into this, Brad. This is between you and me."

He looked toward the telephone. "Aren't you going to answer that?"

"No," she said flatly. "Not until you answer me."

Brad threw up his hands. "I can't talk to you when you're like this," he snapped, rising. The phone rang again as he crossed to it.

They weren't through yet. For once, she wanted a resolution instead of letting things just remain tangled until they faded away. "Whoever it is can leave a message."

"It might be a patient, trying to reach me."

Stacey got up, following him. "*I'm* trying to reach you," she insisted.

But Brad was already picking up the receiver.

"Hello? What? Yes, this is Dr. Sommers. Could you repeat that, please?"

She sighed. Work had pulled him away from her again. Crossing back to the table, she picked up her mug and carried it to the sink. She was about to turn on the water to rinse the mug out when Brad held out the receiver to her. She looked at him quizzically.

"It's for you." His expression was grim.

CHAPTER 8

Stacey suddenly felt very cold. She was aware of the hairs rising along her arms and the back of her neck. Her fingertips were damp as she wrapped them around the receiver. Her imagination hit the ground running.

The neighborhood her son had moved to was considered unsavory and dangerous.

"Is it about Jim?" she asked hoarsely. When he didn't answer immediately, she made a second guess. "Is it Julie?"

Brad merely shook his head. But his expression remained grim. Was that pity she saw in his eyes? Sympathy? A sense of panic mounted in her chest as she brought the receiver to her ear.

"Hello?"

A deep, resonant voice with a hint of a British accent asked, "Is this Mrs. Stacey Sommers?"

With lightning speed, her brain attempted to make an instant voice match. And failed. She didn't know anyone with a British accent, slight or otherwise.

"Yes."

"Mrs. Sommers, this is Ian Bryanne. I am—I was Titus Radkin's attorney." He paused, as if to allow the words to sink in. Her grip on the receiver tightened. Instinctively, Stacey knew what was coming. A sadness pooled through her. "I'm sorry to have to be the one to have to tell you this, but your uncle died last night. He went peacefully in his sleep."

"Uncle Titus?" She said the name numbly.

The image of a tall, thin, gaunt-faced man with flowing, shoulder-length salt-and-pepper hair materialized in her mind's eye. Titus Radkin wasn't actually her uncle, he was her great-uncle.

By last count, he'd been ninety-four and still going strong. Last Christmas she'd gotten a card from him. He'd included a picture of himself and his newest mistress, a woman of thirty-eight. "She's a little old for me, but she has some very fine redeeming qualities," he'd written across the back of the photograph.

Eternally young, that was the way she'd thought of her father's uncle. He'd embraced a completely different generation, one in which people wore flowers in their hair, rioted in the name of peace and drove around in air-polluting VW buses while preaching about saving the environment and doing their damnedest to procreate and perpetuate the species one lovefest at a time.

As she recalled, Titus was a zealous advocate of free love.

Everything else, however, the man had put a price on. A rather dear one. Which was how he was able to buy his very own island approximately twenty years ago. The world had modernized too quickly, going in directions he had no desire to follow. So he had founded his own world. For the most part, or so the story went, he had left the demands of society to live out the rest of his years the way he wanted to.

It hadn't been quite so because he'd gone with a full staff

and had a great deal of money for his every comfort. She'd visited the island once, when the children were still very young. Titus had paid for the four of them to fly out. Brad had had to pass because of previous commitments.

"Does he treat you well, Stacey?" Titus had asked, looking at her with those piercing blue eyes of his.

"Yes," she'd declared perhaps a little too quickly.

He had only smiled a half smile, the left corner of his mouth rising while the other remained stationary, and shaken his head. "In the end, that's all we have, you know, the people who love us. Make sure he doesn't take you for granted."

At the time she'd thought those strange words to be coming from a man who had never turned his back on making love to as many women as he could.

Good-bye, Uncle Titus. I hope you died in the saddle and not peacefully, the way your lawyer said.

Stacey took a breath, processing what she'd just been told.

"How?" she finally asked. "How did he die—besides peacefully."

There was a long pause, as if the man on the other end was trying to ascertain whether or not she was on to the truth. And then the attorney said, "He died of natural causes."

Which could have meant, since this was Uncle Titus, that he died making love. Or that he simply died of being ninety-four. At least the germs he was so vigilantly on guard against hadn't managed to fell him, she thought. Her mother had always joked that they had their own personal Howard Hughes in the family.

The irony of the whole thing struck her. Because Uncle Titus was so well off, her father had mentioned more than once that he looked forward to the day Titus went "to his reward and left us with ours." Uncle Titus had wound up out-living both of her parents, she thought sadly.

And with his death, the last of her extended family was gone.

Granted, there was still Brad's family. Brad had two brothers, one older, one younger, and a younger sister, all mar-ried—all with children and all living within the state. Two of them were only ninety miles away in San Diego, while the other lived up north in Santa Barbara. They all tried to get together for the holidays and on other occasions as well, but it still wasn't quite the same thing.

Titus was the last of the family she'd once had. At forty-seven, she suddenly felt like an orphan.

"Will there be a funeral?" Her voice echoed back to her, sounding shaky. Stacey took another deep breath, trying to regain her composure.

"Yes. The services will be held this Thursday. On the island," the attorney added. After another pause, he told her, "Mr. Radkin expressed the hope that you would attend."

"Of course." Stacey felt an odd hollowness forming at the pit of her stomach. Then it spread, taking in every inch of her and lacing it with sadness.

Other than the unexpected Christmas card, there had been almost no contact between them for years now, at least none that had been reciprocated. She sent Christmas cards and received none in kind. It got to the point that Brad teased her about sending them to the dead-letter office and cutting out the middleman. But she never stopped, always hoping that Titus would respond. He had sent a card and a fifty-dollar savings bond when each of the children had been born. And he'd included a handwritten note.

The note had meant far more to her than the bonds. She dutifully banked the former, which was the beginning of each of the children's bank accounts. The latter she had placed in her box of treasures, things that she had collected over time. Things that meant nothing to anyone but her. She'd placed Uncle Titus's last Christmas card there, along with the photograph.

"I'll be there Wednesday," she told the lawyer.

"I will have the airplane tickets forwarded to you."

"There's no need—" she began.

"It's per Mr. Radkin's instructions," the lawyer told her.

"Oh. Well, then, all right," she agreed. "Thank you for calling." She was still fighting the numbness as she hung up the receiver.

Brad had remained beside her for the duration of the conversation. "You'll be where Wednesday?" he asked.

"Attending Uncle Titus's funeral." It felt so strange to say that. She had gotten accustomed to the idea that the man was going to live forever. The way he'd always thought he would.

She realized that Brad was frowning and shaking his head. "I can't make it, Stacey."

Brad and Titus had met twice, once at a family Christmas and once at their wedding. Brad had thought the man odd, a throwback to another era, but she needed his support now. He couldn't be falling back on prior commitments. Didn't she mean *anything* to him?

"What?"

"The funeral. I can't make it," he said. "I have a six hour surgery scheduled for Wednesday. I cleared my calendar completely to accommodate the time it needed. The patient's already given his own blood. Everything's been set in motion. It can't be rescheduled."

She knew how difficult it was coordinating everything that went into performing a surgery. But this was her uncle Titus. The last living relative in her family. She needed Brad with her.

Stacey tried to think. "Could you fly out right after the surgery?"

Brad's immediate response was to shake his head. "I've got another surgery for Thursday morning." But then he paused, thinking. He didn't want to be the bad guy twice in her eyes in such a short duration. "Maybe I can get Harris to cover for me—"

Stacey knew that neurosurgeons didn't "cover" for one another. Not unless something like an earthquake or hurricane was directly involved. Each had his own area of expertise, his own small kingdom.

She banked down the bitterness that had prompted her to think the last part. "That's okay. I'll go alone."

Brad peered at her face, his own uncertain. "Are you sure?"

She didn't want to argue about this, too. Especially since she knew how it would turn out. Why waste the time? "I'm sure."

Off the hook, Brad still didn't like the idea of her flying alone. "Maybe Jim could go with you—"

She looked at him sharply. "Jim's busy setting up his new life. I'm perfectly capable of flying on my own." She blew out a breath, the impact of the news hitting her all over again. "God, I can't believe that Uncle Titus is really gone."

Brad nodded as he absently checked his pockets for his car

keys. "I thought your uncle would go on forever." Their eyes met for a moment. "Outlive us all."

"Yes," she said quietly, waiting for the ache to set in, the one that always came when she lost a loved one, "me, too."

There was an awkwardness in the air. Brad felt he should say something more. He had no idea what. "He never married, did he?"

"Not officially, at least, not that I know of," she amended, then smiled. "He was too much into 'free love.' Thought that monogamy was a waste of time, although he was pretty faithful to his 'lady of the moment' as he used to call them. When I was little, my parents used to have him over for the holidays because they kind of felt sorry for him." There was irony for you, she thought. Titus was always smiling. Her parents never were. "I think he enjoyed life a lot more than they did in the long run."

"At least he got to do it for longer." Brad glanced at his watch. "Oh, hey, look at the time. I should have already been halfway to the hospital. I need to make my rounds before I go to the office," he told her, striding toward the threshold.

He was halfway to the front door before he stopped and turned around. Hurrying back to the kitchen, he caught her off guard.

"Did you forget something?" she asked.

In response, he took her into his arms and kissed her forehead. "I really am sorry about Titus."

He could have knocked her over with a feather. Stacey smiled up at him. She doubted that he realized it, but that was worth far more to her than the two hundred dollars he had left on the counter.

"Thanks," she murmured.

Brad released her. "I've got to rush."

She followed him to the door. "That really meant a lot to me."

Brad nodded as he left the house. But he really didn't understand why Stacey had said that.

CHAPTER 9

The long flight from LAX to Titus's small Pacific island gave Stacey the opportunity to read for more than five minutes at a clip. She'd almost forgotten how to savor and enjoy a lengthy story. Everything these days came at her in tidy, bite-size pieces. Magazine articles ended within two pages. News stories came with highlights that summarized their content quickly for the rushed. The end result was that she no longer really knew how to immerse herself in something she was reading, had no patience to wade through deep prose, no matter how beautiful. Her brain seemed to lack staying power.

The first half hour of her journey was spent trying to keep her mind from straying as she struggled to focus on the written words before her. At the end of that first half hour she realized she'd been reading the same page over and over again. It took more effort than she would have ever guessed. So was keeping a lid on the impatience drumming through her. She kept wondering about things that she had left behind. Not the usual did-I-leave-the-stove-on anxieties, but misgivings about how Brad would fare in the house without her. He'd assured her he'd be fine, but she had her doubts.

And what if Jim needed her while she was gone? Or Julie?

She took a deep breath. They were all adults, all three of them. Even Brad. They would be fine. But would she?

Stacey propped the book up on the tray before her, trying again to lose herself in the pages of the mystery she'd purchased expressly for the trip. There was a time when she would curl up on any available space and read for hours on end, losing herself in whatever story—romance, mystery, historical biography—she selected. When had there stopped being time for reading for pleasure? For reading "just because"? When had life changed for her?

She couldn't pinpoint a moment, an earth-shattering event, that had transformed her. It had happened in tiny increments, stealthily, so she hadn't really been aware of the change. Until it had overwhelmed her.

The same was true of her marriage, she supposed. They'd started out being partners, two crazy-in-love partners, sharing every moment, every thought with each other. Living on love and dreams and not much in the way of creature comforts, but it didn't matter. As long as they had each other. Now they were like two strangers who met at the same bus stop every morning. There was recognition, an exchange of a sentence or two, but very little else. Certainly no feeling of communion, or even camaraderie.

She hadn't changed, had she? Not in the way she felt about things. Not about any of the things that truly mattered to her.

But Brad had.

Brad had changed, oh so much. Her mouth curved in a sad smile. She had married James Dean and woken up one morning to find herself sleeping next to Dennis the Menace's Mr. Wilson. Conservative, grumpy and so not a risk taker.

She missed James Dean more than she could possibly put into words.

Stacey looked down at her book. She was twenty pages further along than she had been earlier—and couldn't remember a single word of the story that had transpired, or how the mystery's feisty protagonist had wound up standing in a grave.

Annoyed, Stacey flipped back twenty pages, hoping to be more successful in keeping her mind from wandering this time around.

C'mon, Stace, you can do this. You can read this book. You remember what it was like to read, don't you? To block out everything else except for the characters in your book? Strike a blow for the not-so-distant past. Do it for Uncle Titus.

She smiled to herself. Uncle Titus loved to read. It was one of the forms that his rebellion took as society conspired to take its citizens away from the printed word and place them in front of a digital display.

For Uncle Titus, she thought, amused.

Buckling down, Stacey narrowed her eyes and forced herself not to think about anything except the novel she had before her.

Ian Bryanne looked exactly the way he sounded over the telephone.

Tall, thin, faded blond hair worn just a tad longer than the norm in deference to his chief employer. The former citizen of Great Britain was all angles and sharp points in a subdued gray Armani suit. The only splash of color came from his red tie. And from his electric-blue eyes.

The commercial flight she'd taken from California only took her as far as Honolulu. Ian had chartered a small local plane to bring her the rest of the way to Titus's island. The trip had roughly been a hundred miles. Roughly because the weather had turned inclement just before she'd boarded the small aircraft. Her stomach was in complete upheaval by the time they landed.

She hadn't been this nauseated since she'd been pregnant with Julie. Disembarking on very shaky legs, Stacey was convinced she would have been subjected to less turbulence had she made the short trip riding inside of a blender.

It felt like a full-fledged tropical storm by the time they touched down in the field where Titus kept his private Learjet. The moment she stepped out of the plane, Ian introduced himself, leaning forward to give her the benefit of the shelter afforded by the huge black umbrella he had brought with him.

Gusts of wind had the rain falling almost sideways, sailing beneath the umbrella and soaking her, but she appreciated the gesture. Together they walked side by side, careful not to slip on the metal steps of the ramp that had been pushed up against the plane.

"Welcome to the Island," Ian told her crisply, raising his voice above the wind.

Attention focused on getting down to ground level, Stacey only smiled and nodded in response.

The Island. Her uncle hadn't liked naming things. When he had purchased the fifteen-mile-wide island, rather than fixing some vain moniker to the tract of land, he referred to it by its description.

"Keep things as simple as you can," he had told her more than once.

He had the same attitude when it came to everything. The stray canine he'd taken in some five years ago answered to Dog. She had no doubt that if Uncle Titus'd had a son or a daughter, he would have named them Boy and Girl. Unless there were more, and then he would have affixed numbers to them. Boy 1, Boy 2 and so on.

He'd been one of a kind, she thought fondly, reaching the bottom of the stairs. She hunched her shoulders as she hurried to the sleek waiting black limousine. Holding the rear door open for her, Ian waited until she'd gotten in before closing the umbrella and slipping in himself. Once inside, he tapped on the glass that separated their section of the car from the chauffeur.

The limousine came to life.

The rain pounded on the windows as Stacey sat back, trying to relax.

"I trust your trip was pleasant and uneventful," Ian said to her.

It turned out to be fraught with unexpected soul searching, but there was no point in saying that. Instead, she nodded. "That about covers it."

Ian eyed her knowingly. "You will be dry in no time. There is fresh clothing to be had at the house."

Stacey looked at him. "How would you know what size…?"

"I don't," he cut in smoothly. "But your uncle had many of his lady friends stay the weekend, or longer. There was always clothing for them to change into. When they left, the clothing often remained. I am certain that you will be able to find something acceptable."

As long as a G-string isn't involved, she thought, bracing herself.

The trip to what Titus had whimsically referred to as his shack, a structure that could have rivaled a medium-size palace, took only ten minutes. As they drew closer, Stacey became almost speechless. The house had doubled, perhaps tripled in size since she'd last been here.

It struck her as ironic that her late, flower-child oriented great-uncle's house was infinitely more modern and incredibly larger than the house she was living in with her more-than-successful neurosurgeon husband.

You sure knew how to live, Uncle Titus.

"The funeral will be tomorrow at ten," Ian informed her as the limousine pulled up onto the stone-paved driveway.

The driveway was huge and could have easily been converted into a small parking lot. He might have espoused the simple life, but there was definitely a side of her uncle that cleaved to affluence.

Not as simple as you wanted everyone to believe, were you, Uncle Titus?

"The reading of the will will take place shortly after we return from the service," Ian was saying as he slid out of the vehicle, then proceeded to hold the umbrella at the ready for her.

"The will?" Stacey echoed, getting out of the limousine.

In the rush to prepare for her trip, she hadn't even thought that there might be a will, or that she was in it. Her uncle had been eccentric. She'd just assumed that he would be leaving his money to some organization.

"Yes." Lightly placing his fingers against her elbow, Ian guided her toward the front door. "Your uncle left strict instructions that he wanted everyone named in his will to be present for the reading. If they weren't—" safely under the shelter of the roof, the lawyer closed the umbrella with a dramatic gesture "—they would forfeit their inheritance."

Inheritance. That made it sound official. And expensive. Titus had favored threadbare clothing that looked as if it had come directly from a Salvation Army outlet store. The two images didn't jibe.

Ian rapped once and the door instantly opened. A petite, dark-haired woman in a maid's uniform stood almost directly behind the door. She offered Stacey a shy smile before she took three steps back, admitting her.

"Are there going to be many people at the service?" Stacey asked the lawyer.

"Enough."

How many is enough? she wondered. A lot, she hoped.

"Good." Stacey allowed a smile to blossom on her lips for the first time since she'd heard the news of his death. "Uncle Titus always liked a crowd gathered in his honor."

CHAPTER 10

Stacey covertly scanned the open field.

There appeared to be about thirty-five people in all. Thirty-five people standing in the inhospitable rain, listening to the rhythmic recitation in a tongue they couldn't begin to comprehend. The words were said over a sky-blue urn, uttered by a Cheyenne shaman who had been flown in for the service.

The chanting seemed to go on forever, just as the rain did.

Titus had opted to be cremated, and after the funeral services, he had requested that his ashes be scattered to the winds.

Plenty of that today, Stacey thought. A little too much, actually.

As the shaman continued, Stacey leaned in toward Ian. The lawyer had taken the position beside her just before the ceremony had begun.

"Maybe we should wait with the scattering," she suggested. When he made no comment, she added, "It's raining," feeling foolish even as she said the words. Any idiot could see that it was raining. Her point was that the rain would hinder the scattering of the ashes.

After a beat, his eyes focused on the ancient, white-suede-clad shaman, Ian shook his head. "This was your uncle's favorite kind of weather."

Was it her imagination, or did a fond note enter the man's voice? She liked the thought of Titus not being alone, of having a friend to share things with while he lived here. Someone who wasn't just traveling through the old man's life.

She nodded in response. It wasn't her place to go against her uncle's wishes, and Ian would have known him better than she did. The man had always gotten his way when he was alive. Death shouldn't change anything.

Stacey felt a pang that she hadn't made more of an effort to keep in touch. Now it was too late. Would her children have these very same thoughts someday about her? Oh, God, she hoped not. She hoped they would miss her because they had been in such close contact all the time and now she wouldn't be part of their lives anymore.

And Brad, how would he feel if he were standing here and those were her ashes in the urn? Knowing Brad, he'd be applauding her for being so efficient, for not taking up space in the ground, or requiring him to shell out a great deal of money on a casket.

Last night, when she'd called him to let him know that she'd landed safely, she'd gotten his voice mail on his cell. She'd fallen asleep, waiting for him to call back. He probably decided that two Hawaii–Southern California calls were too costly. Why waste money when he would be talking to her soon enough as it was?

She shook the thought off.

All around her, Stacey heard gentle sobbing. She looked

around again. The people attending Titus's service were almost all female. From what she had picked up last night at dinner and again this morning, they were the former and not-so-former lovers of her uncle.

Except for the man in the business suit, at the back of the gathering, Ian and herself, Stacey doubted that anyone in attendance was over forty. Or perhaps thirty. Uncle Titus liked them young, willing and pretty. Their spirit, he liked to say, matched his own. He never thought of himself as old, even when he turned ninety. Like George Burns, he had espoused the philosophy that everyone had to grow older but they didn't have to grow old. He lived by that philosophy.

Finally, the shaman, who looked to be about ninety himself, concluded the ceremony. The moment he did, Stacey found herself being shepherded along with everyone else into waiting vehicles. Once inside, they were driven en masse to the only cliff the island possessed.

There, they disembarked and gathered around the shaman as the ancient man concluded his part of the ritual, more chanting.

The winds had picked up and, along with them, the rain. The shaman appeared to be oblivious to both as they lashed along his face and body, soaking him. What he was about transcended such earthly things as wet clothing.

Stacey was grateful that Ian held the big umbrella for both of them. She had visions of taking off like Mary Poppins had she been given her own large umbrella.

The chanting ceased.

Stacey held her breath, watching.

With remarkably strong-looking hands, the shaman took the sky-blue urn from Ian. Removing the lid, the shaman said a few more words, then tilted the urn so that its contents could be swept over the cliff, down to the sea below or wherever it was that the winds would take the ashes, sowing Titus's essence now that he was no longer able to sow his seed.

Titus, as far as Stacey knew, had produced no children, not even one. Titus was sterile, her mother had once told her in whispered tones. It was a direct result of being exposed to some chemical at the plant he'd worked in as a teen. The same incident that was to render him heirless had also set the course of his life. It caused him to become a nonconformist, ever thumbing his nose at the establishment, except when it came to making money.

The winds shifted just as the shaman finished shaking out the contents of the urn. Stacey suddenly felt something in her eye.

The mourners began to retreat from the cliff, moving quickly to the shelter of the waiting vehicles.

Ian was about to take her elbow, then noted the way she was blinking her eye. "Anything wrong?"

Because she hated a fuss, Stacey was about to say no. But to do so was dumb. There *was* something obviously wrong. Whatever she'd gotten in her eye was stinging now. Her eye was tearing up.

"I'm not sure, but I think I just got some of Uncle Titus in my eye."

She glanced with her good eye to see the lawyer's reaction. It was the first time she saw the sober man smile.

"Tug on your eyelid," he advised, ushering her down to the limousine, his lips twitching. "It'll pass."

Stacey tugged, but the strange feeling in her eye persisted. She and Uncle Titus had apparently melded. At least for the time being.

She wasn't comfortable.

Sitting there in the study a hour later, Uncle Titus now safely out of her eye, she just wasn't comfortable. It wasn't just the straight-back chair that Ian had guided her to, a chair that she just couldn't make herself believe that Titus would have even wanted in his house had he found it in a Dumpster, much less paid good money for. She just felt as if she didn't belong in this gathering.

She supposed that was because she felt that there was a lot about her uncle she didn't know. In the final analysis, she was a stranger and strangers didn't belong at funerals.

Covertly, she looked around the packed room. The array of faces gathered in the study told her that her uncle must have had a great deal of fun over the past years of his life. And, apparently, was willing to pay for it. Why else would he have left all these women something in his will?

She didn't belong here. Aside from the man in the suit, a Geoffrey Daniels from some institute she had never heard of—the Institute for Cryogenics—the room was filled with Titus's lovers, past and present, and his household staff.

One by one, the endowments bequeathed to faithful servants and to the women who had brightened his life for a space of time were read. It seemed to go on endlessly. Stacey shifted in the chair, trying to find a comfortable position.

Had there been some mistake, requesting her presence here?

And then she heard her name, announced in Ian's clear, crisp voice. "And to Stacey Radkin Sommers, my only living relative, I leave my faithful companion for these past few years—"

Stacey tightened her grip on the chair. Uncle Titus was nothing if not unpredictable. He couldn't be leaving her his last mistress, could he?

She said a very fast prayer the nuns at St. Catherine's had drummed into her head.

"—Dog," Ian said as he continued reading the will. "'I know, because of her loving heart, she will give him as good a home as I have and take care of him in his declining years.'"

Stunned, Stacey blinked. Ian's voice echoed back in her head.

A dog.

Dog.

Oh, God, Brad was going to be furious, she thought. He wasn't going to accept having another animal in the house. When the kids were a lot younger, they had both gone through the usual begging-for-a-pet stage. Brad had turned a deaf ear, then finally, feeling guilty, he had compromised and told her to get goldfish.

Julie had seen that as a stepping-stone to bigger, better pets, pets with a discernible pulse. She'd cajoled him into agreeing to let her have a hamster.

"Howard" had been part of their household for less than a month, when he'd cleverly escaped his cage after Jim had left the top off. It took six days to locate the wayward hamster, who finally turned himself in by showing up on Brad's pillow. Brad was sleeping on it at the time.

But not for long.

That abruptly drew a close to their foray into the land of pets. Until two years later when Julie prevailed on her father to get Rosie. After much pleading and tears on Julie's part, Brad had relented. Eventually, he'd been grudgingly won over by the Labrador, but had made no bones about the fact that Rosie was never going to have "friends," nor would she be succeeded once she passed on to her reward. Brad stood firm by his decision.

Stacey raised her hand, attempting to stop Ian before he could get any further. "Um, I really don't think it would be in the dog's best interest to—"

She got no further as Ian raised his cool blue eyes to hers. "I'm not finished, Mrs. Sommers," he informed her crisply.

She lowered her hand. "Sorry."

They could talk about the dog later. But there was absolutely no way she was going to return home with a dog. Besides, how was she going to transport the animal? In a crate in the bottom of an airplane? Depending on how old the dog was, the experience could kill him.

Ian raised his voice, enunciating each syllable clearly. "And, in gratitude for taking care of Dog, I also leave her the sum of $250,000."

Stacey's jaw dropped as if the temporal mandibular joint had disintegrated.

There had to be some mistake.

The other bequests had all been around the same amount of money: ten thousand dollars. It appeared that Uncle Titus loved all his women equally. But, be that as it may, he was awarding these sums to women who had obviously given him pleasure. She and Titus had hardly connected once she was in her teens and even less than that after he had bought his island.

"She is to use the money as she, and only she, sees fit," Ian continued reading. He paused for a second, pushing his slipping glasses back up his nose. "'Those are my terms, Stacey,'" he quoted. "'I want you to use the money the way *you* want, not for anything that your husband or children tell you they want. I know you have a warm, giving heart, but if that happens, you are to forfeit the money and it will go to the institute, along with my island and the rest of my worldly possessions, which, according to my lawyer, is equal to the sum of—'"

Stacey wasn't listening. She was too busy trying to absorb the sound bite that had been intended solely for her. And to remember how to breathe.

CHAPTER 11

Twenty-four hours later, as she disembarked from the private airplane that had brought both her and Dog from Titus's island back to the mainland and Southern California, Stacey still struggled to get her bearings. Still tried to get used to the idea that she had a quarter of a million dollars at her disposal.

And still tried to figure out how to tell Brad about the money and the dog.

She had attempted to get in touch with him twice since the reading of the will. Both times she'd gotten his voice mail. He hadn't answered either message.

Lucky for me I don't need him as a surgeon, she'd thought as she hung up the second time, just before takeoff.

A warm breeze swept over her now as she wrapped Dog's leash around her hand. The pilot had gotten permission to land the small aircraft at John Wayne Airport, which meant that she didn't have to suffer through the famously huge L.A. traffic snarls in order to get back to her home in Newport Beach.

However, there was still the matter of making the ten-mile trip with a dog. Cab drivers frowned on anything with four feet entering their vehicles. She tried to think who to call to come get her. Jim was in L.A., or so she surmised, and there was no way she could reach Brad. Even if she could, he wouldn't be able to get away.

As if reading her mind, the pilot smiled as he placed her only piece of luggage on the ground beside her. "Mr. Bryanne hired a private car to take you home."

One less problem to deal with, she thought, relieved. She wondered if the lanky lawyer had worked out a way to spring the dog on her husband. But even fairy godmothers were known to have their limits. Transportation home was enough magic to hope for.

Dog was intently sniffing at her luggage, acting as if she'd packed away a giant-size treat dipped in bacon. "Mr. Bryanne thinks of everything, doesn't he?"

The pilot nodded, pausing to pet the lively animal. "Pretty much."

"Make someone a wonderful husband someday," she murmured to herself, or so she thought. And realized otherwise as she looked at the pilot.

The smile on the man's rugged face had turned into a grin. "Yes'm." And then he looked past her shoulder at something in the distance. "Looks as if your ride might be here."

Turning, Stacey shielded her eyes as she tried to peer in the distance. A large, burly man came toward them. He seemed to know his destination, or maybe that was just his commanding aura. He raised his hand and waved at her.

Stacey waved back as Dog barked a greeting. Or a warning. She wasn't sure which, since she hadn't gotten in tune to the animal's behavior and sounds yet.

"Mrs. Sommers."

Stacey couldn't tell if the man was asking, or greeting her. She acted as if it was a question and replied, "Yes."

The driver grinned, stooping to pet Dog. "I'm Jake. I'll be driving you home whenever you're ready."

She took a breath. "I'm ready," she told him. But even as she said it, she knew she wasn't. Not in the full meaning of the word. She was ready to go home, but not to take on Brad, which was what it was going to amount to. At least she had a few more hours to prepare. With luck, Brad would be called in for some emergency surgery, the way he had on almost every single important occasion in their lives.

"Lead on," she said.

To her surprise, Jake took the leash from her and picked up the suitcase with his other hand. "This way," he told her.

After thanking the pilot, Stacey fell into step beside Jake.

"Lot's crowded this morning," he commented. "I had to park the limousine a distance from the building."

"Limousine?" Didn't these people believe in economy cars? Everyone was supposed to be acutely aware of the price of gasoline these days.

"Yes'm. Mr. Ian likes nothing but the best for his guests."

As she slid into the dark, spacious, air-conditioned vehicle, she had to admit that this was nice. Very nice, she thought as Jake closed the door behind her. Dog began to explore the almost bowling-alley distance between the rear seat and the front of the limousine. She could get used to this.

Originally, she'd made arrangements with Brad before she'd left. He was to come pick her up at the airport and drive her home. That was when she'd assumed she was coming back on a commercial flight and landing in LAX. The change of plans made no difference, at least not to Brad at any rate.

Just before the reading of the will, she'd discovered that her husband had left a message for her on her cell phone, saying that he wasn't going to be able to make it and to call up one of those airport transport services when she landed. It was a cool, distant message, devoid of any of the personal touches and endearments she placed in hers. With Brad, life had become very businesslike. She could hardly get him to unwind in private, much less communicate a private message on something he considered as public as an answering machine device.

Not able to make it.

The phrase echoed back in her brain, even now. For the past few years, for one reason or another, Brad had been unable to "make" most of his life. Only in this limousine was his absence working in her favor. At least it allowed her to put off explaining why she'd returned with a four-footed companion.

All she had to do right now was brace herself for Rosie's reaction to this newest member of the family.

Rosie was not a typical Labrador. While most Labradors were created exceedingly friendly, eager to please and more apt to hand a burglar his tools than to guard the house against invasion, Rosie had been born with that rarest of entities for a Labrador: a suspicious nature. It did not dissipate as she grew older. If anything, it became more intensified. Everything new had to be closely scrutinized until she was satisfied that there was no threat to her from this quarter.

So the second Stacey opened the door and entered the

foyer with Dog, Rosie came bounding over, barking as if she meant to set off all the burglar alarms within a fifty-mile radius. The onslaught of teeth-jarring noise lasted all of three minutes, but to no avail. Dog was not intimidated. He didn't even move, not even when Rosie finished circling him and barked right into his muzzle.

Stacey would have said that the animal was deaf if it wasn't for the fact that he obeyed the slightest command that Ian had issued in his low, calm voice. She held on tightly to the leash, in case Dog had second thoughts about his pacifistic approach, but the animal continued with his peaceful resistance.

"Uncle Titus would have been proud of you," Stacey told him, finally dropping her suitcase next to the door.

The posturing and barking having failed, Rosie obviously decided that it wasn't worth the effort. She opted for investigation next. Circling again, she began sniffing loudly. Sniffing every inch of the mongrel statue. Stacey watched uneasily, still holding on to the leash, wondering what it took to get Dog to react.

Dog remained oblivious to Rosie's intense investigation.

Stacey could only shake her head and laugh. "Either you're older than you look, or you've been married and learned how to tune things out."

Finally, Rosie tired of her aggressive posturing and made a funny noise that Stacey could only interpret as a greeting.

"So, you're accepting him?" she asked the Labrador.

In response, Rosie trotted out of the room, leading the way to the kitchen. Both her food bowl and her water dish were there.

Following behind the animals, Stacey went to make sure that the Lab hadn't suddenly turned devious on her. She stopped at the kitchen's threshold and smiled to herself. The two dogs were at the water dish. Rosie was inviting Dog to lunch.

At least this had gone better than she'd anticipated. After picking up her suitcase in the foyer, she went straight to the staircase. She absolutely hated unpacking. The sooner she got it over with, the better.

Rosie had been won over with little fanfare. Now if only Brad could react in a similar manner. She could hope. After all, Brad did surprise her once in a while.

When the land line rang nearly ninety minutes later, Stacey stopped grooming the new addition to their family and got up off her knees. Reaching the closest telephone, she picked up the receiver and glanced at the LCD screen. It registered "private," which could have meant anything from an unlisted number, to Julie's cell phone, to a crafty telemarketer or a charity. The latter two groups had gotten clever when it came to getting their calls through. More than once she'd found herself listening to either a pitch for some indispensable object she couldn't live without, or a plea for a donation. She could handle the latter. Especially now.

"Hello?"

"Stace?"

The sound of the deep male voice had her both smiling and stiffening in anticipation as she glanced at the dog who'd lain down docilely at her feet.

"Brad? What are you doing calling home?" He never

called home, not since his early residency days. "Is everything all right?"

"Yes." His tone told her he didn't understand her concern. "I had a few minutes between patients and I thought I'd check in to see if you'd gotten home yet."

The rare display of thoughtfulness stunned her. It also made her feel guilty about what she was going to spring on him.

"I'm home," she answered, sounding so cheerful she hurt her own teeth.

"I picked up on that." She heard the rustle of papers. That was more like it. She knew the man couldn't take a complete break. "I wasn't sure if you'd be there yet. Traffic must be light."

She decided to work backward, telling him about the ride first, then about the private plane, which would lead her directly to the dog. "Actually, I came home by private car—" She got no further.

"A taxi?" Brad cried, annoyed. "That must have cost much more than an airport shuttle. Stacey, you know how I feel about wasting money."

Stacey closed her eyes. God, if she knew nothing else, she knew every single one of his policies about money. The man resisted turning on the air-conditioning unless the temperature hit over eighty-four degrees outside.

"You didn't waste any," she answered tersely. "Uncle Titus paid for it. Or rather, his estate did."

There was a slight perplexed pause on the other end. "Oh, well then, that's okay, I guess. That was nice of him." The silence was awkward. "How was it?"

"All right," she replied, her voice struggling to rise through a throat that was tightening. "For a funeral."

"Yeah, well…"

His voice drifted off. Stacey took the opportunity to jump in. Now or never. "Brad, there's something I have to tell you."

"'Fraid it's going to have to wait, Stace. I've got to get to my next patient."

She wanted to get this over with. The anticipation was wreaking havoc on her stomach. "They won't bolt if you talk to me for a minute longer."

"No," he replied in that patient voice she had grown to hate, "but that'll put me one minute behind, which will lengthen my day and make me come home late. You know how you hate my coming home late—"

"One minute late." When had he ever been one minute late? With Brad, it was always a matter of hours, not minutes. "That'll be a record," she murmured under her breath.

"What?"

She shrugged to herself. She had no desire to get into a heated discussion with him. God knew there was time enough for that when he got home. "Nothing. I'll see you at home tonight."

"Count on it," he said before hanging up.

"I do," she said to the empty receiver before she replaced it back in the cradle. "I always do." The man was nothing if not faithful.

She looked down at the dog, who was still contentedly parked at her feet. "Looks like the execution's been postponed for a few hours, Dog."

But not indefinitely.

CHAPTER 12

"No. Absolutely not. I forbid it." Brad's raised voice echoed about the living room.

Stacey stared at him. She'd been at a loss as to what to say. Until he had uttered the final sentence.

Unconsciously squaring her shoulders like a woman bracing herself to step into a major battle, Stacey raised her chin, unaware of exactly how defiant she looked. But Brad wasn't.

"This is not the Middle Ages," she informed him, "or even the 1960s, Brad. You can't say words like 'forbid' and expect to be taken seriously anymore. At least, not by your spouse."

His eyebrows drew together as if he couldn't follow what she was saying. Angry, Brad looked dark and formidable. "Stacey, we talked about this."

She didn't know whether to laugh or scream. The worst part of it was, he believed what he was saying.

Dog watched her as if he expected her to rise to the occasion. She rested her hand on his head. Since the animal was approximately the size of a miniature pony, she didn't have to bend to do so.

"No, Brad," Stacey replied wearily, "you talked, everyone else listened. Or you expected them to." She could tell by the expression on her husband's face that he didn't see the difference. "And besides, that was in general."

Brad's unenlightened look lingered. "So?"

"So, this is specific. When you nailed your edict to the Brandenburg Gate, there wasn't another dog standing in the middle of your living room, in need of a home."

"And there won't be one for long." He pointed to the closest phone, the one beside the sofa that faced the large bay window. "Call the animal shelter, they'll take him off our hands."

The animal shelter in Irvine was one of the few shelters that did not dispose of strays two to three weeks after they'd been taken in. She doubted Brad knew that when he made the suggestion. She doubted he even knew where the animal shelter was.

"I don't want Dog 'off our hands,'" she informed him, throwing his words back at him. She could see the surprise that registered on his face. Brad was used to her agreeing, to her giving in after only a few words of protest. But not this time. With Dog, there were promises involved. Silent ones, but that didn't make them any less valid. By taking Dog with her, she'd agreed to Uncle Titus's terms to care for the animal. She didn't intend to go back on that.

"Uncle Titus asked me to look after the dog in his declining years."

Brad's frown deepened and she could tell what he was thinking. That Dog would grow incontinent and ruin the rugs. "Your uncle is gone, Stacey," he pointed out tersely. "He's not exactly going to know if you take the dog to the shelter."

"No," she agreed, not giving an inch, "but I'll know." And she would hate herself for it. Besides, over the course of the day, she and Dog had bonded. It was nice having an animal who made her the focal point of the world for a change. "Look—" she gestured to the Labrador, who had shadowed him the moment he'd walked through the door—just before he first laid eyes on Dog "—if Rosie can accept him, why can't you?"

He looked at her uncertainly. "Are you comparing me to the dog?"

You'd come up wanting if I did. "No, just comparing your compassion to Rosie's." She didn't see what the big deal was. They weren't dealing with allergies. Brad had a number of them, but none included dogs. Only cats. She thought herself fortunate that Uncle Titus hadn't asked her to watch over a feline. "Brad, you're hardly ever home, anyway. What does it matter if we have another dog?"

By the look on his face, she had given him something else to fight about.

"I'm hardly ever home, as you put it," Brad informed her tersely, "because I'm working to provide you with a home."

Stacey looked him squarely in the eye. "That's secondary and you know it. You love what you do—"

Brad immediately took umbrage at the tone she was using. "And that's a crime?"

Where did he come off with that idea? She wasn't saying that at all. "No—"

"Would you rather that I was miserable, going off every morning to a job I hated?"

The dog drew closer to her, as if to shield her from the words. She stared at Brad, mystified. How had they veered so drastically off course? "No, of course not. I want you to be happy—"

"Okay, if you want me to be happy, then get rid of the dog.

We don't need two. One is more than enough and Rosie was here first."

Hearing her name, Rosie came alive and trotted over, waiting to play. After a moment, as if realizing it had been a false alarm, she sighed, spreading her paws out before her as she got back down on the floor. The dog's eyes fluttered shut and she resumed her impromptu nap.

"I can't," Stacey insisted. "It was one of Uncle Titus's dying wishes."

Blowing out a breath, Brad shoved his hands deep into his pockets. He moved restlessly around the room. This was clearly not how he had envisioned his evening going. For once, he'd gotten home early enough to have dinner with Stacey. Which meant that he could also indulge in the single drink he allowed himself. One was his limit, not because he couldn't hold his alcohol, but because he felt that more than one might impair his keen reflexes.

He'd needed the drink to unwind, but he made it a policy never to drink when he was angry. He'd seen his father do that. Had seen the man's temper flare, turning him into a man he didn't recognize. He'd vowed never to let that happen to him. He never wanted to be threatening to Stacey the way his father had been to his mother that one time.

He shook his head in disgust. "Titus always was a weird bird, having you travel all that way, only to come back with a mangy animal."

"He's not mangy," she said defensively. Brad looked at her sharply. She ran her hand over the dog's head. "He was better taken care of than a lot of people I know." If telling him about the dog was hard, this next part was going to be even worse. Because she had to shut him out. "And Dog wasn't the only thing Uncle Titus left me."

Brad spun around on his heel, alert. Listening for strange sounds. "What? Is there a chimpanzee in the bedroom?"

She frowned at the flippant question. She'd thought he was serious. "No—"

Brad cut her off, pointing to the far left. "A giraffe in the garage?"

She braced herself. "He left me money."

Brad frowned again, disgusted. "What, to buy dog food with?"

Stacey paused, pressing her lips together. "Not exactly."

Something in her tone caught his attention. Brad eyed his wife. "So how much was it?" When she made no answer, he crossed to her. "More than a couple of thousand dollars?"

"Yes."

His eyes held hers. She couldn't tell what he was thinking. "How much more?" he asked.

Stacey built on the word her husband had handed her. "Much."

Sums of money began to bounce around inside his head. No one knew exactly how much money Titus had, but the man *had* owned an island. Brad stopped to stare at her. "Define *much*."

Maybe it was childish—okay, it *was* childish—but she didn't want to tell him how much just yet. "How would *you* define much?"

"Twenty-five thousand." He drew closer to her. "Am I right? He left you twenty-five thousand dollars to take care of the dog?" The thought seemed incredulous to him, but people were strange when it came to their pets. It was getting on in years, there were going to be vet bills. At least this way, the animal wouldn't cost them anything to care for.

Stacey took it one layer at a time and peeled away. "No, Uncle Titus didn't leave me the money to take care of the dog." She took a breath. "And it was more than twenty-five thousand."

His patience was in short supply and ended abruptly. "Stop playing games, Stacey. How much did your uncle leave you in his will?"

She raised her eyes to his. "Ten times that."

Startled, Brad widened his eyes. "Your uncle left you two hundred and fifty thousand dollars?" Stacey nodded. Brad's voice dropped an octave, becoming almost a whisper. "A quarter of a million?"

Again, she nodded.

And saw Brad smile for the first time since he'd entered the house ten minutes ago. The greeting he'd been about to utter then had been swallowed up when Rosie had come bounding over to greet him, closely followed by her newfound friend, Dog. The call for an explanation had come immediately, followed by what could only be referred to as a less-than-friendly interrogation.

But now there was a smile, a genuine smile. Money was not Brad's king, but it definitely existed within the royal family.

Brad placed both hands on her shoulders, as if to hold her still, even though she hadn't moved a muscle. "Let me get this straight. Your uncle left us a quarter of a million dollars?"

"Yes."

Brad pulled her into his arms and hugged her. Hard. And

briefly. When he released her, his brain was racing. He began crossing to the nearest phone. "I've got to call our accountant, have him look into that new IRA I saw—"

He'd taken her completely by surprise. "What?"

"The new IRA—do you realize how far this will go toward financing our retirement? You're not incorporated," he allowed, "but I am and we could—"

She had to stop this before he went any further. "No."

Lost in thought and calculations, Brad looked at her blankly. "What?"

"No," Stacey repeated.

The word didn't compute. "No what?"

"No," she said slowly, "we can't put this money into an IRA."

"What are you talking about? Of course we can. It'll take some doing, some planning on our part—my part, I guess, but—"

She needed him to understand. "Uncle Titus said that the money was mine."

"Of course it is. You can take a few hundred—maybe even a thousand—and do something frivolous, but the rest is going into the IRA," he informed her. "Look, I'm not trying to take it away from you, Stacey. I'm trying to plan for your retirement."

She was so tired of him thinking of them as old before they had a chance to be young. "I'm forty-seven, Brad. I'm not retiring, I'm remodeling."

Flabbergasted, he stared at her. "What did you say?"

"Uncle Titus said I was to keep the money on the condition that I did with it what I wanted, not what anyone else wanted. You or the children," she said, hoping that by including Julie and Jim, Brad wouldn't feel as if she was singling him out. "And what I intend to do with the money is remodel the house."

The silence was deafening.

CHAPTER 13

The silence grew, mushrooming and separating them like some vast, invisible wall.

She was just about to urge him to say something when he did.

"And who is going to know that you don't want to put that inheritance money into an IRA? Titus?" he asked. "It isn't as if you can just call him to tell him what your plans are."

I'll know, Brad. I'll know.

The words remained lodged in her head, flashing in huge neon lights. Vivid, but unspoken.

Finally, in self-defense, Stacey said, "I've already told Ian that I was going to use that money for the house." It was a lie. She hadn't said anything to anyone. She'd been too overwhelmed by the amount to be chatty. But she hoped that it would end the discussion that, even now, she sensed was threatening to get ugly.

"Ian?" Brad's eyes narrowed into small, green slits. He squinted at her, as if that could make him absorb her words better. "Who the hell is Ian?"

Her voice was as calm as his was agitated. As soft as his was loud. It was as if every time he became angry, Brad just assumed that everyone around him had grown deaf and couldn't hear him if he spoke in a regular voice. "Ian Bryanne. He is—was—Uncle Titus's lawyer."

Frost formed in his eyes. He was shutting her out. Shutting her out because she wasn't agreeing with him. "I see."

Oh, God, was he going to sulk again? "See what?"

He said nothing. Instead, he walked past her to the kitchen. Once there, he bypassed the stove where she had a pot of chicken gumbo simmering and opened the refrigerator.

Utterly ignoring her, Brad took out an already opened package of cold cuts, a head of partially used lettuce, a jar of mustard and what was left of a loaf of rye bread. Digging into the utensil drawer, he took out a knife and began to make himself a sandwich.

Stacey held her tongue for as long as she could. She lasted half a minute. Men could be so infuriating. "Why are you making a sandwich?"

He didn't even bother looking her way. Rosie was between them, her attention completely focused on Brad. She was eagerly shifting from foot to foot. Brad took a slice of ham, tore it in half, then held out first one half, then another to the animal. It was gone in less time than it took to tear the slice in half.

"Because I'm hungry."

What would he do if she just started choking him? Just gave in to a wild urge to shake sense into his head by wrapping her fingers around his throat and depriving his brain of oxygen?

Stacey savored the thought for a second before discarding it.

"Dinner's on the stove," she pointed out needlessly. "I just made it. Why aren't you taking some of that instead?"

Again, Brad didn't even glance in her direction, gave no

indication that he heard any of the words. Instead, he placed a lettuce leaf on top of the mustard-slathered ham and capped it off with a second piece of rye bread.

He shrugged carelessly. "I don't know, you might have other plans for it."

She hated it when he threw back her words at her. Hated it when he cut her off like this. "Brad, you're being silly." Which, in her opinion, was putting it damn mildly.

Brad went about his business as if she hadn't said a word. Taking a can of soda out of the refrigerator, he closed the door with his shoulder, leaving the lettuce, bread, mustard jar and what lunch meat he hadn't used or fed to Rosie out on the counter where it would remain a silent testimony to his having to forage for his own dinner until such time as she put it away.

Slighted, Dog whined and looked up at her, waiting for some kind of treat since Rosie had gotten one. Brad walked out of the kitchen without so much as a glance in her direction or a comment in response to her words.

For a moment, Stacey struggled with her inner earth mother. She was tempted to go after Brad, to try to reason with him and at least get him to eat a better dinner than a ham sandwich on rye. But he was obviously into giving her the silent treatment for now. She knew from past experience that it would be futile to try to make him see things her way. He was so accustomed to getting everything *his* way, she was pretty certain he didn't even realize there *was* another way to do things.

With a sigh, she began to clean up and put things back into the refrigerator. She paused to give Dog a thin slice of ham. Eager, acting as if she hadn't eaten for days instead of minutes, Rosie tried to edge the other dog out of the way.

"No, you big bully, you've had yours. It's time for Dog to get a treat."

That made two of them, she thought silently.

"A quarter of a mill? Wow! Cool."

The delighted pronouncement came from Julie in between forkfuls of the salad that she insisted on referring to as her lunch.

Once every week, twice if she could swing it, Stacey and her daughter got together for lunch at one of the restaurants located near UCI Medical Center where Julie put what she'd learned at medical school to practice. The simple lunches were almost the only time she got to see Julie, certainly the only time she got to see her alone. When Julie came to the house and her father was there, he monopolized her.

Even though she was in medical school, preparing for a career that on occasion could mean the difference between life and death, Julie would drop by from time to time, always with a bag of laundry in tow. Time, Julie had learned, was a very precious commodity. She would use that portion that would have otherwise involved doing her laundry at a laundromat, to come home and touch base.

"Base" was always absorbed by Brad, who wanted to know every detail of what she was studying, what she was doing at the teaching hospital where she was working toward a degree that would eventually lead to her becoming certified in internal medicine.

Julie, who looked like a female image of her father, right down to the soul-melting green eyes and his dark brown hair, added with a wide grin, "Too bad Uncle Titus had to die for you to get it. But it's still very cool," she repeated.

Stacey sipped her iced coffee, trying to get her system into gear. She'd been dragging all morning at work. She absolutely hated it when she and Brad were having "difficulties" as he would refer to this impasse.

"Is that word back?" Stacey asked, setting the frosted glass back down on the beige tablecloth. "'Cool?'"

Julie shrugged. She was nonconformist in every way except for the path she had chosen to follow for her life's work. There she was so straitlaced and focused, it was like watching Brad all over again.

"I don't know. Maybe." And then Julie smiled again. "But the word fits."

"Yes, I suppose it does." She glanced down at her plate. The steak she'd ordered was gone. When had that happened? She couldn't remember eating it. "It also describes the way your father's been reacting toward me since I came back."

The words had just slipped out. She didn't ordinarily complain about Brad, not in an actual sense. But this had really been bothering her. Stacey pressed her lips together. A matter of closing the barn door after the horses had escaped, she thought, mocking herself.

Julie watched her, mildly confused. "That doesn't sound like Dad. He likes money."

Stacey laughed shortly. Now, there was an understatement if she'd ever heard one. "Yes, I know. He wants me to put it into this brand-new IRA that he's been reading about."

Finished with her salad, Julie moved the plate aside as she nodded. "Now, that sounds like Dad." She paused for a moment as she studied her mother's face. "I take it you don't want to."

Stacey noticed that Julie said "you don't want to" not

"you're not going to." As if it was a foregone conclusion that, like it or not, she was going to do it Brad's way. Well, what else could Julie think? The kids had seen her as being pretty much of a pushover all these years. Her capitulation to whatever it was that Brad wanted had become an accepted fact of life.

It made her angry.

"No, I don't," Stacey told her daughter with feeling that surprised Julie.

A glint of respect entered Julie's eyes. "Have any idea what you do want to do with the money?" Julie asked her casually.

Someone else overhearing might have taken the question to be a veiled hint. But it wasn't. Julie had no need to lobby for any part of Uncle Titus's bequest. The cost of her education had already been seen to. Unlike some of the other students around her struggling through medical school, all of Julie's bills were paid by her father—at times over Stacey's protests.

Stacey had always thought working hard to pay for something you wanted helped build character. Remembering his own years in medical school, Brad maintained that it just wore you out.

As if she hadn't worked her tail off to put him through school, Stacey thought ruefully as she wrote the checks that were mailed out to the University of California, Irvine.

"Yes, I have an idea," she told Julie. "I want to remodel the house."

Finishing the last of her diet soda, Julie laughed. "Bet Dad hit the roof."

"In several places," Stacey confirmed.

She paused, looking down at the small plate to her right.

Without realizing it, she'd been shredding the roll she'd taken earlier. There was absolutely no room in her stomach for it. But she had this need to take something apart, bit by bit, and the roll had had the misfortune of being right there in front of her.

After dropping what was left of it onto the plate, she dusted off her hands and then looked at the young woman she had raised. In a moment of weakness, she put the question to her, curious to hear her daughter's answer.

"What do you think I should do, Julie? Your father seems pretty adamant."

Julie didn't even take any time to consider. "I think you should do what you want to do, Mom. If you want to remodel, you go right ahead and remodel. It's your money, right?"

Her money. That sounded so odd. There'd never been "her money" or "his money" before. Just their money.

The wording in the will had made all the difference in the world, she supposed.

"Right," Stacey replied quietly.

"Well, then, there's your answer." Wiping her mouth, Julie dropped her napkin in her plate. "That was good and this was fun, but I've got to dash," she apologized. "Got a paper due tomorrow and the instructor's a brutal, mean son of a bitch. He likes flunking eager, would-be doctors." Rising, she moved over to her mother and kissed her. "Stick to your guns, Mom. I think the idea of remodeling the house is great." She winked just before she hurried off and raised her fist in a minipower sign. "You go, girl!"

Stacey found herself grinning back. And belatedly raising her fist in response.

CHAPTER 14

I'm going through with it."

The statement had sounded a lot more confident when she'd told Kathy yesterday morning at work. And Julie over the telephone during her lunch break.

As she said the words out loud to Brad now, they sounded extremely shaky to her. Like something she would utter just before plunging off a cliff in a first-time bungee jump attempt.

Brad looked at her for a long moment over the length of the breakfast table. The way he looked at her made Stacey think of a professional gunfighter from the Old West, eyeing the upstart who had called him out on the street, challenging him. It was as if they were squaring off. Standing on opposite sides of the long, dusty street. Rosie was at his side, Dog was at hers. That both animals were hopeful of handouts was beside the point. They could have easily been seconds. Backups in an old fashioned duel of honor.

God, but she hated the tension that seemed to be in every corner of the room.

"And nothing I've said has made any difference to you?" he asked.

She could have broken icicles off his words. "Don't make this about you, Brad."

"How is it not about me?" The icicles were gone, melted in the sudden flash of heat that rose in his voice. "You're willfully choosing to throw away a fortune, leaving me with the responsibility of providing for our futures when I could very easily just take this money and have it compounding daily—"

Stacey cut in. "It's not about you because I'm not doing it to deprive you, Brad. I'm doing it to enhance something that we live in. Something we can both enjoy when it's finished."

He looked at her as if she'd lost her mind. When he spoke, his tone did nothing to negate that impression. "Do you have *any* idea what's involved in remodeling?"

Damn it, why did he treat her as if she was some backward ten-year-old? She ran the house, for God's sake. And a medical office with seven doctors.

"Yes." And then, because those same green eyes she'd fallen in love with were boring into her, she relented. "Not specifically," she allowed, "because we've never gone through it, but I am aware of the concept."

There was just enough of a smirk on his lips to infuriate her. "You have to find contractors. Decent ones. And when you do, they're already all booked up or they'll disappear for days at a time."

They both knew he wasn't speaking from experience, either. Just from stories he'd heard from others who had gone through it. With a slight incline of her head, she acknowledged, "I've heard the horror stories. Same as you," she added.

He took it as a jab at his authority. Brad glared at her across the table. "Just don't expect me to help, that's all."

"Help?" she echoed, not following. "Help what? Remodel?"

He was kidding, right? Brad was a wonderful surgeon. As

brilliant as he was in the operating room, that was how bad he was with anything that required the least bit of mechanical savvy. That included the proper way to hold on to a saw or a drill. In the final analysis, Brad had to be as unhandy a man as God had ever created.

He could tell exactly what she was thinking. It was there, in her expression, in her voice. He took it as belittling his abilities. Granted, he couldn't build a palace out of toothpicks and twine, but he was handy in his own right. Brad frowned his displeasure. "No, help finding a contractor. I'm too busy to sit around, interviewing guys with more tools than brains."

Whenever he felt threatened or insecure, he had a tendency to hide behind sharp words and criticisms. She didn't bother defending the world where manual labor was king. She was gaining ground. Winning.

She was actually winning.

You go, girl!

Julie's voice echoed in her head, egging her on.

"That's okay," Stacey told him cheerfully. "I can do it. I can schedule the interviews for Saturdays." Actually, with her work schedule, she would have to. "That way, if you decide that you want to be part of the process—"

"I don't," he declared with feeling and finality, like a judge refusing to augment a death sentence.

Stacey pretended he hadn't said anything. "You can." Brad scowled at her. But at least he wasn't lecturing, she thought. Or pouting. That was progress. "And if you're too busy," she allowed, "that's okay, too."

Brad sighed. He'd lost his appetite. Moving aside his plate, he reached for the glass of orange juice she'd poured and took another sip.

"Look," he finally said, setting the glass down again. "If your goal is a new house, why not just do that? Get a new house. One of my former patients is a real estate broker. I could—"

"Brad. Brad, stop," she pleaded, holding up her hand to get his attention. "My goal isn't a new house," she contradicted.

"It's not?

"No, it's to get *this* house to look like new."

She could see that what she was saying wasn't making any sense to him. She tried again. Because she really did want him to understand. Not to accept and walk away, but to understand. It wasn't all that hard.

"I love this house, Brad. This is *my* house. *Our* house. This is where all my memories are." As she spoke, emotions swept through her, intensifying every word she said. "This is where we started out together when you finally got your practice. Where Julie and Jim became tiny people instead of just babies. This is where we celebrated all our Christmases, all our birthdays. Where we had good times and bad." She swept over the last word and the images it evoked. Because lately, although it hadn't been actually horribly bad, it hadn't been good, either. "I love this house," she told him again with feeling.

She searched his face to see if she'd gotten through. But there was no indication that she had. Had they really grown that far apart? Had their dreams, the things that mattered to them, veered that much off course?

He shook his head. "Then why change it?"

It wasn't changing, it was improving, but she had a feeling

that comparison would be lost on him, too. For a brilliant man, he could be so dumb.

"Because," she told him patiently, trying to put it in the simplest terms she could think of, "like everything else, the house needs a face-lift. The bathrooms are in critical need of updating. The patio is cracked in dozens of different places. Patching it is useless. We need a new one."

"Which will crack in turn."

She'd done her homework. "Not if we use pavers instead. They'll give." She smiled, pleased with herself for having collected articles and ads on remodeling for years now. Dreaming. "Our closets could do with some expanding," she continued. "And the bonus room is sagging."

Brad rolled his eyes, the ever suffering husband. "You're exaggerating."

But for once in her life, she stood ground. "No, I'm not."

"The bonus room isn't sagging."

To Brad's surprise, Stacey rose from her chair and came around to his side of the table. She took his hand, tugging it. Urging him to his feet.

"C'mon."

Finishing off his juice, he rose. "What are you doing?"

When they had originally moved here, they had used the bonus room to entertain their friends. But slowly, they had gotten out of the habit of entertaining. Brad hadn't been inside the bonus room for what seemed like years. In the last few, Jim had taken it over, doing all his studying and occasional entertaining there. Brad stayed clear of it and Jim. It was as simple, as upsetting, as that.

"I'm taking you upstairs so you can see what I'm talking

about for yourself." He began to protest, but she didn't release his hand. Instead, she led the way to the staircase. "If it doesn't have a nerve ending attached to it, you hardly notice it."

It wasn't a complaint, it was just the way things were. The longer he was in practice the more he became oblivious to things that existed outside of the work he had dedicated himself to.

Because he didn't feel like arguing about yet something else, Brad allowed himself to be led up the stairs, although he did reclaim his hand.

The bonus room was at the end of the hall. The large, patio-style doors led out to a tiny balcony that in turn looked out onto the cul de sac. Over to the extreme left, there was a desk with a computer and all the peripherals. Adjacent to that and in between the two patio doors, was a rather outdated television set on a swivel stand. Directly opposite the desk with the computer was a leather sofa that had seen better decades.

Most of the furniture in the room, as well as the house, was approximately the same age as her children. Brad didn't believe in getting rid of something until it was beyond saving. The only new thing in the room was the pool table and that was more than fifteen years old.

Brad put his hands on his hips. "Okay, what am I looking at?"

She gestured toward the floor lamp that stood beside the television set and right next to the patio door closest to the computer.

"That, for starters."

Tall, slender, with a shade to match, the lamp was listing

several degrees to the right. Resembling a sailor at least three sheets to the wind.

"And that." She gestured to another floor lamp, an exact duplicate of the first. This one was over beside the leather sofa and it leaned in exactly the opposite direction. "And those."

This time she indicated two tall maple cases filled to capacity with DVDs and CDs. The cases bowed toward each other like two polite Europeans, encountering each other on the street for the first time in months.

"All that proves is that we have cheap lamps and that the cabinets are overloaded. Get new lamps and get rid of some of those movies and CDs. You don't need to have that many."

He stubbornly refused to see the big picture. And trust Brad to find a way to tell her to curb her spending. She might not "need" the movies he dismissed so cavalierly, but she did like having a library of old movies. She liked the idea of being able to rummage through them and find something to lift up her mood when it needed lifting.

"It's not the lamps, which, by the way, aren't as cheap as you think," she slipped in, then hurried along before he could question her about the price. "The bonus room floor needs to be reshored."

He glared at her. It was obvious what he thought of her estimation. "You sure that a quarter of a million will cover everything you want done?"

Stacey had no idea what possessed her to glibly answer, "If not, it'll be a start." But it felt good to say it.

CHAPTER 15

Brad stared at her as if she had completely lost her mind. For a moment, she thought he was just going to get up and walk away, freezing her out. But the next moment, she realized that he was digging in.

He took in a deep breath. Stacey braced herself for the storm.

"Look, Stacey, if you think that I'm going to let you just pour good money after bad into this money pit we're living in—"

Stacey held up her hand like a policewoman intent on stopping the flow of traffic before it got out of hand. "First of all, why would you call Uncle Titus's money bad?" She knew that Brad thought the man eccentric, they all did, but it wasn't as if he'd been a robber baron. Uncle Titus was gone and deserved a little respect. "Second of all, you don't have to worry, I'm not about to go overboard. I might not be as conservative as you are when it comes to money, but I don't exactly run around blowing it on everything I see, either."

The expression on Brad's face did not change. "Until now."

This was still about the IRA, she thought. "Until ever."

Stacey struggled to keep her anger from taking over, making her say things she couldn't take back. She knew where Brad was coming from. Growing up, he had been relatively poor. A lot poorer than she had been. While other kids were hanging out after school, Brad was working any job he could get, not just for spending money to line his pockets, but to put into the bank. Knowing his parents couldn't help him, he wanted to save as much as he could to pay for his college education.

When he wound up getting an undergraduate scholarship to the same university their daughter was now attending, there was no sigh of relief, no symbolic loosening of the purse strings. Not even a little. Instead, Brad seemed to hang on to the money more than ever, always concerned that the scholarship he'd been awarded would be yanked because his grades fell, or because some other, unforeseen event happened.

Brad always made sure that he was prepared for the eventuality of that inevitable rainy day. In a cloudless sky, he was the one always anticipating storm clouds.

Her voice softened and she tried to reason with him, to get past phobias that seemed to her to be deeply ingrained in him. "You know, Brad, we are at a place in our lives where we can actually relax a little." Reaching over, she put her hand on his. "I'm still working, your practice is doing very well—"

He pulled his hand away. And left her isolated.

"We have a daughter in medical school and a deadbeat son who's a financial drain on us." He saw her start to protest. She was always defending Jim. Maybe that was why his son had never tried to amount to anything. He knew his mother had his back. "Don't think I don't know that you've been slipping him money to get by."

She hated the way Brad picked on Jim. Hated the way he tried to push his own goals, his own values on their son. Brad didn't believe in people finding their own way. As always, it had to be *his* way or it wasn't acceptable. "Jim is not a deadbeat."

The look Brad gave her said that he knew better. "He has a part-time job as a delivery boy and spends the rest of the day clutching his guitar and contemplating his navel."

Brad had always thought of the arts as frivolous. Only the world of medicine was important. Everything else took a back seat. And the arts were relegated to the back of the train. She, on the other hand, had always thought that while medicine treated the body, the arts fed the soul.

"You're being insulting, Brad. He is *not* contemplating his navel, he's writing songs."

Disgust filtered over his handsome features. Once, a very long time ago, when he had bought Jim a toy stethoscope and miniature doctor's bag, he'd thought about what it might be like, having his son join him in his practice. Now it was Julie who might someday come aboard. But it didn't ease the sting of disappointment as far as he was concerned.

"The world doesn't need more songs, Stacey. It has damn well enough already."

She opened her mouth, then shut it. Throwing up her hands, she withdrew from the field of battle. "I'm not doing this."

He'd fully anticipated another volley, something about Jim having the soul of a poet or some garbage. She'd surprised him. Again. Obviously, Stacey was going for some kind of record. "Doing what?"

"Getting into another argument with you over the kids. We've had these fights before." So many times that she could have just shouted numbers at him. Argument 307. Argument 119. And just as much would have been resolved. Nothing.

"It's not 'kids,'" Brad corrected tersely. "It's Jim." He didn't bother trying to suppress the sigh. "It's always Jim. Julie is doing great," he reminded her. "And they're not fights."

"Okay," Stacey allowed. "We've had these 'discussions' before and they've all gone nowhere." And before he canonized their daughter, she added, "There was a time, you know, when you thought Julie was a lost cause."

He looked at her as if he had no idea what she was talking about. As if he'd suddenly realized that his wife had had a lobotomy without his knowing about it. "No, I didn't."

"Yes, you did." Stacey glared at him. "She was dating that Goth, wearing nothing but black and looked like a walking magician's wand, she was so skinny. You threatened to send her off to an all-girls Catholic school if she didn't eat something and find an alternative color to wear."

He shrugged vaguely. "If you say so."

Stacey didn't know whether to laugh or cry. "The point is, it happened and you *were* ready to write her off, but she turned herself around." She got to the heart of her statement. "And so will Jim."

"I'm still waiting," he said.

Had he always had this cruel streak? she wondered. Or had she just been blind to it all these years? "Some people take longer than others. He was damn near perfect until his third year in high school," she reminded him. "Every kid goes through a rebellious period. He's just taking longer than most, I guess. But then, he got started later than most, too."

Brad grew quiet for a moment, as if debating on whether or not to believe her. "And you honestly think he's going to go back to school and at least get an MBA?"

She knew Brad wanted her to say yes. That, pessimist supreme though he was, if she said that Jim would eventually go back for at least an MBA, then he would have some hope of his son's success.

But she couldn't lie to him. Not even to make him feel better. Not unless he was on his death bed as well. Then all bets were off.

"Probably not." She saw hope shrink away, replaced with annoyance and frustration as if the two emotions had never been away. "But I know he'll make something of himself."

Brad's mouth twisted. "Yeah, if we're lucky, he'll be promoted to singing waiter." He shook his head. How had this happened? How had his son not inherited any of his genes? "And we'll wind up having to subsidize him for the rest of our lives."

Money. It was always about the money. She was so sick of hearing about money. It seemed to her that was all they ever talked about, when they did talk. How could something so perfect have gone so awry?

For a moment, because she looked so genuinely sorry, he thought she was being serious. "And here you were, planning to take the money with you. I guess it's true what they say about the best-laid plans of mice and men."

It took everything he had not to shove the table away from him. He was trying to look out for her, trying to get a backbone for his son without having to surgically implant it, and she was being flippant and sarcastic.

"What the hell has gotten into you?" he asked. "Ever since you came back from your uncle's funeral, you're a completely different person."

Welcome to the new, improved Stacey Sommers. The one who came with a spine.

"The difference is," she replied tersely, "I've decided to stand up for myself."

The pause was so long, it made her want to scream and climb the walls. When he finally spoke, it made her long for the pause. "And life's been that bad for you. I've been beating you into the ground every night."

"No, you haven't been beating me into the ground, Brad. But you haven't been listening to what I've been saying, either."

"Yes, I have," he contradicted. "The trouble is, what you've been saying hasn't been right."

Second verse, same as the first. "And you would be the only one who knows what's right?"

"Apparently. At least when it comes to the matters that you've been dragging up."

Brad looked down at his watch. He was running late. Even if he wasn't, he wanted to get away from this woman he didn't recognize. Wanted to stay away until the woman he'd married, the one he loved and had promised to cherish, returned to him.

He knew he couldn't hide out at the hospital and his office indefinitely, but he could leave now. For the moment, he gave in. He didn't have time to try to win her over. With a movement that signaled finality, he threw down his napkin and rose from the table.

"Do what you want, Stacey." His voice was no longer heated. It was distant, removed. As removed as a public transportation announcer explaining the reason for a train's delay. "As you've pointed out, it's your money."

"The will made stipulations—"

He continued as if she hadn't said anything. "Just as long as you don't touch our bank account," he warned coldly. And then he spared her a look. "One of us has to be fiscally responsible."

She could feel the hairs on the back of her neck rising again. "Meaning I'm not."

He began walking to the front of the house. And escape. "I don't have time to do an audio replay of our conversation. I'm late." Reaching the door, he looked at her one last time. "And don't expect me home for dinner tonight. I've got a board meeting. I'll grab something in the cafeteria."

He always ate at home, no matter how late he was. "You hate the cafeteria."

He looked at her significantly. "Right now, the cafeteria's looking pretty good."

And with that, he left.

CHAPTER 16

Stacey had always been an organized person.

Organization was the key to how she had managed to juggle a full-time job along with motherhood and being Brad's wife. At times, the latter was a job in its own right.

When she had first taken on the job of office manager at the medical practice where she worked, everything she put her hand to seemed to be in utter chaos. From the patients' files, to the billing system, even to the actual accessibility of the case histories, everything was in such a jumbled mess that it made finding information a feat only to rival the creation of Stonehenge.

Rather than run back to the shelter of home and hearth, Stacey dug in. She had always had more than her share of stubbornness. And so, with patience and perseverance, she managed to bring order to where chaos had reigned. She streamlined procedures, ordered new computers and implemented software that cross-referenced medical data. The physical files that some of the doctors insisted on retaining she color-coded, allowing anyone to know at a glance if the patient was current or if the file had become inactive.

Everything was backed up in case of a power surge. Data was inputted and kept current. In addition to modernizing their systems, she also managed to save the practice a great deal of money, something that caught the attention of all the doctors who worked there. Rather than farm out medical insurance forms to an outside third party, she kept everything in the office. All it took was a new software program and a little more patience. Soon, claims were being filed quickly and more efficiently, patients were happy, doctors received their money faster, making them happy. Everyone was happy except for the third party who no longer processed their claims and held everything up.

Armed with the kind of background that refused to be daunted, Stacey approached this new challenge in her life, the remodeling of her house, in the same fashion.

The first thing she needed was input.

She needed to obtain reliable references before she even began the process of interviewing potential contractors. Who was good? Who was reasonably priced? Who was dependable and showed up? Was there anyone who was all of the above?

"I sincerely doubt it," Dr. Steven Foxworthy, one of the seven doctors she worked for, told her when she put these questions to him the following Monday morning. After working for the medical group for more than fifteen years, the separation between doctors and staff no longer existed. She had seen to that. The fact that she was also a surgeon's wife didn't exactly hurt the situation, either.

Foxworthy, she recalled, had had some major work done on his house a little more than a year ago. She began with him.

"But I do have the name of a pretty decent contractor for you," he told her. "Or at least Margie does." He smiled ruefully. "She handles all that kind of stuff when it comes to the house and the kids." He shrugged dismissively, but he was young enough to be a little embarrassed by this delegation of traditional roles just the same. "You know how it is."

"Yes," she nodded, "I do." *All too keenly*. But she wasn't here to try to redefine roles. She needed information or this project of hers would never get off the ground. She needed to get started before Brad tried to hijack the money into some treasury bond fund. "But you were satisfied, right?" she pressed.

"Well, yeah," he told her with enthusiasm. "The house looks great."

It was all she needed to continue to the next step. Which was talking to Margie Foxworthy.

"It was touch-and-go for a while," Margie Foxworthy told her over the telephone when she called during her lunch break. Margie was a vivacious redhead who talked as much with her hands as she did with her mouth. Stacey could just see the woman gesturing with her free hand as she spoke. "It got so bad at one point that Steven and I didn't talk for a week. We almost separated."

Stacey shut her eyes. *Great. That's all I need, to have Brad go off the deep end.* From everything she knew about Steven, he was easygoing and mild-mannered. If he and his wife had stopped communicating because of remodeling, then she was probably walking onto a minefield.

"We were at each other's throats almost every day," Margie continued, apparently unaware that Stacey hadn't said anything. Or maybe because of it. "But then it got better." Margie's voice grew brighter. "And now, when I look around—" Stacey heard the other woman sigh with absolute contentment "—I feel that it was all worth it." Margie laughed, a private joke tickling her. And then she shared. "That which doesn't kill you, makes you strong, right?"

Or very, very gun-shy, Stacey thought. But she had vowed not to back away from this project. Over the years, she'd given in too much to Brad. Besides, she reminded herself, the money was only hers if she did with it what she wanted to. Ian now knew what that was, since he'd called her just the other day to inquire how things were going and if she'd decided what to do with the inheritance. He sounded pleased when she told him her plans. She had no doubt that somewhere in the not-too-distant future, she would be getting a call from the lanky lawyer, wanting to know the progress being made.

"Right," she echoed belatedly. "Well, thanks for the input."

"Sure thing." And then, just before Stacey hung up, she heard Margie call out. "Hey!"

Bringing the receiver back to her ear, Stacey said, "Yes?"

"You might want to talk to Wanda Brown. Dr. Taylor Brown's wife," Margie added, in case Stacey drew a blank with the name. "They just doubled the size of their house. Couldn't be happier," she vowed. "Let me find her number."

Stacey listened for a minute to the sound of paper being shuffled and searched through. And then, Margie was back on the line, rattling off the heart specialist's home number.

The more the merrier, Stacey thought with a smile as she laid down her pen. "Thanks."

"Invite me over when it's done," Margie told her.

"Sure." *Either to that or the divorce hearing, whichever comes first.*

But she was committed and she intended to go through with her plan. She knew if she didn't, Brad would always bring it up whenever they had an argument—or discussion. He'd have it filed under Stacey's Folly.

It wasn't going to happen this time.

"It took a year," Wanda Brown told her later that afternoon when she finally had a chance to call the woman. Wanda had been reluctant to comment until Stacey had brought up Margie Foxworthy's name—and the fact that she was married to Brad. Then the floodgates opened and Wanda talked and talked, eating up the minutes of her afternoon break. "It got to the point that I thought it was never going to end," Wanda confided. "Like my labor with Donald."

Only vaguely acquainted with the woman—she'd seen an article on the doctor and his family in the hospital newsletter—Stacey had no idea which of the woman's five boys was Donald, or what the names of the other boys even were, but she knew enough to make the appropriate sympathetic noises.

"But eventually, it did end. The workers packed up their tools and left, and suddenly I was in love. With the house," Wanda clarified. "The boys each have their own rooms now, so there's no more fighting about who did what to whom. At the first sign of any trouble, I just send them up to their rooms." She paused for a second, getting her second wind. "Do you have kids, Tracey?"

"Stacey," she corrected the woman. "And yes, but they're not fighting anymore." They got a long rather decently these days, but when they were growing up, there were times she was certain one was going to kill the other. Julie had never been one to meekly stand by and take it.

"Lucky you."

A few minutes later, most devoted to the trials and tribulations of raising five overactive boys with a workaholic husband, Stacey was finally able to coax the name and address of the contractor who had overseen the remodeling of the Brown house.

The process of gathering the names of contractors who had completed better-than-average renovations went on for several days. After work, since she had no one to hurry home to now with Jim moved out and Brad still sulking and working, Stacey would drive around, looking at houses. It amazed her just how many houses had had some kind of work done. Additions, new windows, different masonry in the front. All this while her own house had stayed the same, frozen in the era that it had been built.

At first, she'd tackled her own development, then she began to drive through the neighboring ones. Each time she saw a house that had obviously had work done, she would get out of her car and knock on the door. Once whoever answered was assured that she was not attempting to sell them something, she was usually welcomed and taken for an impromptu tour. Most of the time, the woman of the house conducted the tour. There was always an apology about the condition of the house attached.

But Stacey didn't see the newspapers scattered about, the shoes that hadn't been put away or the dishes sitting on every available flat space. She was too busy evaluating the merits of the rooms, measuring their future aesthetic value against the immediate discomfort she and Brad would be experiencing by having the house in a complete uproar.

Her list of contractors, along with their strong points and detractions, grew. As did her enthusiasm. Rather than feeling overwhelmed with all the data, she felt empowered. And enthusiastic.

The houses she was allowed to view fueled her imagination and gave her ideas as to what she wanted done to her own house. She began compiling copious notes and armed herself with dozens of magazines, everything from *Architectural Digest* to magazines that dealt strictly with do-it-yourself projects ranging from flirty window treatments to dressing up the toilet bowl cleaner.

Her lists continued growing. Both the one that cataloged the contractors she wanted to interview for the job and the one that dealt with the different ideas she had for the house.

Stacey decided that she wasn't going to add on. They didn't need more rooms, they just needed bigger ones. Her plan was to remodel, replace and refresh. There were a few areas she wanted to expand. Ever since she could remember, she had always wanted a window seat in their bedroom. And after living with a long, shallow closet all these years, she wanted one she could walk into. One that would allow her to have all her shoes arranged side by side and clothes hanging neatly instead of squashed together like people in a subway car during rush hour.

And, she thought, pulling her vehicle over to the curb so that she could make another notation, if they expanded the bonus room to extend over the third garage, that would give them more space to house an exercise cycle for Brad.

Even as she had the thought, she could hear his voice in her head: I don't need an exercise cycle. If I want to exercise,

I can always go to the gym. But he didn't go to the gym, which was the whole point.

Stacey jotted down exercise cycle on a third list. She was smiling as she did it.

CHAPTER 17

The surgery had been touch-and-go.

And endless.

The tumors rivaling grains of sand in size were tangled along a three-inch region of his patient's spinal column. It hadn't helped matters that the forty-six-year-old salesman was close to fifty pounds overweight.

Brad had finally gotten them all, but it was too soon to tell if there would be any nerve damage as a result of the procedure. Of course, if he hadn't performed the surgery, paralysis would have been the eventual outcome. Not to mention that one or more of the tumors could have turned malignant.

They still might now. The hospital's pathology lab closed by the time he had the tissues ready to send out.

A car cut him off just as he came to his exit on the freeway. Brad cursed roundly as he veered to avoid getting into an accident.

It took a second to collect himself.

Brad was never in a good mood when the patient's full recovery was not a foregone conclusion. It was no secret that he absolutely *hated* not being able to fix whatever problem found its way to his operating table, to leave his patient faced with a future that was better than his or her immediate past.

"You're not God, you know. I think you lose sight of that sometimes," Alex Lopez, the surgeon who had assisted him in the six-hour procedure, had said after they had finally finished and retreated from the operating room.

Brad didn't remember what he'd said in response. Only that he knew he had no supreme powers that guaranteed success each and every time he picked up a scalpel.

But all the same, he felt a responsibility, a commitment to the patients who put their faith in him. Faith, he thought as he turned down the long, winding street that eventually fed into his development. Faith came from God, so he expected some sort of tie-in on that level. Logically, he certainly didn't expect to place his hand on a patient, cry "Heal!" at the top of his lungs and have whatever was wrong become right.

Turning into his development, he drove toward his house on automatic pilot.

But still, he argued silently, with all his expertise, all his experience and inherent skill, you'd think...

His mind trailed off. Right now, it was far to much of an effort to think. All he knew was that he was bone weary. And hungry.

And in no mood to deal with strangers.

Brad frowned. There was a dusty, oversize white truck parked at his curb. On the side, the letters proclaimed J.D. Construction.

J.D. For no apparent reason, the words *juvenile delinquent* popped into his head.

Damn it, why tonight? She'd had all late afternoon, early evening to do this, why now, just when he was getting home? God knew he got home late enough for her to finish at work and see whoever it was she wanted to see before he walked through the door.

He needed to lay down the law.

That wasn't going very well these days, was it?

Maybe, if he was lucky, the truck belonged to someone visiting the guy across the street. The man owned six cars and they were parked all over his driveway and along his curb. Visitors were left to scout around for parking spaces, taking them where they could find them.

Muttering under his breath about inconveniences, Brad shoved his key in the lock. He didn't have to turn it. The front door was already unlocked.

Damn it, what had he told her about leaving the front door open?

As he walked in, incensed, he forgot that he still wasn't really speaking to her. "Stacey!"

"In here, Brad."

The voice floated in from the family room. It didn't quite sound like her. Oh, it was Stacey, all right, but it was the voice she used with strangers. Which meant that she was either on the phone with someone, or actually *with* someone. The owner of the dusty truck. J.D. Or his representative.

He groaned inwardly, debating just ignoring everything and heading straight for the refrigerator. But even there he was foiled. The kitchen was completely exposed to the family room. He was doomed no matter what course he took.

Stacey was sitting in the family room, perched on one end of the eight-foot sofa. There was a man in tan jeans and a light green T-shirt sitting on the opposite end.

He looked rather slight for a contractor, if that was what

he was, Brad thought. He would have thought contractors had to be big guys with large biceps.

He was feeling punchy.

Twisting around to get a better look at him, he saw Stacey smiling warmly at him. He wasn't sure if he responded. His face muscles felt too tired to be pressed into use.

"Honey, this is J.D. Conrad." She turned back toward the other man. "Mr. Conrad, this is my husband, Dr. Bradley Sommers."

The man was on his feet instantly, shaking Brad's hand. "Nice to meet you," Conrad said with enthusiasm.

The guy was young, Brad thought. Too young. Too enthusiastic-sounding. Dear God, had he ever been that young? That enthusiastic? It felt like a million years ago and he couldn't remember.

Stacey was saying something, he realized, and tried to concentrate. "Mr. Conrad is giving me some estimates," she told him.

Estimates. You only gave estimates when you had input. He looked at Stacey. So, it had gotten that far, had it? She knew what she wanted and had written everything up so that this guy in the tight jeans and faded T-shirt could give her estimates on how much he intended on robbing her.

Though he was still annoyed with her, Brad had to grudgingly admit that he was also in awe of his wife. It hadn't even been a month and she was already starting to get the project off the ground. Whenever Stacey wanted something, she went after it, the personification of confidence. He supposed that was how she'd kept everything running all these years, freeing him up to devote himself to his profession.

"Why don't you sit in on this, honey?" she urged. Taking the hand that was closest to her, she laced her fingers with his and tugged, indicating the space beside her.

She was roping him in, and being none too subtle about it. Why? he wondered. Stacey certainly didn't need his input. She was doing fine on her own steam.

About to beg off, Brad looked down at her face. A look in her eyes silently entreated him not to leave. He'd always had trouble refusing that look. Now was no exception. With a stifled sigh, Brad deposited his weary torso on the sofa beside her.

As he sank into the cushions, it occurred to him that, aside from the short drive home he couldn't even remember, this was the first time he'd been off his feet since before he'd entered the OR.

Days like this made him wish he'd gotten a desk job, pushing papers around. At least you didn't run the risk of having someone's death or paralysis on your conscience. And you got to sit all day. He shook himself free of his thoughts and realized that the man his wife had invited into their home was asking him something.

It turned out to be a polite inquiry about his field of expertise. He answered, then glanced to see that Stacey had a pad on her lap. On it was a list of neatly printed questions he assumed she intended to ask each contractor.

He had to admit, he was impressed with her thoroughness. Impressed that she actually wanted this much information. Until he'd witnessed this, he would have said these questions were too well thought out to have come from his wife. The Stacey he knew usually flew by the seat of her pants. And, at times, came in for some very bumpy landings.

But then, to be fair, that was only a casual observation on his part. Admittedly, he wasn't usually around to watch her do her balancing act between home and work. There seemed to be more to his wife than he would have initially thought. It caught him off guard to learn that after all these years, she could still surprise him.

The session, mercifully, continued for only a few more minutes. Approximately ten minutes from the time that Brad had come in to join them, Stacey rose to her feet. Crossing to him, she extended her hand to the man sitting on the end of their sofa.

"Thank you, J.D., I think we have everything we need." The man rose, obviously not very happy that he hadn't gotten a commitment from them. As if to placate him, Stacey asked, "How quickly can you get started from the time we call you?"

The question evoked a smile. J.D. took out a rather beaten-up-looking PDA from his back pocket. Turning it on, he waited for the light to come on and then tapped with his stylus a couple of things on the tiny LCD screen. Images shifted.

He looked up, addressing only her. "Two weeks." It seemed like a good answer.

Stacey nodded in response, all the while leading the man to the front door.

"That sounds good to me." She opened the door and stepped back, giving him clear access to the outside world. "We'll be in touch. Thank you very much for stopping by. We appreciate it."

Stacey closed the door, securing the lock, and then turned around with a sigh. The first interview was over. She'd know better what to do and say the next time around.

"So, when's he starting?" Brad asked moodily once it was just the two of them again.

Stacey looked surprised at her husband's question. "On our house?"

"Well, yes."

She laughed softly and said, more to herself than to him, "Hopefully never."

CHAPTER 18

Brad looked at her, confused. His wife had sounded so positive only moments earlier when she was talking to the contractor. She sounded just as positive now, except that the conclusion was one-hundred-and-eighty degrees from the first one. Had she finally come to her senses?

"So you've changed your mind about remodeling the house?"

Stacey had begun to walk back to the family room. The contractor had left his estimate on the coffee table, along with a list of references and even a brochure. She would hold on to those. Just in case.

"No," she told him, "just about letting J.D. do it." There had been only about five minutes during the first ten that she'd contemplated hiring the man, but it would have been rude to cut him short and she was open to persuasion.

Brad sighed. He should have known it was too good to be true. Without thinking, he followed her to the other room.

"Out of curiosity, what took him out of the running?" He was too tired to attempt to block the sarcasm from his voice. "Was it his haircut?"

It seemed strange to her that Brad would think she based things on something as shallow as looks. She knew for a fact that looks never entered into any decision that he made when it came to hiring the nurses who worked for him.

"He was too laid back."

Brad thought for a minute, trying to make sense of her comment. "I thought you didn't like pushy people."

"I don't." Nothing turned her off more quickly than a fast-talking salesman. "But I do like people who are enthusiastic about their work. He didn't have a single suggestion when I showed him the drawings. He just said everything was fine."

Now, that might have been just to get on her good side, which was why she'd decided to hang on to his papers. If no one else rose up head and shoulders above the rest after she'd conducted all of her interviews, she might revisit her opinion about Conrad. But for now, the man was going to the bottom of the list.

Brad looked at her. "Drawings?"

She nodded. "Of the plans I worked up." Beckoning him over to the coffee table, Stacey opened the oversize bright yellow folder that was on it.

He'd thought the folder belonged to the contractor. The color had been a definite turn off for him. He'd never cared for yellow, preferring more somber colors. Curious now, Brad turned the folder around to get a better look at the drawings. Sitting on the edge of the table, he went through them, one by one. There appeared to be at least one sketch for each room in the house.

Closing the folder, he turned it back around and looked at her. "I didn't know you could draw."

Stacey half lifted one shoulder carelessly. "I guess the subject never came up."

"We've been together for more than thirty years." He lumped in the time that they had gone together with the years they had spent as a married couple. "How could it not have come up?" He opened the folder again and looked at the top drawing, amazed. "This is damn good."

A compliment. More rare than a perfect day Back East, she thought. That it hadn't always been that way was something she wasn't going to dwell on. She savored what she had.

"Thank you."

Brad looked at the drawings a moment longer. Were there other talents, other facets to his wife that he had somehow missed or was oblivious to?

And then his stomach growled, reminding him that he was miles past being hungry. And exhausted to boot. Any exploratory tours of his wife's hidden talents were going to have to wait.

Stacey looked at him. "Is that your stomach?"

He nodded, closing the folder again and rising to his feet. "Can you get me something to eat? It's been a hell of a long day."

She was already crossing to the kitchen. "Sure."

They could have their differences all day long, but she was still his wife, still liked doing for him. Now that Julie and Jim were gone, Brad was her only excuse to experiment in the kitchen. If there were only herself to cook for, she knew that she would have taken most of her meals standing up, at the sink, eating from something that came off the shelf. It always seemed like too much trouble to cook just for herself.

He found he had just enough strength to turn his head in her direction. "I'm going to get myself a drink." And with that, he made his way to the family room.

More than food, he realized, he needed to unwind. Because

he was both exhausted and uptight at the same time. Maybe once he was relaxed, he'd call the hospital to see how Mr. Simmons was doing. The man should be out of recovery and in the ICU in about another half hour.

Stacey raised her voice so that he could hear her as he walked away. "Hard day?"

"Yes."

A huge sigh had accompanied the admission, saying volumes more than the single word could.

Stacey crossed to the doorway as he poured Scotch into a chunky glass. "Want to talk about it?"

Glass in hand, he sank down into the recliner. He didn't even seem to know she was only a few steps away. "No."

That sounded like her Brad, she thought. Stacey withdrew and went back to the kitchen.

In the beginning, when their relationship was fresh and new, Brad would talk about everything, sharing with her this brand-new world that he found himself in. But it had been years since then, she thought sadly, washing her hands. Slowly, as the surgeries became more familiar, more commonplace to him, as the different paths he trod took on a semblance of sameness, Brad stopped verbally bringing his work home.

She dried her hands on a kitchen towel, then draped it over the back of one of the swivel stools. She wasn't sure if Brad had divorced himself from it, or had chosen to divorce her from it, but the result was the same. She knew nothing about the days he spent, the gut-wrenching, soul-searching moments he endured, both during a surgery and after, making decisions that permanently affected the lives of his patients.

And him.

"Thanks for sitting in," she called out. Opening the refrigerator, she removed the large pot of stew she'd put there less than two hours ago. "I think interviews go better when a man's present."

It bothered her sometimes that this was still a fact of life, but there wasn't much she could do about it.

"Why's that?"

Brad's voice sounded sleepy to her. She started moving faster, reaching into the cupboard for a large bowl. She placed it on the counter.

"Because, no matter what strides we've taken in the workplace, mechanics and plumbers and contractors still have a tendency to take advantage when they're dealing with a woman."

"Advantage?" He said the word as if he were chewing on it. "You mean sexually?"

Stacey smiled to herself as she shook her head. He really did live in a bubble all his own sometimes, didn't he?

But then, as a man, especially one with the kind of presence he had, Brad had never had to encounter this kind of thing. Whenever he entered the room, there was something about her husband that told people he knew what he was about, that he wasn't about to be taken advantage of by anyone. Ever. And no one had ever tried.

She envied him that.

"No, honey, financially." Looking around for a ladle, she found one in the third drawer. "They like to up their fees because they think we don't know what's involved."

Which was why she'd taken a night course at the local junior college on auto repair. She'd taken another course on basic plumbing for the same reason. So that she knew what was involved and, more important, so that none of the repairmen she called in could take her for a ride.

After removing the lid from the cast-iron pot, Stacey ladled out a healthy portion of the stew into the bowl.

She might as well tell him, she thought, and get this out of the way. "I've got two more contractors scheduled for tomorrow night."

She heard him groan loudly from the other room. "How many of these contractors are you planning on seeing, all told?"

"As many as it takes." Until she found the man she felt was right for the job. "Right now, I've got the names of six altogether, but I'm still looking around." Finding the right contractor was turning out to be almost as important as finding the right man to marry.

"Uh-huh."

Putting the lid back on the large pot, she smiled to herself. There was a definite lack of enthusiasm there, but at least Brad wasn't shutting her out the way he'd been doing for the past two weeks. She opened the microwave door and put the bowl inside, then put a large plastic cover over it. She tapped in a minute and a half, then pressed the start button. Brad didn't like anything to be too hot, but she didn't think he'd want to have parts of his dinner ice cold, either.

Unaware she was doing it, she caught her lower lip between her teeth, thinking. Maybe whatever had happened today at the hospital that he wasn't talking about had put things in perspective for him. Or, at the very least, had consumed all of his energy so that he wasn't railing about her lack of fiscal responsibility anymore.

The microwave bell went through its paces, counting off the last three seconds audibly, then chimed, announcing that it had finished its part of the dinner ritual.

Stacey opened up the door and used pot holders to remove the bowl. She poured the stew, steaming now, into yet another bowl. This way, he wouldn't accidentally burn his fingers.

You coddle him too much.

"Yes, Mother," she murmured softly to the voice in her head that echoed what her mother had told her more than once. "I know."

"Okay," she announced, raising her voice, "dinner's ready. It's stew. The meat and vegetables are so tender, they'll melt on your tongue. You won't have to chew a thing," she promised. Stacey placed the bowl on the dining room table in front of his chair.

There was no response from the other room. "Honey?"

Still nothing.

In no mood to shout, Stacey walked into the family room. "Didn't you hear me, honey? I said that…"

Brad had fallen sound asleep, the chunky glass half filled with alcohol still clutched in his hand. He'd had maybe a couple of sips, no more.

Stacey smiled to herself. "Poor baby," she whispered. Very gently, she removed the glass from his hand and placed it on the coffee table.

CHAPTER 19

"I found one," Stacey announced late one evening in the dining room nearly four weeks later.

Coming in from the kitchen, she set a plate in front of Brad and took a seat opposite him. The steak's aroma wafted up, moving around the still air.

Though tempted by the sight of the steak, he glanced up at Stacey. "Found what?" He wasn't terribly interested in the answer at the moment, but he knew that he was supposed to ask.

Her own portion was half the size of his and she didn't even want that. Her appetite tended to wane this time of the evening. "Not what, who."

"Okay," he amended gamely, taking another bite, "found who?"

She had spent every free moment she had going over her notes as well as tracking down references and reviewing estimates. She had a multitude of pros and cons lists, one for each contractor who had been to the house. "A contractor."

He couldn't refrain from allowing a light note of cynicism to enter his voice. "How could you have missed them? There's been a different one underfoot every time I came home."

He was exaggerating. It wasn't an everyday event. She only

scheduled appointments for Thursday and Friday afternoons after work. The rest of the time she'd spent doubling up at the office. Not by choice but by necessity. Andrea, the woman she'd taught to do the medical group's insurance billing, had gone into labor almost a full month before her due date. With Sheila, the other receptionist, on vacation, she'd had to do her own work and cover for Andrea until such time as the new mother felt strong enough to get back on her feet and back into the office.

Stacey didn't bother correcting him. Brad hated being corrected, and her need for tranquillity was greater than her need to be right.

"I meant that I found *the* one." Was that a wary look in his eyes? She listed the winning contractor's attributes. "Someone who comes highly recommended. Who'll do a good job—and who's reasonably priced," she said, saving what she knew Brad would think of as the best for last.

He blew out a breath, feeling a little like a freedom fighter discovering that the occupation of his country was finally at an end.

"So this means that you're finally going to stop interviewing contractors."

She took a small sip of her wine. She didn't normally drink at dinner, but tonight she felt like celebrating. Phase one was over and she was going to be moving on to phase two shortly. Could a beautiful, new-looking house be far behind?

"Yes, thank God."

He laughed shortly. There was no humor in the sound. "Just when I was getting used to coming home and trying to find a parking space within walking distance of my front door."

Reaching across the table, Stacey moved the serving dish of diced, roasted potatoes glazed with Parmesan cheese closer to her husband. He tended to have tunnel vision when it came to food, and right now, all he could see was his steak.

When he looked up at her, she offered a tight smile in response to his sarcasm.

"I guess now you won't have to."

He inclined his head, as if to agree with her. "So what's this saint-with-a-tool-belt's name?"

"Alex Stone."

The name was unfamiliar to him, but then, he hadn't committed any of the names of the contractors to memory. That was her job, since this was her project. He was just the outsider she refused to listen to.

Still, he thought the last name rather appropriate, given the man's chosen profession.

"Let me guess." His mouth twisted in a half smile. "He likes to work with masonry."

She and Alex hadn't even discussed her plans for the patio. That would come last, after everything inside was taken care of. "No."

As if suddenly becoming aware of the potatoes, he picked up the serving spoon and transferred the vegetable from the bowl to his plate. "Too bad, he could get a lot of mileage out of that. No Stone Unturned, things like that."

Retiring the spoon, Brad sampled the potatoes as if he'd never had them before. They were good and he began to eat with pleasure. She could see it on his face even if she rarely heard it expressed verbally.

Brad wasn't prone to wasting words on compliments. He'd

pointed out long ago that if he didn't like what she served, he wouldn't be eating it. She knew better now than to ask if he liked a meal.

She was just about to fill the silence when he raised his eyes to hers and asked, "I take it he commented on your drawings."

She was surprised he remembered that, her reason for not being keen on the very first contractor she'd interviewed. She smiled at him. "Yes, as a matter of fact, he did. And he had a lot of good suggestions." Her enthusiasm emerged and took over. She'd promised herself to remain low key around Brad, because he didn't share her feelings, but she couldn't help herself. "That's what sold me. He's on the same page as I am."

"Sounds like a prince. Which one was he?"

Stacey shook her head. "You didn't meet him. I interviewed him the day you came home from the hospital after eleven."

He nodded grimly. He knew exactly the day she was referring to. There were times when his days all seemed to run together, but not that day. Because on that day he'd lost a patient. A patient he'd fought to keep alive. He took failure hard.

No matter what his former instructors and his colleagues said about distancing himself from the people who came to him seeking help, he couldn't do it. Couldn't stand apart and pretend it hadn't happened or that it hadn't affected him. Deeply. A life had dribbled through his hands. One moment, he'd had a firm grip, certain he was winning the battle. The next, it was gone and he had lost.

Just like that. His patient had expired.

And he'd been left with a guilt that he had never learned how to cope with. So he'd buried it, denying its existence.

He vaguely remembered coming home that night and just crawling into bed, praying for oblivion. He didn't remember driving. Luckily, the car knew the way.

Brad took a breath, realizing he'd allowed the moment to haunt him. The moment that he'd looked down at Bart Johnson's face, discovering that no amount of chest compressions, no amount of volts traveling through the paddles that he'd been applying to the man's still heart, was going to bring him back.

He shook it off. Stacey was watching him. There was sympathy as well as confusion in her blue eyes. Sympathy was second nature to Stacey. If he'd wanted to, he could lay his burden down before her, put his head on her shoulder and for a second shrug off the intense weight of his guilt. Stacey would be there for him. But he couldn't do it. Men were supposed to suck it up and just continue with their lives. It was almost the only thing he remembered his father saying to him.

He looked back at his dinner. The steak, what there was left of it, was getting cold. He began to eat again. "So when does he start?"

Something had just happened here, Stacey thought. It seemed to her that Brad was withdrawing from her more and more these days. And she had no idea what to do about it, how to get him to talk to her. All she could do was wait it out. And pray that it would change.

"As soon as possible, I hope," she answered.

Brad looked annoyed. "That's the 'date' he gave you? 'As soon as possible?' Seems to me that this answer-to-a-prayer would have been a little more specific."

"He would be, if I gave him the green light."

Mild interest nudged at him. "So, what's stopping you?"

"I want you to meet him first."

"Why?"

Was he baiting her, or was his apathy really that pronounced? "Because you're the husband. You should be more involved in this process. It's your house, too."

Brad shrugged. If it was his house, then he'd have a say in this and they wouldn't be dealing with contractors. But he didn't feel like arguing with her. At least, not just yet.

"Make the appointment," he told her.

CHAPTER 20

It took less and less these days to tire Brad. He was getting old, he thought as he drove home from the hospital. Though a little after six, there was no sign of evening.

He would have preferred the darkness. He wanted shadows.

Forty-eight was old, and he didn't care what Stacey kept saying to the contrary. Stacey lived in some pretend world. She didn't have to face what he did on almost a daily basis.

Cars whizzed by him on the freeway, their owners intent on getting home. He steadfastly maintained the speed limit. And was the slowest vehicle in all three lanes.

In the operating room, God wasn't his co-pilot like that old classic movie title maintained. Death was. God didn't seem to be anywhere around, especially today. But Death had stood there, looking over his shoulder, waiting for a chance to snatch away his patient. Waiting for a chance to undermine his confidence.

Both had happened today.

He knew that at times, the odds were against him. That he would lose some of the battles. But he didn't like losing. And he didn't like having his confidence in his abilities, in himself, shaken.

What made it worse was having his confidence sapped away in his own home as well.

This time, it wasn't the ever-present aura of death that was responsible. It was a contractor. *The* contractor, to put it in Stacey's terms.

As he arrived home, he felt like turning around again. If he wasn't so tired, maybe he would have. But then, it was only postponing the inevitable. Stacey would just reschedule. Her tenacity astounded him. He knew she was stubborn about little things, but this was the first time that her stubbornness had pitted her against him. Against his wishes.

Frowning, Brad got out of the car, slammed the driver's side door harder than he should have and made his way up the walk. He tried the doorknob before reaching for his key. She'd left it open again. Sighing, he walked in.

And was immediately greeted with joyful dissonance and some drooling by not just Rosie, but Dog as well. He fondly petted his pet and then grudgingly petted the other animal, who appeared ecstatic at the attention. He hated to admit it—and certainly not to Stacey—but the mongrel was winning him over.

"Down, guys," he ordered in a voice that was far too friendly to make an impression on either animal. "I've got to get this over with."

He absently wondered how Stacey's contractor would react if he were rushed by both dogs. Would he leave and not look back? It was something to consider....

Brad followed the sound of voices from the rear of the house. And a deep male voice, laughing.

He disliked the contractor immediately.

Alex Stone sat in his family room, obviously making himself comfortable on his recliner, looking more like the Hollywood version of a construction worker than someone who actually made his living driving nails into drywall.

The man was too damn good-looking, Brad thought, annoyed. And too muscular. Stone wore a long-sleeved shirt that had been rolled up as far as it could go, poetically emphasizing his biceps, which seemed to flex as he breathed.

Introductions were made and Alex rose to shake hands. The man had a hell of a grip. Damn, it had been a long time since he'd been to the gym, Brad thought as he took a seat on the sofa, suddenly aware just how out of shape he was in comparison to the man on the recliner. Maybe he could lobby for an extra hour to be added to the day. Or better yet, find a way to manage to do without sleep.

Just thinking about it made him tired.

His mind was wandering. Stone had talked almost the entire time. Brad tried to focus.

"You won't regret this," Stone was saying. His broad smile took them both in, but predominantly, Brad noticed, the contractor had addressed most of his statements to Stacey.

He was regretting this already, Brad thought. But then, it wasn't as if he had any real say in the matter, no matter what Stacey said about wanting to pull him into the process. The inheritance was hers and she was rubbing his nose in it. Nicely. The way she did everything. Nicely.

Somehow, that made it sting all the more.

"So—" Stone looked from him to Stacey "—when would you like me to get started?"

Instead of immediately giving him a date, the way Brad fully expected her to, Stacey turned and looked at him. "Brad?"

Never.

What would stud-man think of that, he wondered. What if he said exactly what was on his mind and could make it stick? If he told the man to pack up his reference book of pretty pictures and get the hell out of here, never to come back?

The thought made him smile.

But there was no sense dwelling on it. That wasn't going to happen. So instead, Brad shrugged casually in response.

"That's pretty much up to you," he told Stacey. His eyes shifted to Stone for a moment. No, he just didn't like him. "The two of you come up with something?"

Stone took the initiative. "I can have the crew out on Monday, bright and early if there are no objections." He looked from one to the other, waiting.

The crew. It sounded like a wrecking service, Brad thought. It also sounded as if no one was hiring stud-man despite his biceps.

"Work a little slow?" he couldn't help asking.

Stone had a two-thousand-watt blinding smile. And perfect teeth. Something else not to like him for. God, was he having a midlife crisis? Couldn't be. He was too old for that. If it were a midlife crisis, that meant he intended to live until he was ninety-six.

"Actually, no," Stone told him. "This crew that I'm calling in is busy finishing up work on a house in Tustin right now."

"This crew," Brad echoed. Even though he wanted no part of this conversation that he felt should have remained strictly between Stacey and Biceps Boy, he couldn't help letting himself be reeled in. "You have more than one?"

Stone nodded. His biceps flexed as he leaned forward. "Two, actually, although I'm hoping to put together one more by the end of the year. The other crew's working on renovating a church in Corona Del Mar."

A church. He supposed that made the man reputable. Brad laughed shortly.

"Guess you'd better do a good job there, or you'll be in trouble with the Boss." Stone was looking at him as if he didn't quite follow his meaning. "You know, no cutting corners."

Embarrassment welled up inside Stacey. The smile on the contractor's face tightened just a little. What the hell had come over Brad? He didn't act this way.

"I never cut corners," Alex told him, his voice mild, even. "That would be shoddy. And dishonest. A contractor relies on word of mouth, which has to be good. Anything else and his reputation goes down the tubes."

Brad shrugged, uncomfortable with his own behavior. He wasn't entirely certain what had come over him. "Sorry, didn't mean to offend."

But he had, Stacey thought. What had gotten into him? He was always polite, if distant. This behavior was completely out of character for Brad. He was acting like a common, ignorant lout. Brad had faults, but the need to build himself up by putting someone else down had never been one of them.

"No offense taken," Stone replied.

But she knew there had been. Lines had been drawn in the sand, even if she couldn't see them. She did her best to gloss over the incident.

Turning to face the contractor, she asked, "What time on Monday?"

He didn't pause to think. "Seven. My guy likes to get an early start."

"And just exactly what is your 'guy' going to be getting an early start on?" Brad asked.

Alex glanced down at the notes. "Your kitchen."

Brad scowled, looking toward the area beyond the family room. It was a small kitchen by modern standards, yet satisfactory enough to him. His opinion didn't matter, though, so there was no point in voicing it. "I guess I'd better get my breakfast early, then."

And then he paused as another thought occurred to him. One of the doctors at the hospital had issued condolences to him when he'd heard that he was about to begin remodeling. "How long is this going to take?"

This time, Stone did pause, doing mental calculations. "Depends on how fast everything gets here. Four, five weeks."

Brad looked at Stacey. "What's everything?"

"Cabinets, sink, the granite for the counter. Tile for the floor," Stone enumerated. Leaning forward, he reached into his back pocket and pulled out several sheets of paper, folded in fourths. He handed them to Stacey. "When you called me back the other day, I took the liberty of jotting down the names and addresses of some of the stores in Orange County that carry the materials you'll need to look at."

Stacey tried not to notice that the papers were still warm. She felt something odd and disturbing moving through her. Forcing herself to glance down at the names, she couldn't make out a single one. It had nothing to do with Stone's handwriting, which was crisp and perfect, and everything to do with the fact that her pulse had accelerated.

Belatedly, she realized she hadn't said anything. She forced a smile to her lips. "That was very thoughtful. Thank you, I'm sure this is going to be very helpful. We're novices at this."

"Hey, even God had a first day," Stone told her.

Brad looked from his wife to the man he was allowing to invade his house. He felt completely shut out, like an outsider in his own home.

CHAPTER 21

Because I don't want to," Brad retorted with an air of finality, "that's why."

Annoyed and frustrated, Stacey stared at Brad and wondered what she ever saw in him. Whatever it was, there was no trace of it in the man sitting at their kitchen table, absently poking at the remains of the vegetable omelet on his plate. His eyes and most of his attention was focused elsewhere, on an article in the local section of the *L.A. Times*.

Stacey struggled to rein in her irritation. Losing her temper wasn't going to get her anywhere. She'd learned that years ago. Brad did not respond well to hot words or displays of temper. And coaxing, when he was being stubborn, had to be conducted with a light, delicate touch, as if she were painting a face on the head of a pin.

You'd think she was asking him for his last pint of blood instead of asking him to accompany her to do something that affected both of them. But at times, trying to get Brad to cooperate was like trying to teach a seal how to walk upright. A miracle or two was seriously needed before that could occur.

Eight in the morning and she was tired already. She thought back almost fondly to the hectic years when she'd been raising both overenergetic kids without two seconds to rub together. Back then, she couldn't wait to have them grown. Now they were gone and she missed them terribly. And she wasn't out of the infant-raising game, either. The care and feeding of a husband was far more difficult than nurturing two children had ever been.

Stacey tried again, hoping to appeal to that sympathetic side of him that had initially sent Brad to medicine, seeking a career. "I don't want to go and pick everything out by myself."

He raised his eyes from the article only for a moment. "Then don't."

"You're not like other husbands, Brad. You actually have good taste."

Setting the paper down—he was pretty close to finished with the article, anyway—Brad raised an eyebrow at the statement, wondering if she was complimenting him or if this was some kind of hidden put-down. Stacey wasn't given to being nasty, but lately, she seemed to be changing from the woman he thought he knew. The one who never rocked the boat.

"And this is your house, too."

So she said. But he was beginning to have his doubts about that. "If it's my house, then why can't it stay the way it is?" he challenged. "Without sucking in everything your crazy uncle left you."

Her immediate response was to defend Uncle Titus. But that would only lead her from the path she was trying to walk. She blew out a breath, wondering if she was just beating her head against the wall, trying to get Brad involved.

"We've been through this so often, I feel like I could put numbers to the conversations." Even so, she went over it again, this time in summary form, hoping that it would finally put a dent in that thick head of his. "Because things are falling apart and need to be fixed, so why not fix them in a way that's pleasing rather than putting Band-Aids on the problem? Because Uncle Titus said I should spend the money the way I want. And because—" and she knew that for Brad, this was the clincher "—we signed a contract with Alex. We can't back out without forfeiting the down payment."

That had gotten to him the second she'd told him about it. He'd thought she had more sense than to be taken in this way. "Which I wouldn't have given him until I saw some work done," he underscored.

"It's the way things *are* done," she pointed out. She removed his empty plate and placed it in the sink, fighting the urge to throw the plate instead. Lately, it felt as if her temper came only one way—frayed.

"No, they're not," he contradicted with feeling. "I don't ask my patients to put money up front before I do the surgery."

She closed her eyes, searching for strength. Running water over the plate for a second, she left it where it was and sat down at the table opposite him. She was afraid that if she sat next to him, she'd be tempted to strangle him. He was being so damn thick-headed and stubborn.

"It's not the same, Brad." No, she wasn't going to let this dissolve into another argument. She wanted them to be a team, not opponents. "Now, we need tile, granite, cabinets, appliances, fixtures, all that good stuff." She saw him wince. "Please, please, *please* come with me to start picking things out."

Brad muttered something unintelligible under his breath, then drained the last of his coffee, now very cold. Setting the cup back down on the saucer, he looked at her. "Why don't you get 'Alex' to go with you?"

Her eyes never left his. "He offered."

She saw Brad's complexion grow just a shade rosier. It had nothing to do with a healthy glow. "What?

"He offered," she repeated with absolutely no feeling, no indication one way or the other as to her reaction to the contractor's offer. "When I gave him the check for the down payment, he offered to come with me to help choose some of the materials if you weren't able to go. He said most of his customers usually valued a second opinion."

That was probably not all they valued, Brad thought darkly. He felt something stirring inside of him, something unsettling he couldn't name. Exasperation, probably, he guessed. And possibly the beginning of an ulcer.

Disgruntled, Brad looked at his watch. It was a little after eight-thirty. "I guess I can give you an hour."

He was due on the golf course today at eleven. It was Saturday and one of those rare days when he actually had no patients recovering from surgery at the hospital, so there was no reason to go in and make his rounds. He'd planned on unwinding with three other doctors.

"An hour?" she echoed.

The man had no clue as to what was involved, did he? She'd already done a little preliminary scouting, heading up the clogged San Diego Freeway after work on two separate occasions. It amounted to getting her toe in the water. She was going for the full leg today, or at least more than just an ankle. That was going to take longer than an hour, even if they were quick.

"Take it or leave it."

Definitely not the man she fell in love with and married, she thought.

And yet she smiled at him, inclining her head the way she always had when she'd given in to him. "I'll take it, of course."

Once they were there, he couldn't very well just leave her and go back home, could he? she reasoned. Having gotten him to agree to look, she intended to take him to as many places as she possibly could today. God only knew, between his work and his stubbornness, when she would get another opportunity to get him to go with her.

"Why in God's name would anyone make so many different kinds of tiles in so many different shapes and colors?" Brad grumbled just as they walked into the third store devoted to surfaces found within bathrooms, kitchens and pools.

Or maybe it was the fourth.

By his own admission, he'd lost count as to how many stores they had actually entered. Squares of ceramic, marble and God only knew what other kind of material were dancing before his eyes. It was worse than a blinding migraine. Instead of bolts of zigzagging light, he was seeing an infinite number of patterns set in some kind of stone.

"I guess it's for people who are having trouble making up their minds," Stacey replied.

Like you, she added silently.

Talk about a woman having trouble making up her mind, Brad had turned out to be ten times worse. There was something wrong with almost every piece he looked at. Too rough, too slippery, too busy, too bland. Too something. And that "something" was the deciding factor that ruled out one sample after another in store after store.

To say she was stunned was an understatement. After the second store, Stacey had fully expected her husband to announce that he was tired and that he wanted to go home, or at least drop her off there before he headed for the golf course. But thoughts of the golf course had apparently vanished from his mind as Brad pored over one tile after another, as intent as if he were searching for the Holy Grail.

After they had left the second store, he'd mumbled something about the third place being the charm. Mystified, she'd gotten into the car and pointed out a third store that was part of "tile row," the unofficial name for a cluster of tile stores that ran along a busy thoroughfare in Anaheim. There seemed to be stores that handled nothing but tile in one form or another for as far as the eye could see.

And now, here they were, entering their fifth store. The daunting side of their pilgrimage through Tile Land, Stacey thought wearily, was that they were still tileless.

She'd expected too much by hoping for an instant rapport. It certainly wasn't for lack of trying. The back of their car now contained an abundance of samples, with the promise of more to come. If this kept up, they would be able to do all three bathrooms in an eclectic mosaic motif, using all different pieces.

She'd learned something today. She'd had no idea that Brad could be so terribly fussy. Married all this time and she'd just learned something new about the man. The realization, even about such a minor thing, took her breath away. She would have sworn that she knew him inside and out.

Brad made no response to her comment about there being so many different tiles due to the inability of some people to make up their minds—he knew it was directed at him. It wasn't that he was having trouble making up his mind. His mind knew it didn't like what it saw. Not really. Nothing stood out. Nothing struck him as being exactly right. As being pleasing enough to live with.

Odd, he supposed, since he didn't actually care one way or another.

Still, since she'd asked and he was going to all this trouble, Brad wanted to feel satisfied with what he picked. So far, the feeling had eluded him. After several hours' worth of traipsing from one store to another, the only thing they managed to agree on happened completely by accident.

One of the stores dealt with the complete kitchen instead of just the counters, walls and floor.

"Nice wood," Brad commented out of the blue as he stopped to take in one display.

"I like the stain," Stacey agreed. It was something fancifully called "breezewood," she discovered, reading the name out loud. Specifically, breezewood with caramel tones, applied to maple.

Stacey breathed a huge sigh of relief. "Looks like we have a winner."

Brad looked at her, confusion knitting together his eyebrows just over his eyes. They were looking for tile and she was pointing at the cabinets. Had he missed something?

CHAPTER 22

Brad stared at her as if she'd just gotten sunstroke. "What are you talking about?"

Stacey indicated the pleasing display arranged around an island. The thought of an island in the center of her kitchen intrigued her. They'd have to do away with the kitchen table, but stools could be arranged around one side of the island. Her mind began to race.

"You like the cabinets, right?"

He'd already told her that, but his response was tentative, halting, as if braced for something more to pop out of the closet.

"Yes."

"Well, so do I." She looked at the cabinets again, envisioning them in her kitchen. "The first thing Alex is going to need once his crew rips out our kitchen are cabinets to put in their place. And I don't see why we need to look around any further since we both seem to like these."

It was nice to stumble across an unexpected bonus like this. Mentally, she'd allotted a minimum of five hours of going from store to store, not to mention more time paging through the catalogs that Alex had left her, looking for just the right cabinets. And here they were, right in front of them.

As if he couldn't quite believe what he was hearing, Brad

stared at his wife. He recalled stories he'd heard from other doctors. Stories about how their wives could never make up their minds about things. That it always took multiple trips to the mall before a single item was finally purchased.

And here she was, saying she was satisfied.

He'd always known Stacey was different. Maybe he hadn't appreciated just how different. "You don't want to look any further for cabinets?"

"No. Why should we? You like them, I like them, they'll make the kitchen look brighter and breezier." Her lips twisted slightly at the play on words. Until now, she'd never heard of a color called "breezewood." It seemed almost like serendipity.

"So would a new coat of white paint," Brad couldn't help pointing out, "and it wouldn't wind up costing nearly as much."

Brad had come a long way today. She couldn't fault him for a little backsliding. "The new coat of paint is part of the deal," she told him matter-of-factly. She could see that he hadn't even considered that. "They're going to be ripping all the cabinets out and putting new ones in."

She paused to open one double-hinged door and saw that the shelves inside spun around, affording easy access to whatever was stored inside. No more getting down on her hands and knees, foraging for a pot that had gotten lodged at the back of the shelf. Funny how such little things could matter so much. But it made her smile. She closed the door again as she went on.

"That's going to wreak havoc on the paint job we have in the kitchen—especially since," she added pointedly, "if I recall correctly, the last time we had it painted was more than seven years ago."

She kept harping on how old everything was. The furniture, the rugs, the paint job. "What's this obsession with getting rid of everything because it's past a certain age?" he asked. Before she had a chance to answer, he laughed shortly. "I'm surprised you haven't tossed me out."

She smiled at him, batting her lashes comically. "Don't be silly, Brad, I put in too much time and effort into you. I'm not about to start from scratch with someone new."

Wandering from one store to another had sapped what little sense of humor he had. "I didn't say anything about replacing me."

Her expression was totally innocent. Turning her back on him, she tested the drawers. They rolled beautifully. Unlike the drawers in her cabinets at home. Those kept getting stuck, moving like square wheels along concrete. "I thought that was what you implied."

"No." He moved, blocking her way so that she was forced to look at him. "Is that what you were thinking?" he pressed.

"Have you found something you like?" the salesman asked smoothly, picking that moment to join them.

"As a matter of fact," she said, pausing to smile at her husband before continuing, "we have."

This was going to be a joint effort, and she was going to drag Brad into it, kicking and screaming, even if it killed her.

When it was done, they left the store. The whole ordeal of filling out forms had taken a little more than three hours. Way over the time limit he had set for her.

Although weary, she still felt a sense of triumph dancing through her. They'd placed their first order. The remodeling had begun. She could hardly believe it. After all this time, it was finally happening.

Thank you, Uncle Titus. I couldn't have done this without you.

Brad was scowling as he walked to the car. She would have thought that he'd be relieved. High on the triumph of finding the right cabinets, she'd decided to postpone looking for tile until another day. For all intents and purposes, the man was free.

"What's the matter?" she asked, then braced herself for the answer.

He looked at her over the hood of the car. "I don't like handing my credit card to a stranger."

Brad was quick to point out every article he came across dealing with identity theft, always asking if she was being careful with her cards. So far, they'd never had a single problem. She was fairly optimistic that it would remain that way. And realistic enough to know that the cards were a necessity of life.

"In our case, it's safer letting the salesman run the card through than handing it to a family member—Julie," she added when he looked at her, puzzled. His expression indicated no enlightenment. "Remember that first credit card statement we received her first month away at college?"

And then it came back to him. Brad shuddered. He'd forgotten all about that. Forgotten the misgivings he'd initially had, letting his only daughter leave home and go somewhere where he couldn't have daily contact with her. When the outlandish credit card statement had arrived, he'd blown up over the amount she'd charged in one month, but in his heart, though he admitted it to no one, he knew that it had been a matter of displacement. The real reason for the fit of temper was that his baby girl was growing up and he felt cast off. That his role had suddenly diminished in her life and that he was only to take care of the bills, but not the girl.

Brad cleared his throat, pushing the memory away. Like everything else, he'd dealt with it. Fought his war quietly and gone on. "Julie outgrew that."

Stacey laughed. "Lucky for us, not so lucky for the economy." Brad's expression gave no indication that he saw the humor in her words. She addressed his complaint, hoping to put it to rest. "This is a reputable business, Brad. We just placed a sizable order and they require payment. We can't exactly carry around the kind of cash that we'd need to buy those cabinets."

Cash was his payment of choice, but he had to admit that it was inconvenient when they were dealing with the amounts this remodeling venture was necessitating. "There are always checks."

Stacey did her best to look sympathetic. "And if we did that, we'd be giving him our checking account number." She managed the statement with a straight face, only to see the light dawning in his eyes. Oh, God, the next thing Brad was going to do was try to clamp down on the checking account. "I was only kidding, Brad," she insisted wearily. "In this life, we have to take some risks. We can't just hang back, afraid to venture out."

"I take more than my share of risks on the operating table," he informed her, his voice distant. "I've got someone's life in my hands, Stacey. Do you realize what kind of pressure that is? One wrong move, one wrong decision on my part, and life as that patient knows it is over."

She knew the kind of pressure Brad was under, knew that it didn't lessen as the years went on. Because each case was new. Each case was like the first one, except he had a little more experience to fall back on. That allowed him a measure of control that had been missing in the early years.

"Then this should be a cakewalk in comparison," she pointed out. When he said nothing in response, she tried to tap into the cheerful feeling she'd had a moment ago. "I think maybe we've seen enough for one day. We bought the cabinets. I'd say we've made a great start."

In response, Brad moved his shoulders restlessly in a half shrug. And then, as if her words played back in his head, he looked at her.

"A start?"

"Well, yes. A start," she repeated. "We're not finished. We haven't picked out the tile for the bathrooms or the kitchen. And then there's the granite for the countertops and the tub for the master bathroom." She enumerated the items as they came to her in no particular order. "Not to mention the fixtures—"

"Then don't mention them," he barked, fishing in his pocket for his key. Any sense of contentment he'd fleetingly entertained was gone. The process wasn't over.

"Brad—"

Finding his key, he unlocked the driver's side door, then took a deep breath. "We're going to have to do this again, aren't we?"

When he wasn't snapping her head off, when he looked like just a tired husband, struggling to keep his end up, she could feel her heart softening toward him. "I'm afraid so."

He frowned. "You know, there are people who get paid to shop for other people. Have you thought of getting someone like that to pick out all that stuff you just mentioned?"

"You mean like an interior decorator? No." And they both knew why. Neither one of them would be happy with someone else's choices. "Because you just demonstrated that you have very specific tastes. If we do all those renovations and you wind up hating the way the house looks, then what's the point?"

He sighed, glancing down the long block. There were tile stores as far as the eye could see. Tile stores that they would probably be entering sometime in the foreseeable future. "I hate it when you talk logic."

Amused, Stacey laughed. Impulsively, she rounded the car and came to his side. She kissed his cheek. It occurred to her that it had been a long time since she'd experienced that impulse.

CHAPTER 23

Stacey drew the calendar away from the kitchen wall and tugged until the nail gave way. It was the last thing she removed from the kitchen.

Calendar in hand, she stood back and glanced around.

The kitchen looked so barren. Just like when they first moved here. Except for the refrigerator, which was their first major purchase together. Up until that point, they'd lived in furnished apartments that could have easily doubled as shoe boxes.

The only thing they had brought with them in the way of furniture was a secondhand sofa that had long since met its demise. But before she'd called one of the local charities to pick it up, she'd moved it from room to room until it had finally found its way into the garage. The kids had loved it there, turning the space into their own special area. Julie had read books there, and Jim—he'd still been Jimmy at the time—had waged endless battles between his army of action figures.

The reason for the meandering path of the sofa was because she hated giving things up. Even as much as she wanted this remodeling, she was having trouble letting go.

"Stupid," she murmured to herself. It was stupid to get sentimental over pressboard cabinets that were too dark for the kitchen and a floor that had seen many better days.

Putting the calendar into a drawer in the family room, she glanced at her watch. Almost seven. Stacey pressed her hand to her abdomen. She had no idea why she felt so jittery and unsettled. This was a good thing that was happening. She supposed maybe she was nervous because she'd been waiting so long for this to come about. Nervous that perhaps, just perhaps, the remodeling wouldn't go as well as she hoped. That had to be it. There was no other earthly reason for the existence of wild, dueling butterflies to be dive-bombing in her stomach.

Brad had left early this morning. Earlier than usual. He's said something about getting out before the chaos began. She laughed softly to herself, shaking her head. As if it was all going to be cleaned up by the time he returned home again tonight.

No, order wasn't going to be magically restored by the end of Brad's day. It wouldn't be back for a very long time. She made no attempt to drive the point home this morning as he left. With so much to do, she didn't have time for another heated discussion. And she was secretly glad he'd left when he did. Otherwise, Brad would be underfoot, questioning every move that the contractor and his people made.

That was just his way.

She opened the pantry doors for the third time, to make sure everything was gone.

Whenever he did get involved in something, Brad had a tendency to take it apart down to its smallest part, its lowest common denominator. Most people didn't appreciate the kind of intense questioning he was capable of. If they were being paid, they usually grinned without feeling and put up with it. Usually. She wanted nothing scaring off the workers. She'd waited too long for this to happen to suffer yet another delay.

They'd already had one. The order for the cabinets had taken longer than anticipated. The starting date for the re-modeling had to be moved over. But Alex assured her there was no problem. Brad had laughed under his breath and assured her that there would be.

The doorbell rang. Stacey felt her adrenaline soar.

She took a deep breath to steady her nerves. At the sound of the chimes, the dogs began barking in unison. Dog was clearly taking his cue from Rosie.

"You two be quiet or you're both going to be locked up for the duration." For good measure, she added a glare to her words.

Both dogs quieted down and trotted obediently behind her as she went to open the front door. Whenever Julie stopped by, she always had something to toss the dogs and they loved her for it.

But it wasn't Julie on her doorstep this morning. It was Alex. He'd brought two people with him. Apparently his crew consisted of a man and a woman. The woman was a head taller than the man and looked as if she could beat him in an arm-wrestling contest with little to no effort.

As for Alex, whom Stacey was trying hard not to notice, he wore a work shirt and jeans. The jeans were worn and had molded themselves to his body, acting like a second skin. And the sleeves were missing from the work shirt. The man had more arm definition at rest than most men had after a two-hour workout at the gym.

Her mouth went dry. Stacey wondered if she could get one last drink of water from the sink before it was ripped out.

Alex sipped coffee from what looked like one of the largest containers she had ever seen. When he saw her, he stopped drinking. Lowering the container, he flashed her a bone-melting, sunny smile. His eyes as well as his lips were involved.

All of her was involved.

"Good morning, Mrs. Sommers. Beautiful day, isn't it? Ready to get started?"

Stacey took a deep breath before answering. "Absolutely."

He laughed and the sound bathed her. She wondered if he was married. And what did that have to do with the price of tomatoes? He was her contractor and all that mattered was that he did a good job and hired good people. If he was married, single or having an affair with a turtle in no way figured into the job.

"Good to hear," he said. Turning, he stepped to the side as he made the necessary introductions. "This is Joe and Alba." He nodded at the man, then the woman. Looking back at her, he grinned. "They're here to trash your kitchen."

Joe nodded his greeting without saying a word. He looked to be in his own world. Alba was his exact opposite. Flashing a friendly smile, the woman reached over to give her a hearty handshake. It was only then that Stacey saw the woman had a sledgehammer with her, its head resting at her feet while she held on to the shaft with her left hand.

"I just had a difference of opinion with my teenage daughter about the length of her skirt—I thought it should have some—so I'm dying to get started and work off a little tension," she confided. Alba's gray eyes gleamed with anticipation.

"Okay," Stacey murmured, hoping that the woman knew when to stop swinging that hammer. "This way."

Alba picked up her sledgehammer as if it was hollow. Stacey turned on her heel and walked back into her denuded kitchen. Alex kept pace and entered the room right beside her. He held up his hand to keep Alba and Joe from starting.

Stacey looked at him, curious. "Is something wrong?" she asked.

Alex shook his head as he slipped his hand along her shoulder. "I just wanted you to take one last look around. Remember what it was—and envision what it's going to be. Are you envisioning it?" She slowly nodded her head, wishing that she didn't feel as if she should be gulping in air in order to sustain herself. "Close your eyes and see it with your mind, Mrs. Sommers."

One of the scenes from the old movie, *The Rainmaker*, came back to her. A young Burt Lancaster, as Starbuck, was standing beside a very spinsterish looking Katharine Hepburn as Lizzie, one hand on her shoulder, the other sliding along the air as if to create images, weaving a spell and telling Lizzie to envision the possibilities that lay ahead—if only she'd risk a little.

Stacey's breath caught in her throat. She could see herself and Alex in those roles, as those characters. Except that he wasn't a rainmaker, and she wasn't a spinster.

With effort, Stacey shook herself free of the image and returned to her life. It was far from easy. She laughed, although it sounded a little fluttery to her own ear. "I'm afraid that right now, I'm having trouble envisioning getting dinner ready tonight." Her pulse had accelerated, she suddenly realized. Just a beat faster than it normally went.

The contractor flashed her another one of what seemed now to be his endless supply of grins. "Have your husband take you out."

Brad didn't care for eating out. Once, when they were

first together, eating out was special. Even grabbing something at a fast-food restaurant, their knees touching beneath a small table, had been special. But now, if they weren't going to a fund-raiser or some kind of function associated with the hospital, meals were taken at home. Or on the fly, separately.

She shrugged away the suggestion. "Most likely he'll probably get something at the hospital before he comes home," she speculated.

"He can still take you out. You deserve it after all the work you put in," he told her.

"Work?" Was he talking about her emptying out all the cabinets in the kitchen?

"Looking for someone to renovate your house," he explained. His eyes swept over her once. A warmth shimmied up and down her spine in response. "Your husband's a very lucky man."

Stacey sincerely doubted that Brad felt that way, especially after this last month. "Maybe you'd like to put that in writing," she joked. When he looked at her curiously, she added, "So I could show him."

For a long moment, Alex said nothing. He just looked at her. She had no idea what he was thinking. The grin on his lips softened into a smile that seeped into her bones and created havoc within her. "Anytime, Mrs. Sommers, anytime."

Had it suddenly gotten warm in here, or was it just her? She moved to open a window. Normally, she left the windows on the first floor closed when she went to work, but Alex and his crew were going to be here, so she supposed it was safe.

Stacey cleared her throat, telling herself she was being silly. "I think under the circumstances you should call me Stacey."

"Fine. Stacey."

He said her name as if he was trying it out for size on his tongue. It was obviously a perfect fit because he nodded his head. And smiled.

The next minute, he turned to the two-person crew he'd brought with him purely for their expertise in demolition work. The man handed Alex a crowbar. He wrapped his fingers around it and gave the order. "Okay, Joe, Alba, time to get cracking."

Stacey tensed as she heard the sledgehammer make contact with her pantry doors. The resulting sound reverberated through her whole body.

At least, that was why she told herself her body was vibrating.

CHAPTER 24

"What the hell is all this?" Brad demanded when he walked into the family room that night. Or tried to. The room was so packed, he almost needed a shoehorn to enter.

It was past seven in the evening. Since Stacey's contractor had started in at seven in the morning, he felt it was safe enough to come home and not encounter any workers. He wasn't in the mood to try to conduct his life amid deafening noise and debris.

The deafening noise was absent, but the debris was another matter. It was definitely present and accounted for. To such a degree that he hardly recognized either room involved. The kitchen looked as if it had been gutted by a flameless fire. The fluorescent lighting fixtures were hanging at half mast, a shattered remnant of their plastic covering crunching under his foot as he walked in to survey the area.

In the center of the room, on a small, wooden folding TV tray, Stacey had set up what looked like a hot plate. The microwave and some kind of grill was on the floor. Beyond that, the kitchen was stripped of everything.

The cabinets, sink, appliances—including the refrigerator—and the table with its accompanying chairs had been pulled out, leaving the kitchen looking like a hollow memory of its former self. Everything but the cabinets had found their way into the living room, strewn every which way.

Brad stared into the family room, trying to discern shapes beyond the refrigerator and stove. He liked to sit on his recliner and unwind in the family room. Now he couldn't even find it. His frown deepened. This had been a bad idea from the start. He'd known that in his gut. There was nothing wrong with the way things had been.

Damn, he should have put his foot down. Now it was obviously too late.

"Everything's out of the kitchen," Stacey said, walking in from the dining room and answering his question.

Brad turned around to look at her.

He seemed lost, she thought. He'd left before she'd gotten even one pantry shelf emptied. Now the large coffee table in the family room was completely covered with as many of the smaller items from the pantry as she had been able to cram into the space. Butted up against it was yet another wooden TV tray, this one holding the coffeemaker and the toaster.

There wasn't as much as an inch of unclaimed space available in the area. Maneuvering was tricky, especially with the refrigerator taking up a large section of the area in front of the coffee table. If he were claustrophobic, this would have been his worst nightmare.

As it was, he wasn't exactly thrilled about having to see it.

"Just how long is it supposed to look like this?" he asked, waving an already impatient hand at the clutter.

A lot longer than he would like. She already knew that. Stacey braced herself for his reaction. "Alex says about five weeks. Maybe more."

His eyes widened. Brad reacted as if she'd just declared that she intended to stage the reenactment of the Invasion of Normandy and play all the parts herself.

"Five weeks!" The idea was entirely unacceptable.

"Maybe more," Stacey added in case the last part of her statement had escaped him. She offered him what she hoped passed for a soothing smile.

Numbers flew through his head. "Do you have any idea how much five weeks' worth of eating out is going to cost us?"

When they were both poor and struggling, it didn't always used to be about money. Why had the focus changed now that they were well off and the ends not only met, but went around the block several times before rejoining again? When had he become such a miser?

"We don't have to eat out," she told him quietly.

"We have to eat," he countered. "Unless, of course, you plan to put us on some kind of weird starvation diet."

Because she was feeling sensitive, she couldn't help wondering if that was intended as some sort of comment about the fact that she'd gained a few unwanted pounds since they'd gotten married.

For the sake of peace, she let that go and addressed only the main problem. "I can cook." As a matter of fact, she already had. Challenged, she'd been creative and managed to make dinner in a minimum of space by rummaging through the garage and taking a few forgotten appliances out of mothballs.

But before she could tell him that, he discounted her suggestion. "How? The stove's not plugged in and you can't just stick the plug in anywhere. It needs a special line."

"You'd be surprised what you can do with a hot plate and

one of those indoor grills." She took his hand, leading him into the dining room. Chaos had not quite reached there yet. "I've got the meals covered," she told him. "All you have to do is show up." She nodded toward his chair. "Think of it as camping out."

But he wasn't ready to sit down yet. He was still trying to process the fact that his kitchen looked like the aftermath of Dorothy's thrill ride to Oz.

"Camping out," he echoed. "Where? In a sardine can?"

"We can have the meals in the dining room. Or on the patio." She gestured vaguely in the direction of the back of the house. "You'll find a minimum of stuff out there," she added in a voice that was a tad more quiet. Alex had set up a makeshift work table out there and had begun cutting some of the molding to size for the kitchen.

He frowned, but she had managed to placate him to an extent. "I guess I can put up with it." Instead of sitting down, he went back into the kitchen and surveyed the area. "This isn't such a big space," he pointed out. "Why does it have to take so long?"

Mainly because the workers weren't going to be there, she thought. A great deal of waiting would be involved.

"Everything has to be coordinated," she told him. And it would be arriving in stages. "The appliances, the cabinets, the floor—" Her eyes widened as her oversight dawned on her. "We haven't picked out a floor yet."

He groaned. More tile places. "Why don't you take some time off from work?" he suggested. "That way, you can devote yourself entirely to finding a floor."

Her first thought was to say she couldn't do it. But juggling the remodeling and the office was becoming a challenge and this was only the first day. And she knew how much Brad hated having unsupervised people in his house. Taking some time off might make things simpler all around. She was going to need to talk to Dr. Reynolds about revamping her schedule.

She nodded slowly, thinking. "Maybe you have something there."

Surprise stirred through him. "Of course I have something there. You're the one who wants all this, so you're the one who should pick it—"

"I mean about asking for some time off—at least during the week," she clarified. "I can try to catch up on whatever needs doing at the office on weekends."

He didn't know if he liked the sound of that. "You're going to work weekends?"

"And after hours," she added. "Just until the house is done." It was beginning to sound plausible. "Alex and his people don't work on weekends, so I don't need to be here for them."

"How about for me?" he asked.

She tried to replay his words, searching for his meaning. "Excuse me?"

"Tool-belt man and his cronies aren't going to be here on weekends, but I am. What if I want you to be here on weekends?"

Stacey stared at him. This was a first. Brad *never* said anything about wanting to have her around. The subject just never came up. Because it was a given, she thought. Brad was so accustomed to having her around whenever he was home that he'd taken it for granted. Taken her for granted. But she couldn't let herself go there now. There was too much to take care of.

She shrugged the topic away. "We'll work something out.

Now," she continued, trying to focus on the positive side of things, "I made you your favorite. Grilled salmon. I've also got baked potatoes and broccoli with cheese sauce."

Skepticism nudged through him. "How?"

She gestured over toward the corner where the TV tray stood. "I've still got my microwave, my indoor grill and that two-burner hot plate I bought at a discount store when we first moved in here."

Very slowly, a smile materialized, curving his lips. "I didn't realize you could be that resourceful."

Yes, I know. Out loud, she said, "Dr. Sommers, I think that there are a lot of things about me you don't realize."

Before this gruesome adventure had begun, he would have argued that he knew her inside and out, knew everything she was capable of and everything she could do. But he was beginning to learn that he was wrong.

Brad looked at her for a long moment, the air pregnant with words that were unspoken. "Maybe you're right," he finally said.

"Why don't you sit down?" she suggested, indicating the dining room. "Dinner's ready."

He did as she asked.

She went to unearth the plates from under the pile of loose sandwich-size plastic bags and wondered what Brad would say if he knew she was discovering things that she'd never known about herself, too.

Including the fact that, until recently, she had been absolutely convinced that she wouldn't so much as look at another man.

Now, she wasn't all that sure.

Because she had looked. Looked for a very long time. And it had left her feeling unsettled. About everything. Most of all, about herself.

CHAPTER 25

Brad put his fork down on his empty plate and finished the last of the white wine that Stacey had poured for them. One glass of alcohol was always his limit. There was no telling when an emergency call might come through, summoning him to the hospital. He had to keep sharp.

But one glass helped to mellow him a little, to take the edge off his day. And, at times, it allowed him to see things more clearly.

Like now.

Sitting back in his chair, he watched his wife for a long moment. Stacey was just finishing her meal. The conversation between them had faded and he hadn't even noticed until now. Sometimes, his own oblivion astounded him.

"You know, that is pretty amazing."

The sound of his voice surprised her. Stacey raised her eyes to his. Something inside her braced for a scene. These days, because of the remodeling, half their conversations were confrontations of some sort. "What is?"

He nodded at his empty plate. "That you can make the same kind of dinner you usually make even with a nonexistent kitchen. Maybe it's not a miracle on par with the loaves and the fishes on the Mount, but it's still pretty amazing."

Stacey stared at him. What was that, two compliments in the past few months?

Slowly, a smile budded on her lips as warmth spread its way through her. "Thank you."

"Yeah, well…" His voice trailed off as he shrugged, not wanting to make a big deal out of the fact that he had said anything about dinner. She acted as if he never paid her compliments. And then he paused. Maybe he didn't. He supposed that he rarely did take note of what she did and compliment her on it.

Rarely? an inner voice mocked him. That would mean that he could actually remember the last time he'd given her one, and the truth was, he couldn't.

But then, husbands and wives were supposed to instinctively know things without having to have them verbally reinforced every few minutes. He couldn't stand around all day, telling her that he thought she was smart and clever and a good wife. She was supposed to know that by now. Know that he appreciated the effort she put into running the house and working as well.

He didn't need any positive reinforcement when he performed a surgery. He just knew whether or not it was good and no words to the contrary would take away from that.

He supposed that women were different.

Brad nodded at the plates on the table. "What are you going to do about the dishes?"

She smiled. What did people usually do with dirty dishes? Wash them."

"How? The dishwasher's in the family room and there's no ink."

"In the kitchen," she pointed out. "But there's one i
the bathroom."

Just before she left, she'd heard Joe saying that while the
were here, he and Alba could take apart the downstair
bathroom as well. She'd nearly twisted her ankle getting bac
to them and vetoing the idea. There was no way she wa
going to be left without running water somewhere on the fir
floor. Otherwise, until the kitchen was back in, every tim
she wanted a glass of water or to cook something or even t
wash her hands, she'd have to go upstairs and then com
down again. While that might be good for her leg exercise
the rest of her wasn't keen on the idea.

The sink in the downstairs bathroom was the smallest i
the house. He looked at her incredulously. "You're going t
wash dishes in the bathroom sink?"

"Not much choice," she answered.

Stacey gathered together the dishes and utensils they'
used and debated taking the glasses, too. She hated makin
multiple trips, but this time, she decided it was more pruden
if she came back for the glassware rather than risk breaking i

Her first stop was the kitchen to clean the crumbs from th
plates. Unlike Brad, she'd left her potato skin. "It's either tha
or throw them away and get a new set every time we run out.

He figured the kitchen would be up and running befor
that happened, but there was no sense in letting the dishe
pile up. "I see your point."

Because he was curious, Brad followed her to the bathroo
just off the family room. Leaning against the doorjamb, h
watched her close the drain and then squirt dishwashing liqui
into the running water. After a moment, he walked away.

Stacey unconsciously listened for the sound of the television set being turned on, thinking that Brad had gone into the living room to watch the news on one of the cable stations he favored. When she didn't hear anything, she assumed that he'd gone upstairs.

He surprised her by returning, with a dish towel in his hands. She raised an eyebrow, silently quizzing him. "It took me some time to find it. The cabinet you used to keep these in is gone."

"Yes, I know. All the cabinets are gone." She couldn't contain her curiosity any longer. "What are you doing with a dish towel?"

"What do most people do with a dish towel?"

"Most people dry dishes with it. But you're not most people."

A hint of smile passed over his lips. "I am for tonight." He nodded at the sink. "You wash, I'll dry." The way he saw it, he had the better part of the deal.

For a second, she was rendered speechless. The last time they had done that—when she washed and he dried—was when they'd lived in that tiny furnished apartment they'd shared just off the campus. Just standing here like this brought back memories. Tons of memories.

She smiled fondly at him. "Sounds like a plan to me."

For a moment, there was nothing but the sound of running water and a dish being scrubbed. He began to feel awkward. A man wasn't supposed to feel awkward around his wife, was he?

"So, five weeks," he said finally, plucking the conversation out of the air.

"Or so," she reminded him. She pressed her lips together, holding her breath and waiting for his reaction. Worried that

the words might in some way set him off. She had no idea
what to expect.

Brad took the first dish from her and began to wipe, his
attention elsewhere. He was trying to remember something.
"Isn't there some kind of penalty clause that states he has to
make a payment to us if he doesn't finish the work by a
certain date?"

"We're having some remodeling done," she told him. "Not
constructing a major office building or housing development."

He set the dried plate down on top of the counter. The
space was limited. "In other words, no."

"In other words, no," she echoed.

He sighed heavily as he took the second wet dish from her
hand.

"Wow, this is major chaos, isn't it?"

Startled, Stacey took her head out of the pantry. On her
knees, she was finishing restocking the bottom shelf in a
quick bid to restore some order to the kitchen before she left.
She'd heard the dogs barking a minute ago, but since the
doorbell hadn't rung, she didn't think anything of it.

Jim stood only a few steps behind her, looking around the
room. He'd obviously let himself into the house with his keys.

Dusting off her hands, she rose to her feet.

The workers had come and gone for the day, arriving at
seven as had become their habit and knocking off at ten.
Before leaving, they'd announced they were going to another
job. Stacey knew that the nature of their business being what
it was, where famine could easily follow feast, a contractor
couldn't afford to turn away any sort of work. In the first four

weeks of remodeling, it had become abundantly clear that Alex had his people working on three, at times four, different projects. Some days she didn't see them at all. If no one showed up by seven-fifteen, she knew that she was facing a nonwork day.

As with everything else that was thrown her way, Stacey had learn to adjust her schedule, working around the construction crew's abbreviated hours. She'd given herself twenty minutes to finish putting things into the pantry before she left for the office. Though the remodeling was slower going than she would have liked and there was Brad's displeasure to put up with, she had to admit that this way was easier on her when it came to her own job. She could catch up on work if she tackled it every day instead of leaving everything to the weekend. Going in after hours hadn't worked out too well, either. Not for Brad or the doctors she worked with.

This was better.

"Not so major anymore," she assured him, stretching up to brush a kiss against his cheek.

It pleased her that Jim had obviously outgrown his "no physical parental contact period" and no longer pulled away. Being a hugger and a toucher all her life, this form of abstinence had been particularly hard on her. Rosie had been on the receiving end of a great deal of hugging during that period.

"At least we've got the refrigerator back in the kitchen instead of the middle of the family room." She'd felt like cheering when the deliverymen had come with the new model. They'd taken the old appliance with them when they left. The family room had instantly doubled in size.

She realized that she'd gotten used to the refrigerator being in the family room. Funny how quickly she could get accustomed to things. Changes just stealthily sneaked up on her.

Like Brad's behavior. She hadn't realized how much he'd changed until she was treated to a glimpse back to how things used to be. Like the dish-drying incident. He'd only repeated it a couple of times in the past four weeks, but it still had the same effect, it made her nostalgic for the people they used to be.

"And I've managed to get most of the things into the new pantry." She was running behind schedule, but she didn't care. Taking his hand, she pulled Jim over to the new cabinets. She wanted to show them off.

Jim looked and nodded, not overly interested in the renovations other than the fact that it obviously made his mother happy to have all this going on.

Standing in the middle of the work-in-progress, he glanced up. The opaque sheeting that had covered the fluorescent lights was no longer there. The fixtures were now opened and exposed. Several components dangled loose. "When's that going to be done?"

"Hopefully before tonight." Alex had said that one of the electricians would be by after five. "I'm having recessed lighting put in. With a dimmer."

"A romantic kitchen." Jim laughed softly. "Seems like a waste."

"As a matter of fact, it's to save on electricity."

Jim shook his head, a knowing expression on his face. "Let me guess, Dad's idea."

It gave her great pleasure to contradict him. "No, the contractor's, smarty pants."

The trite label made him grin. "You never were much

good at name calling, Mom. What other changes are you making?" Then before she could answer, he asked another question, "What's my room going to be?"

"Your room," she replied simply.

Her answer surprised him. He had friends whose rooms were gone before their cars made it to the end of the block when they moved out.

"You're not making it over, or knocking out a wall and turning it into a big study?"

"Nope. Just putting in a few improvements." She was having the closets deepened in all the bedrooms, as well as expanding Jim's and Julie's rooms. "You can stay over any time. Or move back if you need to."

He shook his head as they walked together to the front door. "Not going to happen. I just came by to tell you that the band and I've got a gig at the end of next month. At the Wild Orchid. Three nights—Friday, Saturday and Sunday. I thought if you weren't doing anything…"

He was trying hard to sound casual about this, but she knew how much it meant to him. How hard he'd been working to make something of the band. She shared his excitement. "And even if I was, I wouldn't miss this for the world. Maybe your father would—"

"No," Jim said with finality, cutting her off before she could finish the thought, "he wouldn't."

CHAPTER 26

"**I'll** work on him." She said the words cheerfully, as if ignorant of the animosity thriving between father and son. She hoped it would eventually be a thing of the past.

The steely look in Jim's eyes told her that day had yet to come.

"Don't bother." And then he smiled at her. "Just as long as you can come." Jim glanced at his watch. His languid manner disappeared. "Wow, it's later than I thought. I've got to jet, Mom. I'll see you later."

Later.

The word hung between them, a vague promise without form or structure. But she knew better than to try to pin him down to a time or date.

"Later," she echoed. As he began to leave, she put her hand on his arm. Jim raised his brow, waiting. "How are you fixed for money?"

The shrug was careless. "I have it."

She knew what that meant. That his cash flow had turned into a dribble. "Want to have more?"

It wasn't really a question. She reached into her purse and took several twenties out of her wallet.

Jim took a step back. "Mom, it's not necessary." The protest was without conviction.

Stacey folded the bills in half and stuffed them into his shirt pocket. He wouldn't ask her for money outright, but she wouldn't sleep if she knew he needed it.

"When you get to be rich and famous, you can buy me a summerhouse," she teased. "Right now, that part-time job you have probably doesn't give you enough after taxes to pay for your food."

He shrugged again, his thin shoulders moving beneath his baggy T-shirt. "I don't eat that much."

"Yes, I know." He'd been what was politely referred to as husky until he'd hit his teens and the opinion of his peers became his god. Suddenly, fast food was out, as was anything with sugar, salt or fat. That left very little to choose from. "You can stop by for a meal or two, you know. There's no cover charge."

He laughed. "I'll keep that in mind." He put his hand over his pocket, his eyes smiling at her. "Thanks for the loan."

He was still her boy, no matter how many candles were on his cake. She saw no reason not to slip him a little something extra until he got to his artistic feet. "Consider it a gift for coming by."

Crossing the threshold, Jim turned around and frowned. "You don't have to pay me for stopping by."

She nodded, as if taking his words to heart. Her expression was completely innocent as she told him, "It's just until I find a way to tie you up and keep you in the basement."

"You don't have a basement," he pointed out, trying hard

not to show her how much he missed the banter, the warmth that she represented.

"It's on the remodeling list," she deadpanned.

He laughed, shaking his head. For a second, leaning forward, he almost forgot himself and kissed her. But he stopped at the last minute, moving back. There were images to uphold and independence to hang on to.

"See you, Mom."

"See you," she echoed, closing the door. She needed to attend to one more thing. Already she was running late, a few more minutes wouldn't matter.

"That your son?"

The question came from behind her. Stacey stifled a gasp as she swung around, ready to swing.

Alex caught her wrist before she could make contact. "Hey," he cautioned with a laugh. "Sorry. Didn't mean to startle you."

Her adrenaline slipped down to a more manageable level. She took a breath to steady her pulse. It didn't help. "I thought you'd left."

"I did." He released her wrist. "But I came back. The side gate's unlocked. Just like your patio door. I forgot my book," Alex explained, holding up the thin blue binder in his other hand. "It's like leaving a chunk of my life behind."

Alex struck her as being very up on everything. She was surprised that he was still using pencil and paper rather than the latest electronic technology. "Most people feel that way about their PDAs."

He made a dismissive gesture. "I keep all the records on a computer at the office, but when I'm out in the field, nothing beats the feel of paper. I like seeing things right in front of me without trying to remember what 'folder' it might be in, or worrying that the hard drive might crash."

She'd never had that happen to her personally, but she'd heard enough horror stories to make her take the proper precautions. "You could always back up."

"I could," he allowed. His eyes were smiling at her. "Maybe someday." His voice was significantly lower than the one he used when he was instructing one of his crews about the day's schedule.

Something unexpected rippled through her. Stacey felt a blush creep along her neck. It came out of nowhere and seemed bent on embarrassing her.

Flustered, feeling as if the contractor was hinting at something entirely different, something light years away from a discussion about backing up computer data, she glanced away, desperate for a way to shift the focus onto another topic.

Her eyes came to rest on the gaping hole that had once been her sink.

"Um, the sink still isn't here."

"Actually, it is," he told her, his voice reverting a little to its business-like timbre. "The granite for the counter isn't. We have to mount that before we can install the sink."

"But we picked out the slab two weeks ago," she protested.

It had been a hard-won victory, getting Brad to come out with her again. Looking back, she wasn't even sure just how she managed it, only that he came. Grudgingly, but he came. And they had gone from one granite showroom to another. Five in all.

The only problem they'd encountered was finding a color

they both liked. Brad tended toward dark hues and she liked things light. They wound up compromising on Blue Pearl. And one showroom had the perfect piece.

Brad had found it, actually, pointing it out to her as she'd gone wandering up and down the various rows in the warehouse. The triumphant expression on Brad's face was one she was going to remember for a long time.

"Yes, I know," Alex was saying. "But they cut it backward at the store."

"Backward?" She shook her head. "I don't understand."

"Somehow, they got their hands on the wrong measurements. They cut it to the old specs. The hole was where your old sink used to be."

They had agreed that it was more aesthetically pleasing, not to mention more symmetrical, if the existing window was moved six inches over to the right. The sink's position had to be moved as well. The result was more counter space on the left and less on the right, but she found it more functional that way.

"Don't worry," Alex said, reacting to the dismay on her face. "We still have the major portion of the granite and that's going to be put in tomorrow morning," he promised.

"And the other piece?" she asked.

"It'll be here as soon as they finish cutting it. I've got one of my people overseeing it this time, so there'll be no mistakes. They won't charge you for the new piece, seeing as how it's their fault."

That would make Brad happy, but she wasn't thinking of the cost right now. "The two pieces won't match." She'd seen how different the same stone could be. It all depended on which part of the quarry it was taken from. Blue Pearl could vary as much as by five shades.

"They'll match. I give you my word." He looked so intense, she felt he actually meant it. "I'm having them bring in more slabs from their warehouse in Phoenix. And I don't intend to back off until I'm satisfied."

God help her, she envisioned a completely different scenario when he said that. One that had nothing to do with granite slabs. Swallowing didn't help. She had nothing to swallow with. Stacey abruptly turned on her heel and went to the refrigerator. After yanking the door open, she took out a bottle of water. She'd never been the type to walk around with a bottle of designer water in her hand, but without an accessible sink in the kitchen, she'd given in to the luxury she'd heretofore viewed as pretentious.

Right now, she was grateful that she'd stocked several of those little bottles in her refrigerator because her throat had gone utterly dry. And her tongue was sticking to the roof of her mouth. She almost drained the whole bottle before she felt she could talk.

"All right, then," she said hoarsely, screwing the top back on the almost empty bottle. The next sound out of her mouth came like a croak. She cleared her throat. "I'll leave it in your hands."

The grin on his lips made a beeline for her middle. "Good idea. I won't let you down," he promised. And then he winked. "You look like you're in a hurry. I'll let myself out."

She barely remembered nodding her head in response. What she was aware of was that her stomach had flipped over. Twice.

Grabbing her purse, Stacey hurried to the front of the house and then out the door. As she shut it behind her, she took in a deep gulp of air.

And all the while, she silently repeated a refrain in her head. *I love my husband, I love my husband.*

CHAPTER 27

The front door opened and then closed. Her back to him as she finished preparing dinner, Stacey was aware of Brad's displeasure before he ever said a word. The sigh she heard was akin to a tropical storm.

Now what?

Forcing a smile to her lips, she turned around. "Hi, honey."

He didn't seem to hear the greeting as he glared at the sink that wasn't, and the half-missing counter that still hadn't been delivered.

"You said five weeks," Brad reminded her tersely. "It's been more than six. And they're not anywhere near finished."

Sometimes she wondered if he retained anything but surgical procedures in his head. "I also said 'or so,'" she reminded him not for the first time.

Brad sighed again. He didn't like things that were beyond his control. Dissatisfaction flowed through him.

He wanted his home back. He'd never been as domestic as Stacey obviously was. He hadn't entertained the feeling that some men enjoyed, that his home was his castle. It was just wood and stucco, but it was *his* wood and stucco and he wanted his privacy back.

He wanted to come in at night and not have to anticipate

strangers in his house, tearing out fixtures or running power tools at the maximum noise level.

If all this *had* to take place, why not during the daytime while he was out? That was why he made sure he was gone each morning before seven. This chaos wasn't supposed to dribble into the evening. Evening was for peace and quiet, not hammering, drilling and God only knew what all else.

More than peace and quiet, Brad wanted his wife back.

Half the time Stacey was gone when he came home. She was still back at the office, working in order to make up for being here in the morning to admit the first wave of workers. The other half of the time, when she *was* home by the time he arrived, she was busy talking to those same invasive workers, or to that lumpy graduate of Gold's Gym, the contractor.

The bottom line: she wasn't his anymore. She was this woman he hardly recognized.

The corners of his mouth turned down as he continued staring at the hole where the sink was supposed to be installed. It reminded him of the shape his life was in. Used to be he'd put in a grueling, soul-sapping day at the hospital and his office, and then he'd come home. To a haven of sorts. He hadn't realized at the time that it was a haven, but now he could see that was exactly what it was. And he wanted it back. He wanted his life back the way it had been a few weeks ago. Quiet. Simple. Organized and dependable. Just the way Stacey had been. She wasn't predictable anymore.

And he, well, he felt inadequate now. More than that, he felt like an outsider in his own home, in his own life. He'd never felt that way before.

And it was all because of the remodeling. Damn her hippie uncle for dying, anyway.

"Or so," he repeated with a healthy dose of contempt. "That could mean forever."

He always saw the down side to everything. There were times Stacey wondered how Brad had ever become a doctor. Doctors were supposed to deal in hope, not constant despair.

"More than likely," she began evenly as she took the casserole she'd made in the Crock-Pot and transferred it into a serving dish. "What it means is that it's going to take just a few more weeks." She did her damnedest to smile at him. "Look on the bright side. At least we have the family room back."

She gestured in the general direction of the room. The area no longer looked like a storage place for a pack rat suffering from an advanced case of obsessive-compulsive disorder. The family room, thanks to her intense efforts, now looked the way it once had: pleasantly disarrayed with everything readily accessible.

The only noticeable difference in the room was one that she found very gratifying. Where once there'd been a wet bar, something that dated the house back to the seventies when it was first built, now finely crafted maple cabinets, stained with an eye-appealing honeyed hue, ran along the same wall. A mirrored backdrop broke up the straight line that went from top to bottom. It reflected a granite countertop. The same type of granite they would use for the kitchen counter.

The cabinets had just been installed today and she kept walking by to admire them. Granted, the doors still needed to have the hardware put in, just like the kitchen cabinets, but it didn't matter. She loved every new piece, loved the rooms taking shape.

Brad obviously didn't share her feelings. His hands clasped behind him like an overly tall Napoléon, he went from section to section, scrutinizing each carefully.

Looking for flaws.

Stacey held her breath, waiting. "Dinner's ready," she finally told him.

She might as well have been reciting the opening lines of a nursery rhyme. He didn't appear to hear her.

"At these prices," he complained, waving a hand at the empty cabinets, "they should be perfect."

She actually thought they were. Or close enough to it to satisfy her, at least. In her mind, she'd already staked out a section for the family photographs—a large section because the moments of a family's life needed to be commemorated. Another section was for tapes of family events, such as Christmases and birthdays. The tapes she had dated back to the Christmas before Julie turned two, when they could first afford a secondhand camcorder.

Bracing herself for another sparring match in which she had to defend the contractor, his crew, their work, and her decision to have this done in the first place, she asked, "What's wrong?"

He looked at her incredulously, as if she'd checked her brain at the door. "Can't you see it?"

Today had not been a good day at work. She'd almost lost her temper with the new girl, a temp who had been hired to take Andrea's place while the latter was still on maternity leave. By day's end, she'd seriously given thought to telling

Andrea to bring her baby in and hire the temp to be a baby-sitter. That appeared to be more in keeping with the temp's meager mental abilities.

Doing her best not to let the mood that had been created at work spill out into her home, she answered evenly, "I wouldn't ask if I did."

"There." Brad indicated the extreme left side where the cabinets had been fitted against the wall. The wood surpassed the wall by a little more than an inch.

"And there," he said, pointing to the extreme right where the cabinet came in contact with the opposite wall. There, halfway down the wall, the wood began to edge out the plaster. By the time it reached the carpet, the cabinet had almost a two-inch advantage over the wall.

He glanced at her expectantly. Her expression remained the same. "Don't you see it?"

Stacey moved her head from side to side, still staring at the cabinets. "No."

"Good thing you have me here."

"Good thing," she echoed. She was still clueless as to what he was talking about.

"The cabinet," Brad finally told her, his voice controlled, his expression indicating the disdain he felt. He enunciated every syllable as if she were more than a little mentally challenged.

"Yes?"

"It juts out further than the wall."

She already knew that. She wasn't blind. And she wasn't obsessed, either, she thought. "So?"

"So," he repeated impatiently, "the sides—the cabinet," he

emphasized, "is supposed to be flush with the walls. Both ends are supposed to be flush," he insisted. "Tell them that, those guys with the tool belts. Tell them that I want the cabinet to be flush with the walls. Like the old cabinets were."

"Right. Flush." And then, because she wasn't thinking clearly, because she forgot that this was Brad, who could transform nit-picking into an art form, she made a fatal mistake, she asked, "Anything else?"

She'd fully expected him to tell her that he had no time for this and to finally sit down and eat his dinner. But he didn't sit. He didn't eat. Instead, he unbuttoned his jacket and said, "Now that you mention it..." He eyed the kitchen. The next moment, he was walking into it. "You might want to get a pad to write all this down so you don't forget."

It was either willingly be present at the start of the Third World War, or do as he asked. Stacey chose the latter. She picked up a pad from the newly returned kitchen table and prepared to write.

Ten minutes later, she had her very own list of picayune flaws. Most of Brad's complaints had to do with the cabinet doors. There were an abundance of them in the kitchen, none of which met properly, according to Brad. Some were too high, some were too low, and a couple of sets stuck, rubbing against one another when opened.

The latter really seemed to annoy Brad. "Hell, I could do a better job."

God forbid, she thought. Alex would charge her double to undo what Brad did. When it came to being handy, Brad had a very special place in line. Right behind earthworms and snails. The man hadn't a clue as to which tool was for what. It had always been that way.

Stacey was quick to render the excuse she always used whenever she wanted to call in a professional to do a job that Brad debated tackling himself.

"You know that your hands are too precious to risk injuring. Anyone can handle a band saw. Very few people have it in them to be a skilled neurosurgeon. You get hurt, you might never be able to operate. It's too big a risk," she told him with finality, adding just the right note of pleading. "I can't let you take it."

Brad sighed. And then he tapped the list she still held in her hand. "Then make sure you give Mr. Tool Belt my list."

She'd always hated nit-picking, but she knew that Brad would give her no peace until he saw that his complaints were being addressed.

"As soon as he comes in tomorrow," she promised.

Only then did Brad walk back into the dining room. To his by-now-cold dinner.

CHAPTER 28

"Wow, Mom. You weren't kidding when you said you wanted to remodel," Julie said appreciatively, only remembering at the last second to lower her voice as she took her mother aside to the living room. Initially, her reason for stopping by was to touch base and to hopefully catch her father before he left for the hospital. Although she hated doing it, she needed to ask him for money. She called it a loan against the day she could pay her parents back the cost of her education. She'd miscalculated again. The books for her courses had cost more than she'd allotted on her budget and her cash flow was down to zero.

Less than zero if she counted the money she'd borrowed lately from several equally impoverished medical students.

Because studying made daily commuting next to impossible, she lived with a couple of roommates just off the UCI medical school campus. Pulling up to the curb, she saw that the garage was open and her father's stately Mercedes sedan missing.

She had no time to lament the bad timing or the minor traffic jam she'd been in that had caused it. Her eyes had been taken hostage by the sight of the stud making his way up the front walk. He carried a two-by-four over his shoulder as if it was made out of cardboard. His muscles looked like boulders. Sculpted boulders.

Julie lost no time getting out of the car and in through the open door, right behind him. Her attention entirely focused on the stranger she followed, she almost walked right into her mother.

Stopping just in time, Julie caught hold of her mother's arm. It took effort to look at her and not the man disappearing around the corner. "Who *is* that?" she asked.

More important questions presented themselves to Stacey. The semester was in session. Julie was one of the most conscientious students she knew. For her to be here, something had to be wrong.

"Julie, what are you doing here?" She quickly scrutinized her daughter's face. Was that the new lighting, or was her daughter's complexion flushed? "Is everything all right?" She refrained from putting either her hand or her lips to Julie's forehead, knowing that the girl hated that. Hated to be fussed over almost as much as Jim did. "You're not sick, are you?"

The question brought Julie around for a moment. Questions about the handsome stranger were temporarily placed on hold.

"No, but my wallet is." Even the flippant reference had her flushing a little. "I was hoping to catch Dad before he left."

"You just missed him. These days, your father likes to leave the house before the workers get here." Stacey walked over to the hall closet where she usually hung up her purse on the hook right inside the door. Taking it out, she opened her purse and looked at Julie. "How much do you need?"

Julie caught her lower lip between her teeth. The older she was, the more awkward she felt about asking. "A hundred should do."

Stacey took out her checkbook and held it aloft, tucking her purse under her arm. "Check?"

"Cash?" Julie countered hopefully.

Returning the navy-blue checkbook back into the zippered compartment of her purse, Stacey began to rummage through the rest of it. She found her wallet quickly enough, but not the amount Julie needed. Stray bills turned out to be three singles, nothing more.

She looked up, shaking her head. "I'm sorry, Julie, all I have is a twenty." She tried again. "If you need a hundred dollars, I can write you a check."

"Thanks, Mom, but I really need to have it in cash," Julie told her. "I owe the money to a couple of my roommates and this guy I work with in the research lab."

They had a standing policy about borrowing that was summed up in a single word: *Don't.* But there was no need to belabor that point. "Julie, you should have told me you were short at lunch last week."

A fleeting, contrite smile fluttered over Julie's lips. "I don't like to seem as if I can't handle money, it's just that…"

Stacey nodded, not wanting to make Julie feel guilty. They'd all been there. She could remember the pinch created by lack of funds all too well.

"If you really need the cash, I can make a quick trip to the ATM," she offered, slinging her purse over her shoulder.

"You could write the check out to me."

Both women turned to see that Alex had reentered the room and was walking toward them.

"I might have enough cash on me." He nodded at Julie, but she could see that he was actually talking to her mother.

And that the quick, lethal grin was aimed at her mother as well. "I couldn't help overhearing—all but the amount."

As he spoke, Alex took out his wallet. The worn, cracked leather had more than a healthy bulge. Maybe it was a guy thing, Stacey thought. Brad liked handling cash instead of using credit cards or even checks. And his wallet looked just as beaten up.

Stacey glanced at Julie, leaving it up to her to raise the amount if she needed to. "A hundred."

Julie nodded in response.

He counted out five twenties. "A hundred it is." Finished, he folded the bills and placed them into her hand.

Stacey felt slightly flustered, but banked it down, telling herself that she imagined his fingers lightly passing over the palm of her hand. She came to as Alex started to walk away. "Wait, let me write out the check for you—"

"No hurry," he told her easily. "I know you're good for it." Crossing the threshold to get another tool from his truck, he paused to look at her over his shoulder. "Besides, I know where you live." A wink punctuated the end of his statement.

Stacey banked down another flutter, this one a little more insistent and intense than the one before it. Turning toward her daughter, she said, "Here," and pressed the bills into Julie's hand.

Julie still watched Alex walk down the driveway. And appreciated the way the man's jeans adhered to his anatomy. It took her a second to catch her breath. "Wow." She placed her hand to her chest as she turned to look at her mother. "Is he ever hot."

"Really?" Stacey deliberately moved to the living room, where she knew they would be out of the way. "I hadn't noticed."

"Like hell you didn't," Julie hooted. She grinned broadly, as if she'd caught her mother in a huge lie. A turnaround from when she was a little girl and her mother knew when she wasn't telling the truth. "You got pinker just talking to him."

Stacey shrugged, looking away. Wondering what was wrong with her and why she was acting like some adolescent barely into a training bra. And wishing that Julie hadn't witnessed it. "I'm uncomfortable taking money from people."

Pocketing the money, Julie slipped her arm around her mother's shoulders. "That's okay, Mom. It looks like he feels the same way about you."

Surprised, Stacey looked at her daughter. "Uncomfortable? Really?"

"No. That you're hot."

Had she been eating or drinking anything, Stacey knew she would have choked. "What?"

Julie grinned. Putting her hands into her back pockets, she rocked back on her heels. "You heard me. He thinks you're hot."

Ridiculous. The man was just being polite, nothing more. If she wasn't so starved for affection, her imagination wouldn't be going to places it shouldn't. "Julie, I've got to be at least five, six years older than him."

"Mom, that's nothing. You're a very pretty woman. He's a healthy male. A very healthy male," she underscored, glancing out the side window. Alex was outside, talking to someone in the yard. "Healthy males are attracted to pretty women."

Yes, to pretty women their own age, not to tired war horses who only had misty memories of what romance had been like.

And this conversation was completely out of bounds. "Julie, I'm married. To your father. Remember?"

Julie shook her head. She pursed her lips as she watched Alex bend over and pick up something that had fallen out of his pocket. An appreciative noise escaped her lips. "I really don't think that makes any difference to him."

"You're imagining things." Stacey said the words with finality, hoping to put an end to her daughter's speculation.

But she should have known better. Julie was her father's daughter. Once she had latched onto a subject, she wouldn't let it go.

"Nope, I don't think so." Julie grinned, her eyes sparkling as she seemed to roll the thought over in her head. "You know, if anything did happen between you and—" Rather than say the name, Julie nodded toward the window and the man who was directly outside.

"Nothing's going to happen, Julie, do you understand?"

"But if it did," Julie persisted, placing her hand on her mother's arm, "it's okay."

How could her daughter possibly say that? How could she even think that? Hadn't she raised Julie to think better than that? "Julie, you're talking about my breaking my marriage vows—to your father."

Julie looked at her. Suddenly, they were no longer mother and daughter, exploring a fantasy. They were two women talking about something that both knew was a sad fact of life.

"Dad's always taken you for granted, Mom. Maybe he needs to be shaken up a little." Julie saw the surprised, distressed look on her mother's face. "Didn't think I noticed, did you?" Julie laughed softly. "Just because he and I get along so well doesn't mean that I'm oblivious to the way he treats everyone, especially you. Dad needs to see you as a woman again." Her smile was understanding. Encouraging. "Maybe if he sees someone treating you the way you deserve, he'll wake up."

There were a great many times in the past few years when she had felt lonely, alone in a marriage that was supposed to contain two people, two partners. But she had done her best to hide that from her children. She didn't want them taking sides. It was bad enough that Jim had made certain judgment calls, she didn't want that happening to Julie.

Especially since she knew how much her daughter loved Brad. "Julie, your father loves me."

"I never said he didn't. He just doesn't know how to treat you, that's all." She craned her neck, but Alex had disappeared around the corner and was no longer visible. "I think that hunk would know *just* how to treat a lady."

Stacey tucked her arm through Julie's and drew her over to the front door. She knew for a fact that her daughter had a ten o'clock class and needed to be on the road if she ever expected to make the class on time. "Well, we're never going to find out. I'm too old and too married for him, and you, Julie my dear, are too young."

Julie flashed a bright grin. "Never too old or too young to dream, Mom."

"We'll talk about it next week at lunch," Stacey told her as she walked Julie to the curb where the car was parked.

Just before she got into her vehicle, Julie leaned over and whispered into her mother's ear, "He is hot for you, you know."

The next minute, Julie was in her car, driving away. Leaving Stacey to cope with a whole myriad of emotions.

CHAPTER 29

You know, I'm getting really pretty tired of this, not to mention fed up."

Stacey suppressed a sigh. Brad had barely been home ten minutes before starting in. Granted, his words echoed her own sentiments, but she wasn't about to let him know that. Any agreement would launch a diatribe of monumental proportions about how this remodeling was a huge waste of money, how he had told her that it would be. And on, and on, and on.

There was only one tiny light in the forest. A pinprick, really. Brad *seemed* to have gotten a little more involved in the remodeling process than she'd originally thought he would, although definitely not more than she'd hoped. After much coercion, he'd gone back with her to the tile stores and helped her pick out a style and color to be used for the kitchen floor. Once the decision had been made, she'd heaped an avalanche of praise on him—overkill, sure, but it'd had the desired effect. It got him to agree to look in a couple more stores. At the last one, just as they were about to leave, he'd been the one to point out the black onyx tiles. She fell in love with them and now they were on order for their master bathroom.

Empowered, Brad had even made the suggestion that they

use the tiles on the outside of the sunken tub she had her heart set on. She loved the idea and told him so, weakening his resolve enough to get him to look for new appliances. Alex had given them the name of a discount house he did business with that carried name brands.

Brad had made a snide remark about kickbacks, but he'd come along with her nonetheless.

As they looked over the sea of stoves, refrigerators and dishwashers, for a moment or three, Stacey had recalled the feeling she'd had when they'd first started out. Then they had pooled their money and carefully considered every cent before they bought the refrigerator they desperately needed. The one that had refused repair and formed ice inside the vegetable crisper no matter what she turned the temperature dial up to.

Funny, she didn't realize at the time just how happy they were. How nice those days were in retrospect. Not that they weren't struggling, but even so, they were struggling together. Every challenge encountered wasn't just his challenge or her challenge, but *their* challenge.

When had they stopped being "they" and dissolved into "him" and "her"? She didn't know. It had just happened.

And even though Brad had surprised her by getting more involved in the remodeling, there were consequences for this hard-won victory. There were lists issued on a daily basis. Lists generated because he conducted nightly inspections of everything that had been done that day by Alex's crews—the days they did come to work. When she complained that she had trouble reading his handwriting—which on its own merits would have qualified him to be a doctor if nothing else had—

he began dictating them to her. Frowning and passing judgments, constantly registering his dissatisfaction as he made his way from one item to another.

Stacey wondered if Brad was still capable of being satisfied. She certainly saw no evidence of it.

Now, after making his announcement about being fed up, Brad stood watching her. As if waiting to see whether she would ask him what he was fed up with. Silence seemed pretty good to her right about now, but she might as well play the game instead of aggravating him.

So she took a breath and asked, "And by 'this' you mean...?"

"Those people we're paying to work aren't showing up," he complained. So now "we" were paying them, she thought. Since when? She'd been very careful to put all of Titus's money into a separate account and was only writing checks against that. "What is this, the sixth, seventh time they haven't come when they were supposed to?"

She found it more irritating than he did because she was the one who had to hang around, waiting to let them in. But his tone made her gravitate to the crew's defense.

"They have other jobs."

"Fine, I have nothing against free enterprise. Let them finish ours and then they can go on to their 'other jobs.'"

"It doesn't work like that."

He slanted an annoyed look in her direction. "So now you're a remodeling expert?"

Stacey pressed her lips together, physically keeping words back. She refused to get sucked into an argument. It was Friday night. The weekend was spread out before them. She wanted to be able to enjoy as much of it as humanly possible.

That wasn't going to happen if she had words with Brad that resulted in one of them saying something that couldn't be taken back.

"No, I'm not a remodeling expert," she replied evenly. "But I think you were the one who pointed that no contractor has just one job at a time. It came under your list of cons as to why we shouldn't have any remodeling done."

"And I was right," he announced triumphantly. And then he shrugged, because it didn't matter if he was right or not. They were stuck in the middle of this renovation from hell and would be until it was finished. *Finished* being the operative word.

Brad surveyed the area. The kitchen opened up to the family room, which in turn fed into the living room, which eventually became the dining room. He could see parts of all four if he stood near the front door. And it looked exactly the same as it had this morning.

And yesterday morning as well.

He glanced at her. "They weren't here yesterday, either, were they?"

She had waited until almost ten o'clock before she'd decided that no one was coming and she might as well get to the office. When she'd called Alex's number on her way there, all she got was his voice mail. The low, seductive voice promised to return the call.

She was still waiting.

Stacey shook her head. "No."

Brad had thought as much, but there was a certain triumph in getting her to admit it.

"That makes two days." He held up two fingers, moving them to get her attention. "Two days that they could have used to finish up the family room and move on to the guest bathroom."

It wasn't the guest bathroom. It was Jim's bathroom. Right off Jim's room. The correction rose automatically to her lips, but she clamped her mouth shut. There was no point in getting into a discussion about what to call the room. Obviously Brad had earmarked the room for other uses rather than contemplate that Jim might need to move back.

Brad could call the room Irving for all she cared. Jim's things were staying in the bedroom until such time as Jim came and took them out himself.

She glanced toward Brad, waiting for the next salvo. It was too soon for the sounds of his displeasure to be over. And then she saw it. That look. That gleam he got in his eyes sometimes. The one that transformed him from a highly skilled, highly respected surgeon to a man who was willing to experiment in a field he knew nothing about. He literally felt he knew no boundaries because, as far as his abilities in medicine went, he had none. His feet of clay materialized when it came to other matters. Like fixing things.

The pit of Stacey's stomach tightened in uneasy anticipation.

Brad looked at the light fixture in the family room. Specifically, the switch that controlled it. Or was supposed to. They'd decided to have the ceiling scraped and textured, then had recessed lighting installed to brighten the entire area. Since there were times when all that extra wattage wasn't wanted, she had requested to have a dimmer installed. That part was still pending.

Alex had given her a list of dimmers that could do the job and told her she could find them in the hardware store. She'd gone the following afternoon, after work, comparing switches until she found what she wanted. For good measure, she got a dimmer for each room in the house, just in case she decided to change over everything. She really liked the way the recessed lighting looked.

But neither Alex nor any of his crew had been around for the last couple of days to install the dimmer. She'd put her hopes on Monday.

In the meantime, the family room was technically out of commission, at least during the evening hours. The illumination from the one floor lamp she had in the corner of the room wasn't nearly strong enough to decently light up the entire area.

"I can do this," Brad declared with no small conviction.

Oh, God, here we go. "Do what?" she asked him, praying he was talking about something else entirely.

He glanced at her impatiently. "Install the dimmer."

"No, Brad, you can't," she told him kindly but firmly. "You can do a great many things and I'm always the first to stand and cheer you on, but I've known you forever and you are definitely not handy when it comes to fixing anything but the human body."

His attention was focused on the protruding profusion of wires that pushed their way out from behind the single metal strip that held them and the defunct light switch in place. He regarded it from several angles, coming to the same conclusion each time.

"How difficult could it be?"

Very. Out loud, Stacey said, "I don't know. If I knew, maybe I would have done it myself."

"Get me one of the dimmers you bought."

She gave it one last try. Maybe he'd be struck by a bolt of common sense if he met with any resistance. "Brad, no."

No bolt came.

"Stacey, get me a dimmer switch," he repeated, impatience weaving into his voice. This was a man who had infinite patience while performing an operation that, by necessity, had to be conducted at a painstakingly slow pace. But with anything else, he had less than a normally allotted share.

As she watched him stride toward the door that led to the garage, she knew it was useless to dissuade him. He was going to do what he was going to do. And right now, he was getting his toolbox where he kept a very handsome, complete set of tools that gleamed whenever he opened the box. Gleamed because in the five years since he'd bought them, they had hardly ever seen the light of day.

And when they did, the result was never good.

Like the time he had tried to install the garbage disposal and they had wound up, much to the plumber's joy, with a small lake in their kitchen.

"I'll get the dimmer," she told him, bracing herself for disaster.

CHAPTER 30

"You sure you want to do this?" Stacey asked her husband for the third time in as many minutes.

She held onto the dimmer she'd brought in from the garage, reluctant to surrender it. She supposed she could have bought herself some extra time by saying she didn't know where the bag of dimmers was, but he would have seen through that. She almost always knew where everything was located in the house at any given time. As far as she was concerned, it was all part of being a good wife and mother.

Besides, he would have gone into the garage like a bull in the proverbial china shop and hunted for the dimmers himself. And she would have been left with sorting out the chaos.

Brad still wore his good suit. These days, unlike when they were first married, all his suits were good instead of just a precious one. She doubted he knew she'd packed that suit away instead of giving it to charity the way he'd instructed. That was the suit he'd worn on all his medical school interviews. The same suit he had on when he graduated four years later. And then worn when he'd applied for his residency.

These days, instead of only one good suit, he had only one set of worn clothes that he wore on those rare days when he had some extra time to spare. Still, old habits died hard. And she had been very careful of his one good suit.

"Don't you think you should change?"

"Yes," he said, answering her first question about whether or not he was sure about trying his hand at installing the dimmer, "I'm sure about this and I don't think I'm going to get all that dirty working with a handful of small wires, attaching a dimmer." He took the switch from her and pulled off the plastic wrapper around it. "You're my wife, Stacey, not my mother."

She hated being compared to his mother. On any level. There wasn't a compassionate bone in the woman's body.

"I know who I am, Brad."

He spared her a look. "Do you? Then why do you keep treating me as if I were some little kid you needed to supervise?"

She would have loved nothing more than to let him play the big, brave, capable husband. But while Brad might have been one and two, he definitely wasn't number three. Not capable by a long shot. Yet, armed with the knowledge of a dozen misadventures on his part, she was still enough of an optimist to hope that this one time, he would luck out and somehow manage to connect the wires correctly.

"Sorry," she murmured. "I didn't realize I was treating you like one of the kids."

"Worse," he corrected. "At least you have faith in them." He shrugged at the apology, his expression telling her that it was accepted.

Reaching for the screwdriver, he began to work the secondary screws along the light switch. Or attempt to. The tip of the screwdriver kept slipping out of the screw's slot.

Stacey waited a second for him to catch on. When the screwdriver slipped out again, she gave him a hint. "I think you need a flat one."

Perturbed, Brad looked at her over his shoulder. "What?"

"You're using a Phillips head screwdriver." She pointed toward the offending tool. "I think you need a screwdriver with a flat head."

She didn't think, she knew. Stacey rummaged around the toolbox a little and then found what she was looking for. She took out a medium-size flat-head screwdriver and held it out to him.

He took it much the way he took a scalpel. "I was going to try that next."

Stacey managed to suppress a smile.

As he went back to work, she said, "Jim stopped by the other morning." She waited, but Brad made no comment. "He had some good news."

She saw Brad stop for a moment, but he didn't turn to look at her. "He's decided to go back to school for a real degree?"

"No. He told me he has a gig."

This time, Brad did turn around. His expression was quizzical. "A what?"

"A gig," she repeated. And got the same results. She knew she'd used the term before, but Brad completely shut out what didn't interest him. She could probably repeat the term a dozen times and it still wouldn't register. "A job performing at a club. He and the band," she added. Still no response. She gave Brad another sound bite of information. "At the end of the month. He wants us to come."

Brad moved his shoulders in a dismissive gesture. "So go."

"Us," she repeated with feeling. "The pronoun is 'us.' He wants *us* to come hear him."

He turned around, a screwdriver in his hand, a scowl on his face. "I don't like that kind of music."

She was pretty sure that Brad didn't know what "that kind of music" was since he'd never listened to Jim play. But that wasn't the important point.

"But you like your son, right?" When he said nothing, frustration made her press on. "Right?"

Brad sighed. It was an old battle, fought with bent swords and no promise of victory for either side. A truce was the best that could be hoped for.

"Yes, I like my son, I just don't like the course his life is taking." He thought of the boy who'd been such a sponge, soaking up information faster than it could be dispensed to him. Where had that boy gone? And why, why had he gone? "He's wasting all that intelligence, all that potential."

Brad was looking at it from a father's vantage point. Had he completely forgotten what it had been like to be young and starting out? A twenty-two-year-old who wanted something different? Who wanted to grab life by the waist and hang on, hoping for a wild, exhilarating ride?

"If your father had said to you that going to medical school wasn't sensible because you'd be going heavily into debt and it would take years before you could actually earn a livable wage, would you have listened to him? Would you have gone into the family business because that amounted to immediate gratification and an immediate salary?"

The family business had gone belly-up years ago. He'd

never thought of it as particularly stable, or a way to go. Even as a kid. "No, but—"

She grabbed what she could, not letting him continue and negate the point she was trying to make. "Everyone has to do what they feel is best for them. You can't live Jim's life for him."

He wouldn't have if he could. But he would have liked to lay down the groundwork, the ground rules. "No, but I don't have to approve of it, either, and by going to listen to him play, I'm telling Jim that I approve of the way he's throwing his life away."

Stacey looked at him, shaking her head. For an intelligent man who graduated first in his medical class, he could still be as dense as split pea soup. "No, Brad, what you're telling our son is that you love him and you support him even though what he's doing wouldn't have been your choice for him. Everyone needs to hear that. Even people who claim to be hard-nosed about it."

"Support," Brad echoed, saying the word as if it left a horribly bitter taste in his mouth. "That's what it all boils down to, doesn't it? Support."

"Emotionally," Stacey emphasized. "Not financially, emotionally. Jim needs to know we're behind him." Because Brad had turned away, Stacey moved around him until she was in his face. She hated talking to the back of his head. Especially when she was pleading. "At least tell me you'll think about it."

Brad's hand tightened around the screwdriver. He felt cornered and he hated feeling his shoulder blades against the wall. But Jim was his son and beneath the layers of misunderstanding that had begun to thrive between them, blood did count for something.

The memory of a small boy, looking up at him eagerly, hanging on his every word, echoed back to Brad. He missed those times. Missed that kid.

Brad blew out a breath, temporarily surrendering. "Okay, I'll think about it."

These days, a little bit went a long way for her. A very long way. Impulsively, she threw her arms around his neck and hugged him. "Thank you. That's all I ask."

With the screwdriver in his hand, Brad didn't trust himself to return the hug. His right hand hung limply at his side. He patted her back with his left.

"No, that's not all you ask," he told her. "You ask a lot more than that."

Turning back to his "work," Brad took out first one screw, then another. Tiny though it was, a sense of triumph began to build. He put both screws down on the coffee table. Without the restraining metal bar, the profusion of colored, plastic-coated wires appeared as if they would shoot out of their confining hole at any second.

There was still the switch to deal with. The screws holding it in place were smaller. He went in search of a smaller screwdriver. Once he found one on the bottom of the toolbox, he applied it to the two screws.

Watching him, Stacey held her breath.

Brad continued, "You're asking me to go."

"Well, ultimately, yes. That's what I hope your heart will get you to do."

The relationship that he and Jim had enjoyed had long since died. "He doesn't care if I show up."

"He does care," Stacey insisted. Mentally, she crossed her

fingers as the lie passed her lips. "He said so. He told me to invite you. Us, remember?" she said, referring to what she'd said earlier about Jim's invitation. Brad's look was deeply scrutinizing, but she held fast, refusing to back off. "He did."

The exact opposite was true, but saying so wouldn't help mend the torn fences between father and son. She'd been doing this verbal balancing act for almost a year now, lying to one about what the other had said. She hoped that if she issued enough little white lies, she would manage to draw the two men together close enough to have them willingly carry on a dialogue instead of avoiding each other.

But this time, Brad laughed shortly, shaking his head. Ordinarily, Stacey didn't lie. He could bet his life on her truthfulness. But this was something that was too close to her heart and it blinded her to everything but reaching her goal. Getting him to talk to Jim again, even though his son showed him no respect.

"I don't believe you," Brad told her a second before he put two wires together. He could hear her draw in her breath, could feel her eyes widening as she watched. He grinned in triumph, twisting the ends of the wires together. "See, nothing to it."

The next second, darkness had swallowed up the entire house.

"Apparently," Stacey commented under her breath.

CHAPTER 31

She heard Brad muttering a curse under his breath. "Damn it, maybe if I just adjust—"

"*No!*" Stacey cried with the same feeling she uttered the time Jimmy had stood on the edge of the glass-top coffee table, a towel tied haphazardly around his neck, and declared he was going to fly. He'd gone crashing through the table the next moment. But Jimmy had been four at the time. Brad was twelve times that and hopefully at least twice as smart.

"No," she repeated when she heard no outburst of pain or saw any sparks flying from the general vicinity of Brad and the light switch. "Don't adjust anything," she told him, trying hard not to sound as if she were lecturing. But what else could you do with an ordinarily intelligent husband who had taken leave of his senses? She couldn't very well stand by and egg him on.

She liked being married and had no desire to suddenly find herself a Merry Widow at the age of forty-seven.

"But—" Brad protested.

"Brad, please. The last thing in the world you should be doing right now is *anything* with live wires. There's no light. You can't see what you're doing," she tried to reason with him. "You could get electrocuted."

"Small chance of that happening," Brad muttered under his breath, but audibly enough for her to hear. "It looks like the whole house lost power."

She looked around. No light came from the hallway, which she'd been told by an electrician was on a different circuit. "I'd say that's a fair guess."

She thought she heard Brad rummaging around in the toolbox. For what? Besides, he couldn't recognize anything by touch. This wasn't the operating table. As far as he as concerned, this was no man's land.

"Honey, wait," she cautioned.

The rummage noise ceased. "For what?" Brad asked.

For common sense to come back to you. "I'm going to get a flashlight," she told him. "I started putting things away in the new cabinets in the family room this morning before I left. I remember storing a couple of flashlights in one of the upper cabinets."

She'd thought about leaving everything for the weekend and was now glad that she was on the obsessive side when it came to restoring order. Putting things away had been slow going, but she refused to just haphazardly toss items into the cabinets and hope for a day when she would find the time to reorganize.

"All right," Brad agreed. "I'll wait until you get the flashlight. If I see what two colors I inadvertently connected, I can remedy that and—"

"Brad, you're not a professional," she insisted. "Why don't you just leave—Ow." she cried as pain went surging up and down her leg, so intense that it felt as if the top of her head was coming off. Her kneecap, the point of contact, was throbbing.

"What?"

Brad's voice was utterly alert. As if he was ready to spring into battle and defend her. The pain began to recede, allowing her to smile to herself.

"I walked into something." She took a deep breath, willing the rest of the pain away. "The recliner, I think." It had wood trim around its edges.

She heard the rhythmic sound of nails hitting tile—and sliding. Mournful sounds of dogs followed. Despite their sliding, it was obvious that the four-footed creatures could maneuver far better in the dark than she could, Stacey thought.

"I should be the one getting the flashlight." Brad's voice was closer than it had been a minute ago.

She bit back the instant command that rose to her lips. He wouldn't appreciate her ordering *him* to "Stay," or saying that he had done more than enough for one night.

So she asked him a simple question: "Why?" Because his statement made no sense to her.

Her outstretched fingertips came in contact with something hard and smooth. The cabinet. She felt around the surface, making her way toward the far right. The cabinet closest to the right wall was where she'd placed the flashlights. She hadn't checked the batteries before she'd put them away. Stacey mentally crossed her fingers that they worked and that God didn't have a nasty sense of humor.

At least not one he wanted to exercise now.

Finding the wall, she worked her way back to the cabinet door. There were two cabinet doors at each of the locations, one above, one below. The cabinet with the flashlights was approximately chest level.

"Flashlight-finding isn't particularly gender-oriented," she pointed out as she opened the cabinet door.

"No, but you're bumping into things."

She turned her head in the direction of Brad's voice. "And you wouldn't?"

"Yes, I would," he admitted grudgingly. "But I don't want you getting hurt."

Because of something he'd done, Stacey surmised, filling in the unspoken part of her husband's sentence. At times, understanding Brad required a great deal of second-guessing.

"I'll live," she assured him cheerfully. "It wasn't a rabid recliner."

Where had she put those flashlights? She reached in farther. The cabinets were a lot deeper than the old ones had been. Until just now, that had seemed like a good thing. She would have to remember to keep the flashlights in the front.

Her hand slid over something she didn't recognize. She tried to remember what else she'd put away in this particular cabinet and came up blank.

"What's taking so long?" he asked her.

"I'm being careful. I have X-Acto knives stored somewhere around here and I don't want to slice open my fingers."

"Look, let me—"

Just then, her fingers came in contact with the long, smooth shank of the last flashlight she'd bought. Metallic-blue and sleek, it would have gladdened the heart of any night watchman on patrol. "Eureka."

"Stacey, what's the matter?"

He sounded, tense, worried. "That was a good cry," she told him. "I found one of the flashlights." Withdrawing it from the cabinet, she fumbled around, searching for the on-off switch. Finding it, she flipped it to the on position.

A strong beam of light emerged. Stacey grinned in triumph. The batteries *weren't* dead. "And the Lord said, let there be light, and it was good. For at least three hours," she added, remembering what it said on the hard plastic that had encased the flashlight.

She turned the flashlight toward Brad and saw that he no longer stood by the defunct light switch. He crossed to her, his project temporarily forgotten. "What happens in three hours?"

"The batteries die." The instructions had warned that the light was particularly strong and that it drained batteries rather quickly.

The news didn't seem to faze him. "I'll have it fixed by then."

God, but he was a stubborn man. She hadn't found the flashlight just to watch her husband electrocute himself by its light.

"No," she told him firmly, digging her feet in to take a stand, "you won't."

And it was much too late to get an electrician in at that hour. There were a few around-the-clock emergency services, but she and Brad weren't at that life-and-death stage. Because they'd want immediate service, it would probably cost an arm, a leg and half a head to get someone out here before Monday morning.

Taking out the second flashlight, a smaller rendition of the one she was now holding, she handed it over it to Brad before aiming her own at the kitchen. "I'm going to get some candles from the kitchen and you're going to have dinner before it turns into a Popsicle."

"But what about the power failure?"

She liked the way he made it sound generic, as if something had befallen the entire city and was not the result of his playing Mr. Fix-It.

"The 'power failure' can take care of itself," she told him.

He followed her, not because he was hungry but because standing in the dark that he had inadvertently created intensified his feeling of inadequacy.

"I know how to fix it," he protested. "I just crossed the wrong wires—"

Stacey looked over her shoulder just before she took out a dinner plate. An amused smile played on her lips. "You think?"

He scowled, his fingers tightening around the flashlight. "You're not being very supportive."

"Why? Because I don't want you playing with tools and possibly hurting yourself?"

She could see by his expression that she'd said exactly the wrong thing. That she wasn't supposed to say he was "playing" with tools or that she anticipated him hurting himself. But facts were facts and he was always the first one to point that out to her.

She tried to ameliorate her words, if not her sentiment. "Brad, honey, you have got a million attributes and I'm very proud of you. But none of those attributes involve being mechanically inclined—and why should they?"

Setting the flashlight on the counter on its end, with the beam of light hitting the ceiling, she sent out a pool of dim light while she retrieved two long tapering candlesticks from the cupboard next to where she kept the dishes and glassware. After returning to the dining room, she placed one candle into each of the two white ceramic candlestick holders on either side of a very fragrant arrangement of flowers in the center of the table.

Carnations and baby's breath. Her favorite, he vaguely recalled.

Brad's eyes narrowed as the flower arrangement registered. "Who are the flowers from?"

"Not you," she replied mildly.

Taking a match from the book she kept on the first shelf beside the candles, she struck it. The flame sizzled before it settled down. She lit first one candle, then the other.

"I know that," he told her between his teeth. "Who are they from?"

For some perverse reason, Stacey was tempted to string him along, to make him think that perhaps someone else found her attractive. Attractive enough to send her flowers. But that was juvenile, she told herself. And she was beyond those kinds of games. Or should have been.

"Me, Brad." Satisfied that the light would remain, she straightened up and softly blew out the match. "The flowers are from me. Because I like pretty things." *And waiting for you to send me flowers would mean that I would probably have to be dead.*

He looked at her as if he was having trouble processing her words. "You sent the flowers?"

"No, I *bought* the flowers. The store has a delivery charge." And she wasn't a spendthrift, no matter what he thought of her, she added silently.

Returning to the kitchen, Stacey opened the now-dormant stove where she'd kept the dinner warming until Brad had killed the electricity. Taking out the pan, she placed it on top of the range.

"I tried something new with seafood," she told him. "I thought you might like it."

He looked over her shoulder as she arranged the food on a single plate. "Will you join me?"

The invitation surprised her. Ordinarily, he didn't think anything of eating alone. His hours were such that most of the time, meals were taken without him, even when the kids were growing up.

She didn't care for the fish she'd prepared for him. Salmon was his favorite. It wasn't hers. But this was the first time that he'd actually asked her to join him in years.

She didn't have the heart to turn him down. Especially while his ego was still suffering. So she smiled and nodded. "Sure. That'd be nice."

CHAPTER 32

And it was nice, she thought a little while later. Surprisingly nice to linger over a meal. To have a conversation that didn't dissolve into sound bites because one or the other of them was in a hurry to be done. Or because an argument was pending.

They sat and talked. About the house, about his day. About hers. If she didn't know better, she would have said they'd both walked through a time warp that went back some twenty years or more. When they were first starting out. When Brad had been willing to share his day and been curious about hers.

Maybe it was the candles, she mused. They'd shut off the flashlights to conserve them and used just the candles for light. They had cast just enough illumination to make the meal spectacularly romantic.

She'd even forgotten she was eating salmon.

"This was good," he told her, retiring his fork on top of the plate.

She smiled. He barely noticed what he ate these days. Had she known he'd be this nice, she would have handed him a screwdriver and pointed him toward a light switch years ago.

"Glad you liked it."

Leaning over, she took his plate and then placed it on top of her own. Silverware clinked together as she started to get up.

Brad placed his hand on hers. "Don't go yet."

"It's just to the kitchen. To do the dishes," she said, as if she hadn't done this a thousand times before. Although, she'd never done it in a Brad-generated power failure.

Brad shook his head, his hand still on hers. "The dishes'll keep."

"The dishes'll get crusty," she told him.

Releasing her hand, he rose and took both plates in his. He walked into the kitchen with them. Stacey was on her feet, two steps behind him. "Wait, I didn't mean for you to do them."

The light from the dining room faintly seeped into the kitchen. He placed the dishes in the sink, then picked up the larger of the two flashlights she'd left on the counter, turning it on. Leaving it on the counter, he turned on the water in the sink.

"I know," he told her. Once he opened the cabinet beneath the sink, he rummaged around for the detergent, knocking over containers. "Not exactly much I can do in the dark. Watching the news is out."

Stacey squatted down beside him. Her hand went right to the detergent. They rose to their feet together.

"You could try reading," she told him, squirting a little of the detergent on the top dish.

"Eyestrain," he countered. "Besides, looking at you is easier on the eyes than trying to read newspaper print in limited light." Crossing his arms, he leaned his back against the counter. Watching her. "Have you noticed they're using smaller print these days?"

The hazards of getting older, Stacey thought, passing a scouring brush along the surface of the first dish. She'd given up the fight against reading glasses just this spring. Brad had followed suit not long afterward.

"Yes, I noticed." A smile played on her lips. "Someone should write to the editor, make him aware of that," she added, tongue in cheek.

He nodded. "Someone should." After picking up a dish towel, he took the wet dish from her and dried it. "I'm sorry about the electricity."

She shrugged, not wanting to dwell on the mishap. "The governor is always saying we should cut back on our consumption of electricity."

Brad laughed. "I doubt if this was what he had in mind." And then, as he continued drying the second dish, all but massaging it, he grew serious. "But I really am sorry."

He paused as a sigh escaped his lips. He debated saying more, or just letting it drop. But tonight, he didn't feel like letting things drop. Tonight, standing here in the dark, he remembered another time when there had been no electricity. When there hadn't been enough money to pay the bill and they had spent the weekend in darkness until Stacey could bring the payment to one of Southern California Edison's branch offices. "I guess I just started feeling inadequate."

She turned off the water and stared at him. If anyone should be the picture of confidence, it was Brad. He had all sorts of plaques in the den, honoring him, honoring his efforts. "You? Why?"

"Because…" Damn, this was hard for him to get out. He was tempted to wave his hand and mumble, "Never mind," But the dark wouldn't let him. He tried again. "Because these people, the men who come to work here—when they come

to work—some of them can't string together two coherent
sentences. But they can *build* something—and I can't even
put in a light dimmer," he said in disgust.

"You could if you ever watched it being done."

He raised his eyes to her face, surprised she came so quickly
to his defense. But then, why should he be surprised? Stacey
had always been on his side. When they were starting out,
she'd been there with him every step of the way. And he had
gotten his degree, and she had gotten—forgotten, he thought
with a pang.

"Brad, listen to me." She took his hands in hers. Her eyes
were intent as she looked up at him. "These people wouldn't
know how to build our shower, or hang doors or even the
right way to paint, without having seen it done once—or a
dozen times." She lifted a shoulder in a gesture that swiftly
dismissed those talents. "You could do the same thing in half
the time, with half the observation."

Brad smiled at her words, at the intensity behind them.
All for his benefit. "You don't really believe that."

Her eyes widened. "Yes, I do. I've always thought that you
could do anything you put your mind to. *Anything,*" she emphasized with such conviction, she almost had him convinced that she meant what she said.

"I suppose," he allowed with a smile so reminiscent of the
man she'd fallen in love with. "I won you."

She laughed. He might smile like the man she fell in love
with, but his memory was certainly present day—and foggy.

"That wasn't exactly 'winning,' Brad. To win, you would
have had to have been in some sort of a contest. As I
remember it, you stood still long enough for me to catch up

and throw my arms around you." Since they were telling each other things, and the darkness seemed to be absolving them of past sins, she shared one more thing with him. Something that had rested heavily on her chest all these years, especially as they grew further apart. "I used to feel that if I hadn't made it so easy for you, maybe you would have appreciated me more."

He looked at her, surprised that she could have that kind of thought. That kind of doubt about his feelings. "I do appreciate you."

She wondered if he actually believed what he was saying. To an outsider, his actions said differently. And all she had were his actions, because Brad was hardly ever vocal about what was going on inside of him.

"Sometimes it's very hard to tell," she told him quietly.

Brad began to protest, but then he shut his mouth. Instead, he took the glass she had just picked up to wash out of her hand and felt around behind him for the counter. He wasn't looking at the counter because he was too busy looking at her.

Remembering the girl she had once been. Remembering the woman she had become. The woman who had given him so much pleasure, when he'd been there to receive it. It occurred to him, just then, that they had grown up together. And then, somehow, grown apart. Couldn't there be one without the other?

It was really silly. Her heart began to race. Race because the man whom she knew better than herself had touched her.

"What are you doing?" she whispered.

She couldn't remember the last time that Brad had made

any kind of romantic overtures toward her outside of their bedroom. And even that was difficult to remember.

When he didn't answer, she asked, "Brad, are you flirting with me?"

"Doing my damnedest," he told her. "I guess I'm out of practice."

She held her breath as she threaded her arms around his neck. Everything inside of her felt like smiling. "They tell me that it's like riding a bicycle. You never really forget how."

"I never learned how to ride a bicycle, either," he told her.

Stacey's eyes widened. She didn't know that about him. They'd never attempted to go bike-riding, never talked about it. When the children had reached that age, she'd been the one to teach them how to ride a bicycle because he was never home.

After all these years, something new. Who would have thought?

She grinned. "And still you went to the head of the class," she marveled. "I guess you were always destined for greatness."

From out of nowhere, like an old friend he'd lost touch with, his love for her overwhelmed him. Brad lowered his mouth and kissed her.

In the background, he heard the two dogs beginning to make noise, each animal jealous of the attention.

He felt Stacey's lips curving against his. Brad drew his head back slightly. "What?"

"First it was the kids, now it's the pets. I'm beginning to remember why it was always such a challenge for us to be alone in the early years."

"Wait right here," Brad told her as he stepped back into the dining room. Both dogs followed closely behind him.

She peered into the next room and saw him extinguishing the candles. "What are you up to?"

"Making sure we're not interrupted by the fire department." Returning, he brushed by her and smiled. "Now, where was I?"

She fully expected him to resume kissing her. Instead, Brad picked up the large flashlight from the counter and handed it to her. As she took it from him, Stacey found herself becoming airborne. He'd scooped her up in his arms.

"Brad?"

"Hold that thought," he instructed, making his way through the foyer to the stairs.

"Brad, put me down," she insisted. "You'll hurt your back."

He gave no indication that he was about to listen to her. "And you'll hurt my pride if you point out any more things I'm not capable of doing."

He was right, Stacey thought. The male ego was fragile. There was no way she was going to damage his, especially not right now.

Stacey held on to his neck with one hand and with the other, illuminated the way up the stairs.

When he came to the landing, Brad was breathing a bit heavier than she was happy about, but she kept that to herself. Underneath it all, he was still the boy she'd married.

"Well, that was nice," she told him once her feet touched the floor again.

Brad said nothing. Instead, he cupped her face and brought his mouth down to hers.

With a sigh, she sank into the kiss, remembering how wonderful it all had once been.

CHAPTER 33

Brad drew her into their bedroom, half of which was still in the throes of being remodeled. The mirrored doors fronting the old closet were still up. They captured the single beam from the flashlight Brad had tossed into the room, casting it back at them like shooting stars.

Just outside the windows, on either side of the California king-size bed, the moon presented its full face, illuminating part of the room more brightly than the flashlight.

They made love like two strangers, familiar with the rituals and what to expect, but completely taken by surprise as the particulars began to emerge.

Stacey found herself moving backward, as if in a dance whose melody she heard only in her head. Felt in her bones. His mouth sealed to hers, draining away her soul, Brad guided her to the foot of their bed.

The eagerness she tasted on his lips was something she hadn't anticipated.

They had known each other and made love with each other since the beginning of time, although far more sparingly in the past ten, twelve years.

The novelty of it had vanished. Lovemaking had become comfortable between them, done by the numbers. There were no longer any unexpected moves, no sudden thrills exploding out of nowhere. Just a steady building until the final satisfying release.

Brad had always been a good lover, a thoughtful lover, whenever he finally got around to it. But those times had grown few and far between and, as time went on, some resentment built within her. Resentment because, however unintentionally, Brad had made her feel like a supplicant in her own marriage bed. As if the act of lovemaking meant far more to her than it did to him. But this time was different.

This time, from the moment he kissed her on the landing, she could feel something unusual taking place. It was almost like the first time. Except that there was no fumbling. Only eagerness.

Rather than languid, the way their kisses had become, the kiss he pressed to her parted lips was fiery. In one instant, his embrace took away her breath, her very ability to think.

Not that she was busy mentally planning the household budget or laying out next month's schedule when they made love. She couldn't solve geometry problems in her head while their bodies were involved with building friction and momentum, but she *was* conscious of the moves. As well as conscious of the sounds coming from somewhere outside their bedroom window. She was never so taken away by what was happening on their mattress that she wasn't able to hear a plane flying overheard. Or a car screeching to a stop to avoid a near collision. Or the neighbor's dog barking, answering some imagined challenge in the distance.

But this time, as Brad's skillful hands roamed along her body, tantalizing her, drawing away her clothing one article at a time until she was rendered completely nude, her heart began to accelerate until it hammered wildly in her chest. She wasn't even sure how it managed to remain within her body. It felt as if, any second, her heart would break free.

Her pulse echoed the rhythm, deepening, intensifying, until her body literally vibrated with anticipation. With effort, she focused, forcing herself to concentrate instead of allowing her mind to completely surrender to liquefaction. As much as she wanted to absorb, to ride out the hurricane in all its glory, she needed to be an active participant.

Mimicking Brad's movements, she tugged his shirt out of his pants, undoing the buttons one at a time so that she could push the material off his shoulders. With one sharp movement that visibly stole his breath and gave her a sense of empowerment, Stacey unhooked his belt, then opened the catch at the top.

When they'd first gotten married, he'd had a twenty-eight-inch waist and she'd faced the challenge of trying to find dress pants for him with that waist and thirty-four-inch inseam. It hadn't been easy. Nothing about their early life together had been easy, but the memories that lingered were wonderful.

In twenty-six years, Brad had only gained three inches on his waist, even though he no longer worked out the way he once had. Then it had been almost a religion for him, a way to release the pent-up tension that had no other outlet. But he'd gotten away from that for the most part, like everything else.

Even so, she knew he was still a hell of a catch. Not just because he was a doctor, but because he was still young-looking, still handsome. Still vital.

Still desirable, she thought.

Desire raced through her now. She was eager for the ultimate mingling, yet wanting desperately to savor every nuance of this. It had been years since they had been this intense. Years since this much want had raced through her veins. Had all but brought tears to her eyes. He was making her body sing.

Oh, God, she'd missed this. Missed the teeth-jarring, hot sex that made her feel every inch a woman. As he possessed her, Stacey curled her body into his, her hands raking over all his well-known spaces.

Stacey bit her lip as she felt his fingers delve into her. Catching her breath, her head spinning, she returned the favor and touched him intimately. And heard a guttural sound of appreciation escape his lips. It made her almost wild with desire.

She had no idea why, no explanation for this sudden surge in her veins. All she knew was that the degree of passion she was experiencing had not visited her for a very long, long time.

Her breathing became shallow and she could hardly catch her breath. But if she was going to die this way, so be it. She'd go with a smile on her lips.

Brad had no idea what had triggered this intense surge. He wanted to ravage her. This was his wife, for pity's sake, a woman whose body he knew even better than his own. And yet, there was a newness here, a feeling that had been absent for so long that he hardly recognized it when it reappeared.

Desire, hot and intense. Raw. Branding him as it made its demands.

He didn't know whether it was the lack of light, the fact that half the house seemed to be in a state of upheaval, or that she didn't care that he couldn't wield a hammer. Whatever the reason, Stacey seemed different tonight. More like the woman he'd once known.

She was still Stacey, and yet she wasn't. All he really knew was that whoever she was, he wanted her. Wanted her the way he hadn't wanted her for a very long time.

Maybe all it was was a midlife crisis, he didn't know. He didn't care. Because the feeling was exquisite and he had missed it. Missed feeling this alive. Missed feeling this degree of excitement just over touching her. Over anticipating the final passage into a euphoric state that he knew evaporated far too quickly.

For once in his life, logic did not negate anticipation.

Brad filled his hands with her, enjoying the softness of her skin, the heat of her body as she turned and twisted beneath him. He kissed her over and over again, each kiss building on the last.

Each kiss promising more to come.

This wasn't the comfortable lovemaking he was accustomed to, the anticipated release of tension and stress that waited for him at the end. This had fire and passion and allure. And he found it irresistible.

His mind was a complete blank. All that remained was the wanting. It was pure and unstrained and he marveled at the fact that he had allowed everything else to get in the way. To make him forget just how good it could be between them.

Tucking her body against his, Brad raised his body until he was positioned over her. Her eyes spoke to him, calling to him. He could feel his heart reaching out to hers. Entwining his fingers with hers, he raised his hips and then drove himself into her.

Sheathed himself within her as everything, *everything* else faded into oblivion. Everything but the pounding rhythm that echoed within both of them. He moved faster and faster, until he reached the end.

Crying out her name.

It hadn't been this good in so long that he couldn't recall the last time. Brad held on to the momentum, the sensation, as hard as he could.

And then came the afterglow.

The afterglow clung to him with a tenacity that gladdened his heart even as it surprised him. And made him remember, ever so faintly, another time, another place, when nothing else mattered as much as Stacey did.

When had he lost that?

With every ounce of strength he had available to him, Brad hung on to that feeling, that memory. And let the soft, faint scent of her shampoo, the one that reminded him of almonds and vanilla, fill his head and his senses.

And for a brief, brief moment, it pushed away everything else.

He tightened his arms around her, experiencing emotions that were all but foreign to him.

CHAPTER 34

Only the sound of their breathing and the fading flashlight on the floor broke up the silence and darkness. Neither of them said a word as the euphoria had receded and then dissolved into the shadows. Finally, Stacey took a deep breath. As if that would help shield her from the answer she feared was coming. But she had to ask. Had to know. Hiding her head in the sand wouldn't change anything.

"Are you leaving me?"

Stunned, Brad was certain he'd imagined the question. It was too ridiculous to be real. "What?"

And then it came again, her voice stronger this time. "Are you leaving me?"

He raised himself up on his elbow to look at her. Stacey was staring at the ceiling as she asked the question. The branches of an oak tree right outside their window cast elongated shadows, like grasping fingers, along the ceiling. It added to the surrealistic scenario.

Had he imagined all this? The lovemaking? The passion? The insane question?

"Stacey?"

And then she wasn't staring at the ceiling any longer. Her eyes had shifted to his face. To his soul. There was no mischief, no smile, no indication that she was anything but serious.

"Are you?" she asked again.

For a second, he was utterly speechless. Shell-shocked. And then he demanded, "What kind of a question is that?"

Stacey took another deep breath, which didn't help. Nothing calmed this uneasy feeling. Brad wasn't telling her that she was being absurd. Wasn't even bothering to deny the supposition behind her question.

Something inside of her tightened. Now that she'd had a chance to slip off her cloud and examine what had just taken place, anxiety had a deathlike grip on her. Anxiety forged by an anticipated outcome she didn't want.

An anticipation that wouldn't release her, wouldn't allow her to breathe. Was it a coincidence? Or was this the way things were now done? She ran her tongue along lips that were suddenly sandpaper dry.

"Charlotte Lowe's husband made love to her the morning before he left for the office. She said it was the best sex they'd ever had. That afternoon, just as she was defrosting the pork chops for his dinner, some process server in a secondhand suit served her with divorce papers. She was completely devastated."

He was trying to follow her and figure out what this had to do with them. "By the sex?"

"By the divorce papers." She pressed her lips together. Charlotte had cried through all three of the cocktails she'd had at lunch. "She said she never even saw it coming."

Brad looked at her for a long moment, in his mind's eye

seeing what the shadows blotted out. "And you think I'm divorcing you."

She didn't know. She wanted to think not, but why this sudden change? She hadn't done anything spectacular, anything different from the way she'd been doing things all along.

I love you, Brad. I always have, I always will.

Humor played along her lips as she tried to shut away her suspicions. Her fears.

"Or setting me up for a hit."

Stacey shifted her body toward his, her blond hair spilling out onto her shoulder. For some reason, he found that particularly arousing tonight. He touched her face, wishing he could see into her mind. He couldn't tell, by either her voice or her expression, if she was being serious, or just joking.

They used to joke, he thought. He'd loved the sound of her laughter. When was the last time he'd heard it?

Her eyes delved into him. What was she looking for? he wondered. What did she see? A stranger? Or the man she married? At times, he felt as if nothing had changed, the rest of the time he felt as if everything had. Including him.

"You haven't made love with me like that since before the kids were born," she told him softly.

Toying with a strand of her hair, he wrapped it around his finger, his eyes never leaving hers. "Maybe I thought we were overdue." And then he smiled. "Or maybe it was whatever you put in that seafood medley you served tonight."

Slowly, a smile began to curve the corners of her mouth. "Then you're not divorcing me?"

His voice was solemn as he told her, "Couldn't afford it. I'd lose half of everything."

Stacey felt the foundations of her world slip a little. "Oh."

Brad cupped her cheek. "And you. Mostly you," he told her tenderly. "Especially you."

Her heart did a little somersault in her chest. When was the last time he'd said anything nearly as romantic as that? Who *was* this man?

"All right, now I am worried," she deadpanned. "I need to see some kind of ID. Better yet, I want a DNA test done." And then the glimmer of a smile faded and she turned serious as a new concern assaulted her. One that was even worse. She scrutinized his face, wondering if there were any telltale signs she'd missed. "There's nothing wrong, is there?"

"Wrong?" Because it was Stacey, the word was too broad to attach a meaning to. He needed more of a clarification.

"Yes, wrong," she repeated, emphasizing the word. Her body was turned into his, but she was no longer aware of the warmth between them. Real concern had blocked everything else out. "You didn't just find out that you have something, did you?"

She couldn't bring herself to say the dreaded words. Here she was, a doctor's wife, and she was just as much in terror of the world's fatal diseases as everyone else. Maybe more.

"You mean like six months to live?"

"Yes," Stacey whispered. She searched his face for a sign that she was wrong again. But he looked so serious. Had she guessed it? Was he trying to savor what little time he had left? Her stomach tightened so hard, she could barely breathe. "Do you?"

He inclined his head, as if searching for a way to answer her. "I imagine I do. Have six months. Maybe more."

She looked at him. And saw the smile that was struggling

to curve his mouth. Damn him, he was waxing philosophical—and scaring her half to death while he was at it.

"You're not leaving me and you're not dying."

"No," he answered. "I'm not." He threaded his fingers through her hair. "I'm not dying and I'm definitely not leaving you on my own power."

She blew out a breath, confused. "I don't understand. I like it," she added quickly, "but I don't understand."

He laughed and traced the outline of her lips with his finger. The way he used to, he suddenly recalled. "Maybe you shouldn't. Maybe I shouldn't." Dropping his hand, he drew her closer. "All I know is that for no reason, out of nowhere, I started thinking about what it would be like not to have you in my life." His expression turned serious. "And I didn't like it."

Yes, Virginia, there is *a Santa Claus.* Because Brad was being so honest, so straightforward, she found herself wanting to tell him things that she had been harboring in her heart.

She splayed her hand on his chest. The light smattering of hair tickled her palm.

"I know I pay the bills and figure out our taxes and do the hundred and one things that belong inside of each day, but I didn't think you noticed any of that."

"I guess I didn't," he confessed. "Oh, on some level, I knew it was happening because I didn't have to deal with any of it. Didn't have to deal with making dinner, searching through a pile of rumpled clothes, trying to find something that was clean, or having the phone go out because I forgot to pay the telephone bill. You took care of all that so well, I was only aware of the end results." He smiled at her. "You made life very comfortable for me, Stacey.

"Maybe I got too comfortable. Too sure of myself." He caressed her face. "Maybe it took short-circuiting the house to show me that I'm not a superhero. That I can't handle everything—and I don't."

She could feel her heart being won over all over again. Moments like this—and God, she hoped there would be more—reminded her why she'd fallen in love with him. And why she was still in love with him.

"Nobody can."

He laughed shortly, contradicting her. "That guy who's been strutting around here most mornings acts like he can."

"You mean Alex?" she guessed.

He wasn't much when it came to names. "The head contractor."

"Alex," she confirmed. "And if Alex was *that* capable, then the house would have already been finished instead of just halfway there." She thought of what Brad had said to her when he'd initially complained. "He would have taken it on, one house at a time, completed it and then moved on to the next."

Brad could see right through her. And it was comforting, he realized. For a while there, he'd lost that knack. "You're saying that to make me feel better."

"I'm saying that because it's true," she insisted. And then she grinned broadly. "Just like it's true that you shouldn't be allowed to pick up a tool under penalty of death."

His pride stung a little, even though he knew she was right. "Oh, I'm not that bad."

Stacey gestured around at the darkness. "I rest my case."

"Rest?" Brad echoed playfully. His eyes on hers, he grazed the back of his hand along her nude body, strumming it slowly as if he were touching the strings of a priceless guitar. "Is that what you're thinking about right now? Rest?"

Stacey could feel her body being aroused again. Humming in response to his light touch. She could feel it begin to moisten again in anticipation.

Her voice was husky as she lay back down, threading her arms around his neck. "Actually, no. Just the opposite, if you must know."

"I must know," he told her just before he brought his mouth down to hers.

CHAPTER 35

Still talking on the phone, Julie answered the door, then did an old-fashioned, belated double-take when she realized who was standing in her doorway.

"Um, I'm going to have to call you back," she told the person on the other end of the cordless phone, then terminated the connection. Stunned, she stepped back, admitting her far-from-expected visitor into the tiny communal living room of the off-campus apartment she shared with three other med students. "Mom, what are you doing here?"

Stacey had been here only half a dozen times, always by invitation. This was the first time she'd come unannounced on the off chance that Julie was in. Impulse had brought her here.

It looked as if twelve very messy people were living here instead of just three, Stacey thought, covertly glancing around and hoping that Julie didn't notice. "I thought I'd drop by and ask you for some advice."

For a moment, Julie remained exactly where she was, staring at her mother and rendered utterly speechless. And then she leaned back in order to look out of the second-floor window.

"Was that a rip in the fabric of time I just heard?" Straightening again, she looked at her mother in earnest. "You're asking *me* for advice? You who dispenses advice faster than that Pez dispenser you have on the shelf in the family room?"

Stacey smiled. Julie was referring to the dated candy dispenser her uncle Titus had given her when she was a little girl. Legend had it that the dispenser had been his when he'd been her age. The toy wasn't on the shelf anymore. She'd placed it in a drawer in her bureau to keep safe during the renovations. The renovations in the family room were completed, but the dispenser still remained in her drawer.

Taking no offense because she knew that none had been intended, Stacey told her daughter, "Well, I've come to learn that in some areas, you know more than I do."

Soundlessly, Julie crossed the living room, leading the way to the first bedroom on the right. Her bedroom. A couple more steps had her at her desk. And the calendar that hung on the wall just beside it. She circled today's date. Putting her pen down, she looked over her shoulder at her mother who'd followed her into the room.

"Just in case I ever forget—which I won't," Julie assured her. "Okay, shoot." And then she suddenly became serious. And just a little pale. "You're not leaving Dad, are you?"

It was Stacey's turn to stare. Julie's question had come out of nowhere, with no preamble and, she'd like to think, at least as far as the children were concerned, no basis. The truth was, if she had wanted to leave Brad, it would have been years ago. For some unknown reason, things were finally getting better between them now.

"Why would you say that?" Stacey asked. "And why would I be asking your advice about something like that if it *were* true?"

Relieved, Julie blew out a breath. "Well, I know some things about breakups."

There was no arguing with that. Julie had been drop-dead gorgeous ever since she'd graduated junior high school. And each year from then had been marked by the presence of a different boyfriend. To Julie "long term" meant something that lasted over the summer.

Stacey nodded. "But nothing about relationships that have endured for more than twenty-six years," she pointed out, sitting down on the corner of the unmade bed.

"Okay—" the words dribbled slowly from Julie's lips as her brain examined one theory, then another "—if you're not leaving Dad, then—" Her cornflower-blue eyes widened in surprise and vicarious delight. "You're doing it," she breathed.

"It?" Stacey echoed.

Julie huffed impatiently. "Having an affair with Mr. Tool Belt Guy." Without waiting for an answer, she bounced right to the questions. "Really? How long has this been going on? Don't you think it's dangerous? Dad might—"

Like a traffic cop, Stacey held up her hand, trying to stop Julie and her galloping imagination, the scope of which never ceased to amaze her.

"What's dangerous is that you might wind up getting whiplash from that tongue of yours. It's almost faster than the speed of sound." Stacey shook her head. "I am *not* having an affair with Mr. Tool Belt Guy. Now, if you just keep quiet for a few seconds, I'll tell you why I *am* here."

Julie realized that despite the fact that she was in her mother's corner, she was relieved to hear that her mother hadn't stepped out on her father. Perching on the edge of her desk, she crossed her arms before her and waited. "Okay. I'm listening."

After that bit of drama, this request almost sounded silly, Stacey thought. "I want to work out."

Julie's eyes narrowed. "What?"

"Isn't that what you call it? Working out?" She was out of her element here and felt vulnerable. Naked. And that was the problem. She no longer had the kind of confidence in her naked body that she'd once had. Gravity had seen to that. Getting up, Stacey prowled around the small space. "Some kind of exercise regimen that eventually will yield a better me."

Julie's expression softened. "There's nothing wrong with you."

Maybe on the inside, Stacey thought. But on the outside, there was a great deal wrong from where she stood. "There's more of me than there used to be and I don't want it around anymore."

Julie studied her mother for a second, torn between sympathy and amusement. Relying on love to guide her through this. "Are you sure you're not getting it on with Mr. Tool Belt Man?"

Stacey laughed shortly, shaking her head. "Not unless he's breaking in every night and taking me in my sleep," she said firmly when she saw the faraway, slightly dreamy look in Julie's eyes. "I thought, since you're so trim and being a medical student and all, you might have a few good tips for me."

What was she thinking? She was forty-seven years old. Time to update her frame of reference. Middle age, not teenage. Stacey got up off the bed, picking her purse up from the floor. "Never mind, this was a bad idea."

Moving quickly, Julie got in front of her. She put her hands on her mother's shoulders to hold her in place. "No, no, this is a great idea." Since her mother looked as if she was willing to stay, Julie dropped her hands to her sides again. "But why the sudden interest in looking svelte again?"

"Your father."

Julie frowned. "He's criticizing you?" Her father always was a perfectionist, more prone to point out the one flaw than to applaud the dozen attributes.

"No."

Julie's eyes widened as she jumped to yet another conclusion. "He's straying?"

Stacey rolled her eyes. "No, Julie, your father's not 'straying.'"

It was the one thing Stacey knew she could bet her soul on. She'd had a moment of concern that night he'd short-circuited the house, but she hadn't been thinking rationally. Brad was as steadfast as the day was long. There was no other way to put it. Outside of his family, he was far too interested in his profession even to notice that the world was divided into two genders, much less avail himself to the opposite one.

She smiled at her daughter. "If you ever decide to drop out of medical school, Julie, you might want to consider becoming a fiction writer. You've certainly got the imagination for it. No," she said, getting back to the subject at hand, "I just thought that after all this time, maybe our marriage could use a shot in the arm." Julie was looking at her as if she was speaking in tongues. She tried to make it simpler for her daughter. "If I can get back to the dress size I used to be, that might be a good start."

The light seemed to dawn on Julie. Along with an almost

beatific smile. Her eyes lit up. "Excellent start," she enthused. "And good goal," she added, looking her mother up and down. Stacey Sommers had never actually "let herself go," so there would be no massive amount of backpedaling required. Just a little paring down here and there. Now that she thought about it, the challenge of resculpting her mother excited her. "Okay, why don't I take you to the gym?" she suggested. When she saw her mother demur, she added quickly, "It's right here in the building."

Stacey had just wanted to bounce the idea off Julie. She was running short of time. But she supposed she could work in a quick visit. "You have a gym on the premises?"

Julie nodded. Hooking her arm through her mother's, she began to guide her from the bedroom toward the front door.

"One of the perks of living here. It certainly wasn't the crayon-box-size bedrooms." Julie grinned. All sorts of routines began to suggest themselves to her. "This is going to be fun."

"Fun" was not the word Stacey would have used to describe the workout program that Julie and her friend, a tall, hulking Nordic-looking young man appropriately named Sven, who was, conveniently enough, also Julie's new boyfriend, had come up with for her. Torture, maybe, agony most definitely. But fun? Not a chance.

Her daily torment consisted of a cross-training machine and free weights to be used with and without the regulation-size bench she'd purchased. The first time she was on the cross trainer, a machine that the salesman at the fitness store had sworn would be "so easy on your knees, you won't even know you're using it," she had barely managed to get out five minutes, convinced that she was going to die at any second, her fingers wrapped around the two poles. Five minutes had never dragged by so slowly, not even during her eighteen-hour labor with Julie.

But she was determined and slowly, very slowly, she managed to conquer five minutes and move on to ten, and then to fifteen, until she was doing twenty minutes, which she'd designated as her ultimate goal. Twenty minutes at a resistance that she kept turning up until she found herself feeling like Marathon Woman.

The weights were another matter. They were for building strength, something she'd always thought she had in natural supply until faced with metal plates and a bar. But most of all, the free weights were for toning. Toning her arms, her thighs and a midriff she'd always been so confident would never need any help other than what Mother Nature had initially supplied her with.

What Mother Nature gave, she was more than willing to take away. At the least opportune time. There was a bulge there now, a bulge where once the terrain had been so flat, a miniairplane could have landed on it.

Finding the time to exercise in a day already overflowing with activities and responsibilities proved to be the ultimate challenge for Stacey. Between work, overseeing the renovations to the house and running said house so that things went along smoothly, there was no pocket of time to dash to a gym.

So, she had the gym brought to her.

Relying on Sven for advice, Stacey purchased the necessary weights, bench and cross trainer and had them all delivered to the house. She housed the lot in the downstairs back bedroom, a place where once all things miscellaneous eventually found themselves. Over the years, it had turned into a glorified storage area. Stacey turned it into her minigym.

Because 4:00 a.m. was the only time that had been heretofore unaccounted for, 4:00 a.m. was when she did her workout.

She found that being semiconscious when she started was better for her, anyway. The best part was that Brad was sound asleep. She wanted a chance to set her program in motion before he knew what she was up to.

With any luck, it would be six months before Brad found out what she was doing.

CHAPTER 36

The faint clanging sound broke through the gauzelike haze surrounding his brain, pushing sleep aside.

Noise. What kind, he couldn't tell. Nor did he care. It had woken him up when he didn't want to be woken up. Whatever was left of the dream he'd been having faded almost instantly.

Stretching, Brad turned to his wife. Or the side of the bed where his wife was supposed to be. It was empty. Assuming that Stacey was probably in the bathroom, Brad stretched again before he glanced at the clock on the nightstand. It was a little after four.

Ungodly.

He could remember when four in the morning had arrived to find him still on his feet, half-past groggy as he was putting in the end of a marathon eighteen-hour shift at the hospital. Fervently wishing death would take him and put him out of his misery.

Four in the morning had also been the hour Julie had insisted on waking up for the first six years of her life. Like clockwork.

Had that really been eighteen years ago?

Everything passes, he thought with a faint smile. The smile slipped away a little more as each minute made its exit.

He finally decided that Stacey wasn't coming back to bed. So, where was she?

Curious, Brad sat up and tossed off the covers. No light came from the bathroom. Getting up, Brad looked around now in earnest. The bathroom door was wide open, showing no signs that her departure from their bed had been very recent.

What the hell was going on?

Brad made his way to the room's threshold and looked up and down the small hallway for some sign of her departure.

The bonus-room door was directly opposite the master bedroom and dark as well. He began to wonder what was going on.

"Stacey?"

No one answered him.

Brad raised his voice. "Stacey?"

In response, the dogs, who'd been sleeping at the top of the landing like two mismatched guards, were instantly aroused. Awake, they swiftly padded over to him, each eager to grant him his heart's desire and to perhaps score a treat for the effort as well.

"Where is she?" he asked the furry duo. "Where's Stacey?"

Rosie gave no indication that she knew, or cared, where the rival for her man's affections was. But Dog, with his bright, wide brown eyes, seemed to understand. Barking once, he clattered down the wooden stairs, his untrimmed nails announcing his bounding, uneven descent. It sounded like an unpolished rendition of "Chopsticks."

Brad followed, wondering if Stacey had decided to catch up on some of the work she'd brought home from the medical office the other night. Or maybe get a jump start on tonight's dinner by throwing things together in the Crock-Pot.

He didn't like the idea of leaving something on all day, especially while they were both out of the house. But for some reason Stacey really seemed to like cooking with the Crock-Pot. He'd learned that you had to pick your arguments and leaving a Crock-Pot on just didn't seem worthy enough of an argument.

If he were honest, these days he was more inclined to let ride a great many things that would have once irritated him. He'd stopped letting the little things clutter up his life.

For a while there, those little things obscured the big picture. The only thing that really belonged in the big picture was his marriage and his wife. And what mattered most was enjoying both. But first, he thought, scratching an unexpected itch at the back of his neck, he needed to locate his wife.

The only light coming from the kitchen was the small one they left on before going to bed. She wasn't in the kitchen. Or anywhere else.

An uneasiness slipped over him. What was that clanging sound? Had he dreamed it? Or was it the door, slamming itself shut as Stacey made her way out?

Where would she go at this ungodly hour?

"Stacey?" he called again, this time more loudly. Still there was no answer. Only questions. And increasing uneasiness.

As Rosie followed behind, Dog led him to the rear of the house, to the bedroom that was just off the family room.

Initially, when they purchased the house, the bedroom had been intended to be the servant's quarters. At one point, Stacey had wistfully said it would have been a nice place for a housekeeper. But that hadn't come to pass, either. Neither one of them had wanted a stranger living with them, even if he'd had money to throw away. Which was never the case, as far as he was concerned.

The door to the back bedroom was closed. But that was nothing new. It was always closed. The state of disarray within the nine-by-twelve room was something neither one of them had any desire to see as they passed to use the powder room.

Over time the back bedroom's decor had given way to sheer clutter. Books were placed there in hopes of eventually being given a more dignified home on shelves yet to be built. As were clusters of CDs, clothes earmarked for charity and golf clubs that had outlived their usefulness but weren't quite ready to be tossed away yet. It was, for all intents and purposes, their version of No Man's Land.

It had been that way for the last ten years. Perhaps even longer.

Dog went directly to the back bedroom door and began scratching it.

Brad frowned. So much for a dog's keen sense of smell. "She's not in there, Dog. Look." He took hold of the doorknob and turned it. "I'll show you." Brad opened the door.

And stared.

Stacey didn't immediately realize that her inner sanctum had been breached. She was on the cross trainer, her eyes shut, her concentration intense. To complete the sensation of isolation, she had on a pair of large headphones, which were plugged into the small TV set right in front of her. She had the headphone jack in the set to keep the noise level as far down as possible in order not to wake Brad up.

The longer he didn't know about her exercise program, the

more of a head start she had to get to her ultimate goal: knockout.

Standing in the doorway, his hand resting on the doorknob, Brad felt his initial surprise die away. But he remained there a moment longer, watching her. Marveling at what he witnessed.

The look of sheer intensity on Stacey's face was incredible. How long had she been at this? Days? A week? Longer?

He looked around the room. The clutter had all been shoved to one side, like a guest who had overstayed his welcome and was being urged to leave. The freed-up space had been taken over—every inch of it—by gym equipment.

Seeing his wife in the same place as steel objects intended to reshape the human body seemed somehow incongruous to him.

When had all this shown up? Damn, he needed to take a more active part in his own home. She'd been drawing him in, urging him to help more and he had gotten to enjoy weighing in with his opinion, but obviously there were still areas that had been left untouched.

The cross trainer's wheel was moving faster.

"Stacey?"

Locked away in her private world, her eyes shut, the headphones on, Stacey neither saw nor heard him as he came closer to her. She was completely oblivious to the fact that she wasn't alone in the room.

Until Brad tapped on her arm.

And nearly gave her a heart attack.

Her eyes flying open, Stacey yelped even as she shucked in air. Instantly, her pace was broken, her concentration gone. She very narrowly avoided falling off the cross trainer because the large pedals continued moving even if she didn't.

Gulping in air and trying to rein in her surprise, Stacey pulled the earphones down around her neck. The faint sound of someone talking now softly echoed in the background. Both dogs yapped at her, but she hardly noticed. Her attention was on the man wearing only pajama bottoms and a scowl.

"Brad, what are you doing here?"

"I live here, remember? That means I usually get to know if something's going on." And obviously, she hadn't felt like sharing, he thought. "What *is* all this?" he asked. His wide gesture took in the cross trainer and the red bench with its cluster of various weights underneath it.

She answered as if it was the most common thing in the world for her to have them. "My cross trainer and my bench. I've only got a few free weights."

He blinked, wondering if he'd wandered into a parallel universe. The Stacey he knew considered going for a short walk enough exercise for a year. The one in front of him glistened with sweat.

He had to admit that a part of him found that rather arousing. But that wasn't the point. He didn't like being in the dark.

"Where did you get all this? *When* did you get all this?"

"At one of those fitness stores." Getting off the trainer, she reached for the towel she'd thrown on the bench. Stacey began to dry herself off. She was going to be out of time soon. She'd make it up tomorrow, she promised herself. "Sven helped me out. He told me just what I needed and what I didn't."

"Sven," Brad echoed. "One of the construction crew?"

"No, Julie's new boyfriend." She draped the towel around

her neck. "Sven's studying to be an anesthesiologist. I had no idea so much was involved in putting people to sleep."

Stacey was wearing sneakers, he noticed. She *never* wore sneakers. He couldn't remember the last time he's seen her in anything other than high heels, except when she went barefoot.

There was something kind of sexy about her and he found himself more than a little attracted. "Okay, you answered where and when, now why?"

And suddenly, he had an uneasy feeling he knew why. Because Stacey was trying to catch someone's eye. He'd finally become aware of his wife again and he'd stumbled across that awareness too late.

No, damn it, it wasn't too late. If she was doing this to get someone's attention, or because she wanted to be available again, he'd find a way to deal with that. And to change her mind.

"Because I want to look better," she told him simply.

He took the towel from her, slowly drawing it along her neck. "I think you look fine."

"I don't want to look 'fine.'" Fine was what something was when it hardly measured up. When it was adequate. Mediocre. "I want to look terrific."

"For who?" he demanded, feeling his adrenaline climbing.

"For myself," she answered, and then, because that wasn't the real truth, or at least, not the entire truth, she added softly, "and for you."

He was just about to launch into a tirade. And then she went and took the last bit of wind out of his sails.

CHAPTER 37

"Oh, well, if you're doing this for you," Brad murmured, "I guess I really shouldn't say anything to stop you."

His eyes washed over her. How long, he wondered, had it been since he'd *really* looked at her? It seemed to him that all these years, he'd been interacting with a shadow, an image of her that he had in his mind, without really seeing Stacey.

He looked at her now. And liked what he saw.

She was older than the girl he'd taken as his wife all those years ago, but there was an appeal to her maturity. If asked, he wasn't all that sure that he would have had the same reaction to her had Stacey somehow managed to be caught in a time bubble.

For one thing, she would have looked younger than their daughter. Too young for him.

"But if it's just for me," he told her, "you don't have to bother."

"No?"

If she didn't know better, she would have said she felt a warmth building between them. Something pulling them toward each other. After all these years, it was rather an incredible phenomenon to experience. And then she dismissed it. She was probably light-headed from the last half mile she'd pedaled.

"And why's that?" Her voice sounded a little breathy to her own ear.

"Because I like you just the way you are," he told her simply. The unadorned statement thrilled her. "With a little meat on your bones. Something to hold on to instead of worrying about breaking." He winked at her, evoking a shiver that slid along her spine. She remembered that he used to wink at her all the time, whenever their paths crossed at school. Brad wove his fingers through hers. "It's still early."

That all depended on which side of the clock you were on. She had a workout to finish before she could continue with the rest of her morning.

"Relatively," she allowed.

He nodded, slowly drawing her away from the cross trainer, away from the rest of the exercise equipment. Across the threshold and out of the makeshift gym.

"And I don't have to get ready for another couple of hours," he told her.

Was he saying what she thought he was saying? With anyone else, she would have said yes. But this was Brad, who, except for the first couple of years, had a fairly low sex drive.

She attempted a deadpan line. "You might as well go back to bed."

She watched his mouth curve and felt another thrill shimmying along her spine. "Just what I was thinking."

She would have liked nothing more than to lose herself in his arms. But there were rules to obey, schedules to keep. And that meant continuing with her ritual. Nothing ran on mere whim and luck. "I'm all sweaty," she pointed out. "I'd have to take a shower...." Her voice trailed off.

He grinned, not smiled, but grinned at her as if she'd said exactly the right thing. "We can do that together." He was gently tugging her in the direction of the stairs. "After."

"Together?" she echoed. "You know, we've never done that before." She wondered if he remembered. "In all the years we've known each other, we've never showered at the same time." A slight hint of concern nudged at her. She put the back of her hand to his forehead. "You feeling all right?"

He laughed, moving her hand aside. "Never better." They were on the stairs now, with him one step ahead of her and still holding her hand. She had no choice but to follow. Not that she would have done anything else, anyway. "Maybe it's the black onyx tiles."

He led her to the bedroom.

"Maybe," she mused. Stacey raised both her hands up over her head as Brad slipped her exercise bra from her body.

After Brad had gone to the hospital and she was left to deal with the glass man, who'd incorrectly installed sliding doors on the tub, she realized those lyrics were no longer running through her head, haunting her.

Peggy Lee's song, the one containing the sad question, "Is that all there is?" hadn't popped up in her head in weeks.

Not once.

Not during the busiest of times, and not, more important, during the few lulls, when she had time to think about something other than getting the next project under way and completed. Not even when her nerves had gotten frayed over incompetent suppliers.

The emptiness that always seemed to precede the refrain was absent as well.

It wasn't that she no longer had the time to raise the question, she just didn't feel lost and hollow anymore.

In the middle of pointing out the mistake to the glass installer, it hit her. Somehow, some way, while she and then Brad became immersed in renovating the house, taking down walls and opening the rooms up to the sunlight, they had wound up doing the very same thing with their marriage.

Walls were coming down. Sunlight was coming in, reaching out to the corners that had previously only known shadows.

Oh, they were a long way off from achieving the eternal matrimonial harmony showcased in a classic episode of say, *Ozzie and Harriet,* and most likely always would be, but they *had* undertaken the long journey back from the brink of the abyss where their marriage had been tottering for so long.

And she was happy. It was the kind of happiness she'd always hoped to have in her life. She was content with moments that leaned toward wild happiness.

She couldn't ask for more.

"Is it clear now what I want?" she asked, enunciating her words slowly to the stocky workman. It wasn't that English was his second language. The man didn't appear as if he could have managed more than one. Words of more than one syllable were apparently challenging.

"Yes, ma'am," he said with less enthusiasm than displayed by convicted killers on death row. But at least he was polite. And he was trying. That was all she asked.

Stacey smiled to herself as she got ready to leave for the

office. Leonardo DiCaprio might have been king of the world as he'd stood on the bridge of the *Titanic*, but she was the queen.

At least, she certainly felt that way.

Stacey hugged the sensation to her. "Don't forget to pull the front door shut," she reminded the man. She knew Alex would be by later to check on progress and he could be relied on to lock up once he was done, but it didn't hurt to repeat the warning.

The glass man smiled sheepishly as he nodded his head.

She was tired. Bone-meltingly tired. From her brain on down.

Stopped at a light, Stacey stretched a little, rotating her shoulders to relieve the tight feeling. It did no good. A cramp threatened to move in and take possession of her. The three miles left between her and home felt insurmountable.

And her eyelids kept insisting on drooping.

It was almost eight. She'd had to stay late at the office. Later than she'd wanted to. A virus appropriately named "Gotcha!" had infected their computers early this morning. In before office hours officially began, Gina, the new temp she'd hired to help with the work overflow, had decided to check her personal e-mail and opened an attachment from someone. That was all it had taken.

That was all it ever took, Stacey thought darkly. Just an innocent-looking attachment.

By the time she'd come in to the office, everything was in shambles. Dr. Desmond had acted as if it was the second coming of the plagues of Egypt. Within three minutes of entering the office, she had rolled up her sleeves and sat down in front of the main computer, where she had remained except for two bathroom breaks for the entire day.

She'd fought the good fight, as the old saying went. Valiantly trying to restore patient files belonging to all seven doctors. Every one of them had been corrupted in one form or another, some completely, some partially. There was no rhyme nor reason to it.

The challenge had demanded every bit of her own computer expertise as well as calling in tech support. It had been a tough, hard battle, but eventually she found herself on the road to victory. Little by little, scraps of things were restored, files that had vanished materialized—not in their entirety, but enough to make sense of. And for the uphill battle to continue tomorrow.

When she recovered her own strength and energy. Right now, both were missing in action.

She couldn't remember when she had been this exhausted, this drained. At the same time she felt good. And it was nice to know she was getting somewhere.

As she turned the corner onto her block, a new thought occurred to her. She began to pray that the white pickup truck would be absent tonight. She was just not up to dealing with workers, or even Alex, despite the fact that the contractors were polite and charming. That took energy and she had none.

Might never have any again.

There was no sign of the white pickup on either side of the street. Grateful, Stacey breathed a sign of relief. All she wanted was to kick back, have maybe a glass of wine and rest before she had to think about making dinner.

As was his habit, Brad was probably going to be later than she was.

But Brad wasn't later than she was. He was earlier.

He was here, she thought as she pulled up into their driveway. His Mercedes was visible through the open garage door.

How long had he been home? There'd been no call to her cell, asking her where she was, so it couldn't have been very long, she reasoned.

Bringing the car to a stop, she yanked up the hand brake and got out. On the few occasions Brad had arrived home before she did, he'd foraged through the refrigerator to find something to eat. But she knew for a fact that there were no leftovers in the refrigerator and Brad had no idea what a meal looked like in the precooked stage.

Hopefully, he wasn't gnawing on a box of frozen peas, his stomach growling as he waited for her to get home.

Her exhaustion taking a backseat to survival, Stacey unlocked the front door and sailed in.

"Sorry I'm late," she called out. She tossed her purse onto the closest receptive surface, never breaking stride. Her objective was the kitchen. "I was doing battle with a virus."

It took several seconds for the sight to register. When it did, she stopped dead.

There were candles in the dining room. Candles all *over* the dining room. Not just in the center of the table, but on every flat surface that didn't have something flammable in the immediate vicinity.

CHAPTER 38

Stacey stared, trying to process the scene. The candles flickered and glowed before her. Was she in the wrong house? No, her key had worked in the lock. And everything else looked familiar.

What was going on? And where was Brad?

Stacey heard a noise coming from the kitchen. Brad? The dogs weren't barking, so that was a good sign. She hurried through the dining room and came to an abrupt halt at the kitchen's threshold, where she received a second surprise in as many minutes.

With a dog on either side in attendance, Brad was standing at the kitchen counter, Gulliver surrounded by a dozen Lilliputians. In his case, the Lilliputians came in the form of white bags, their mouths undone and gaping open. A rather fierce red dragon on the side of each bag was exhaling the words China Sea written in delicate red script.

Stacey blinked.

The scene didn't change, didn't disappear. The bags remained. It was enough to make a woman believe in the existence of parallel universes.

Or more likely, given the way her day had gone, she'd

gotten sucked into her own computer, a human sacrifice of the infernal "Gotcha" virus.

Brad, his back to her, was doing something with silverware and plates. Feeling slightly uneasy, Stacey cleared her throat.

"Brad?"

She'd said his name at the exact same moment he'd begun to turn around. Facing her, he held one of the bags in each hand. On either side of him, a dog watched with bated breath, hoping for an accident. Hoping to be able to clean up the mess.

Brad grinned. "Hi."

"Hi," she echoed, too stunned by the candles and the army of take-out bags to form a coherent question.

Taking the initiative, Brad nodded at the bags he was holding. "I think some of this might still be warm." The delivery boy had left a little over fifteen minutes ago, but everything had been steaming at that point.

Well, the voice certainly sounded like Brad's. Maybe she hadn't been sucked into the bowels of her computer after all. But Brad never ordered takeout anymore. He said he didn't believe in it. Too much salt, he maintained sternly.

Still, the bags were here. And it *did* look like Brad. Smelled like him, too. The moment she thought that, she realized that he was wearing his old cologne. When was the last time he'd worn cologne?

Stacey snapped to attention and crossed to him. "Brad, what's going on?"

Turning back to the cabinet, he took out two wineglasses. "Well, I came home and you weren't here."

"So in your frustration, you decided to knock over a Chinese restaurant?"

"I had it delivered," he corrected matter-of-factly. "I couldn't remember if you liked moo goo gai pan or lobster Cantonese better, so I ordered both." Which explained two of the bags, but not the rest. "And then dinner for me, plus egg rolls, fried rice and a few other things they talked me into." He shrugged philosophically. "There's got to be something here you like."

She stared at him as if she'd never seen him before. And maybe she hadn't. Or at least, not this way. Not for a very long time. Affection flowed through every vein. She moved closer to him, close enough for their clothing to brush. Her eyes smiled up into his.

"Yes," she attested softly. "The waiter."

Because the moment called for it and he felt impulsive, he brushed his lips against hers even as he picked up several of the bags. "I'll bring this in, why don't you sit down?"

She caught herself sighing. It was a good sigh, not like so many others that had the sound of defeat or resignation about them. Picking up the plates and silverware, she followed him into the dining room.

He was distributing the bags on the table. "What made you do all this?"

"I ran into Kyle McDermott this afternoon." Bunching up the bags, he left the little white cartons on the table. McDermott was one of the physicians she worked for. "He told me all about the computer bug. And that, like the obsessive soldier that you are, you hadn't left your desk all day." Bringing the last of the bags to the table, he emptied them out. "I thought maybe you could do with a break."

It was too good to be true. But she wasn't going to examine

it any further. Magic had a tendency to disappear when held up to the light of day. Still, because it was so unlike him, she couldn't resist one more question. "And the candles?"

Taking the wine that he had chilling out of the refrigerator, he came back into the dining room and looked at her, one brow raised quizzically. "Women like candles, right?"

"But you see a fire hazard every time someone lights a birthday candle."

After removing the cork, he poured white wine into her glass. "This isn't about me. This is about you."

Wow. Stacey could feel her pulse begin to accelerate. She sank down more than sat down in her seat. "Who *are* you and what have you done with my husband?"

"What do you mean?" Filling his own glass, he sat down opposite her. "I've always been like this."

She took a long sip of her wine. God, that felt good. Setting the glass down, she looked at him for a long moment, then said, "Honey, I love you and I don't want you to take this the wrong way, but—not hardly."

"Well, I meant to be like this," he told her. "I just got sidetracked."

Yes, by the past eighteen years or so. But that was behind them and she had never been one to carry a grudge. A crumb of kindness went a very long way with her.

She raised her glass to him in a silent toast. "Well, all that counts is that you seem to be on the right track now."

Compliments, when not about his expertise in the operating room, had always made him uncomfortable. Even coming from his wife. He pushed two little white cartons toward her. "So, which do you like? Moo goo gai pan or lobster Cantonese?"

She saw no reason to choose. She liked them both. "Yes," she grinned.

Touching the side of the first container, he realized that it was more cool than warm. Dinner should at least be warm. "Maybe I should put these in the microwave for a minute."

She moved the container aside and took his hand in hers. "We can always do that later."

"Later?"

Rising, she began to lead the way toward the living room. The bedroom seemed much too far away. "Suddenly, I don't feel nearly as wiped out as I felt just a few minutes ago."

Amused, he allowed himself to be led. "Must be all that exercising you've been doing."

She pretended to nod solemnly. "Must be."

They were in the living room now. Stacey released his hand and went over to the bay window.

"I've renewed my membership at the gym, you know," he told her.

She drew the drapes, then turned around to look at him. "No, I didn't know."

"Well, I did." When she rejoined him, he slipped his hands to her waist. "That's where I ran into Kyle. At the gym near the hospital." Catching the tie that was fastened at the top of her blouse, he tugged on it lightly, undoing it. "We played a game of handball."

Her eyes widened. At his subtle touch and at the thought of his playing. "Handball? You haven't played that since college."

He shrugged, working the buttons of her blouse loose. "Second childhood."

She began to undo his shirt. "Nothing wrong with that."

She smiled as his shirt and her blouse found the rug together. Trousers and skirt went faster. "We all have an inner child within us."

He kicked aside the material at his feet. Underwear disappeared as if it had never existed. Bodies heated. "My inner child wants to know if your inner child can come out and play."

"Can it ever." Stacey laughed as she threaded her arms around his neck. When her chest came in contact with his, she backed off for a moment, then glanced up at him with mild surprise. "You're right. You *are* working out."

He nodded, bringing her close again. Wanting her and savoring the force of the desire. "I'd be the first to know that."

"But not the first to appreciate it," she guaranteed him. She deliberately lowered her head as he went to kiss her. Playing a little hard to get upped the stakes. Instead, she ran the flat of her hand along his chest. And sighed appreciatively. "Very nice."

He raised her head again with the crook of his finger beneath her chin. "Talk is cheap."

Enough playing hard to get. She wanted him. Badly. Her voice was low, sensual, as she promised, "Then I'd better show you."

And when it was over, when they were spent, exhausted and lying there beside each other on the rug that had taken them six weeks of deliberation to finally agree on, their breathing slowly becoming less audible and more steady, Stacey felt as if she had never been this content before.

Everything was perfect.

Except…

Except for one last thing.

Raising the subject now, especially after this, after he'd been so thoughtful and then so loving, would be pushing the envelope. She knew that. But the question refused to be banked down. Refused to leave her in peace.

She was like the Fisherman's Wife, she supposed. As soon as one thing was granted—even something wondrous and grand the way this was—she wanted something else. She wanted more. But unlike the Fisherman's Wife, she didn't want an empire to rule. She just wanted one last thing to make life complete.

Stacey drew in her breath. Quietly.

Here went nothing, she thought, pressing her lips together before she sailed into the choppy seas. "Brad?"

"Hmm?"

He sounded as if he was drifting off to sleep. They had dinner and candles waiting in the other room. Had he really gotten that relaxed? She found it difficult to believe.

"Have you given it any more thought?"

"Hmm?" Rousing himself, Brad turned toward her, his expression quizzical as he waited for her to give him something more.

"Jim's band is playing at that club on Friday. The Wild Orchid." She realized that she was holding her breath and forced herself to release it. "Have you thought about what I'd said? About going?"

"Yes."

The single word hung out there without any accessories or adornments, giving her no clues. "'Yes' you've thought about it?"

"Yes."

It was like pulling teeth. But every second that went by

she could hope for the right response. "And what is it that you've thought?"

His eyes met hers and held. And time stretched out before them like a feline waking from a long nap, asserting its flexibility.

CHAPTER 39

Just when her patience had reached its limit, Brad asked, "How many different ways do you want me to say it?"

There was a touch of irritation in his voice, but after all these years, she finally accepted that without this annoyance, it just wouldn't be Brad.

"Say what?"

"Say yes," he reiterated. Then, in case she still missed what he was telling her, he said the word again. "Yes, although I'd probably rather sit through a root canal, I'll go with you on Friday night to listen to Jim and his band play."

Even as he agreed, he struggled to bank down a shudder. He didn't care for what he'd heard of the contemporary music being played these days. But he wasn't going because he liked music. He was going because Jim was his son. And because the boy who'd been brought into the emergency room today, a shattered victim of a senseless freeway shooting, had been about Jim's age. And the boy had died. Reminding him that life was far too short for estrangements.

"Most likely," he theorized, "it'll sound like someone gutting a cat without the benefit of anesthesia, but like everything else, it'll be over with and in the past soon enough."

Propped up on her elbow, Stacey had been watching his lips

as they moved. She'd heard only one thing. The important part. That he was going. And that meant the world to her.

"I love it when you talk crazy like that," she told him with a grin.

The next moment, she took his face between her hands and kissed him. Kissed him hard, as if this was the first time she'd ever kissed him and she'd been waiting to do it for an eternity.

"Wow." It was the kind of kiss that would have knocked the socks off a barefoot boy. He looked at her with new, keen respect.

Stacey batted her lashes at him flirtatiously. "There's more where that came from."

His back ached a little from the floor, but he didn't care. Brad tucked her against his body and felt their heat mingling. Whispering promises. He was one of the lucky ones. After all this time, he was still turned on by the woman he'd married. And lately more so than ever.

He cupped her cheek, tilting her head up so that her lips became a tempting target. "Is there, now?"

"You bet." Her eyes sparkled. Lifting her head a little more, she brought her lips a fraction of an inch away from his. "Come and get it."

Brad needed no more of an invitation than that.

Brad's voice preceded him as he walked into the master bathroom. "So, what would you do if I decided to change my mind?"

Stacey never turned from the mirror. She'd been dressed and ready to go for the past half hour. Her makeup, however, had far less staying power and it had already begun to fade.

She'd popped into the bathroom to give it one final boost before they walked out the front door.

It was Friday night and traffic into L.A. was going to be a bear, the way it always was. Since Jim's show began at eight and the club where he was performing was approximately thirty-five miles away, she had allotted two hours for traveling a route that, under normal circumstances, would take them no more than forty minutes.

They were minus three minutes to departure. Time to get going.

Her eyes met Brad's in the mirror as she finished applying a fresh layer of eye shadow. "About the marriage? I'd have to say I'd be pretty upset—however, not nearly as upset as I would be if you told me you'd changed your mind about going to hear Jim play."

He'd only been kidding, although he had to admit it would have been tempting. He leaned against the doorjamb, his arms crossed before his chest. She looked pretty damn good for a woman close to fifty.

"That bad, huh?"

She snapped the tiny compact closed and returned it to the shelf. "That bad," she confirmed. Leaving the bathroom, she switched off the light.

As she passed the bed, she picked up a light gray shawl with silver threads shot through it, and her purse. Brad walked in her shadow.

"You realize you're going to owe me. Big time."

She was at the head of the stairs and turned to look at him over her shoulder. "You might have a good time."

Brad shut out the light in the bedroom as he came out into

the hall. "And I might sprout wings and fly within the next month, but I won't."

Walking down the stairs, she smiled to herself. She had rubbed off on him over the years. The Brad she first knew would have never uttered such a wild exaggeration. That Brad had had no imagination. She liked the new, improved model much better.

At the bottom of the stairs, they were met by both dogs, who sniffed and made small, whiny noises. Rosie and Dog knew they were leaving. The dogs were almost human. She hurried into the family room to check if they both had water in their dishes. Leaving food would just be a waste. Neither dog ate when the house was empty. They needed human companionship.

"He's your son," Stacey told him, rejoining him at the front door. "He wants your approval—"

Brad snorted, opening the door for her. "If my approval had meant anything, he'd be in medical school, or going for an MBA, anything but a strolling troubadour." Taking out his keys, he locked both locks before turning from the front door and going down the two steps.

Stacey laughed and shook her head. "Nobody knows what that is anymore."

"Troubadour," he repeated. "A medieval musician who wanders around, playing on street corners and hoping someone tosses him some money." The look on his face told her he hated thinking of their son in those terms. But he did.

She threaded her arm through his and tugged him toward the driveway, where he'd left his black Mercedes parked. "C'mon, we don't want to be late."

Aiming his key ring with the car alarm at his vehicle, he disarmed it. "'We' don't want to be there at all," he corrected.

On the passenger side, she stopped to give him a look over the roof of the car that was half pleading, half assertive—and all Stacey. He sighed. There was no fighting that. Not if he didn't want his conscience to overwhelm him.

"Like I said, you owe me big time." He pulled open the door on the driver's side. "You know how much I hate to drive in traffic."

She paused before getting in on her side. "We can take the carpool lane, which is usually moving." Stacey looked at him over the roof of the car. "And if you don't want to drive, I will."

"No," he remarked as he got in, "I don't particularly have a death wish tonight." Key in hand, he put it into the ignition but didn't turn it on. "But wait, the evening's still young. Check back with me later after their first set."

"Their first set?" she repeated, and looked at him incredulously. She'd teased him about looking for pods in the garage, but now he was scaring her. "You know what that is?"

"Yes, I know what that is." He struggled to bank down his irritation as he turned on the engine. It purred to life. One hand on the back of his seat, Brad slowly pulled out of his driveway. "I'm not a complete idiot."

"You're not an idiot at all," she was quick to underscore, even though, in her opinion, he was the last man on earth who should have needed to have his ego stroked, "it's just that I didn't think you'd pick up something like that."

"You'd be surprised," he told her. The winding path from their block to the end of the development ended quickly enough. He glanced both ways, saw no oncoming headlights, and pulled out into the main drag.

"All the time, lately," Stacey responded. She looked at him with a broad, leading smile. God, she loved him for doing this. "All the time."

"This doesn't look much bigger than our first off-campus apartment," Brad grumbled.

Stacey's hand was tethered to his as she led him inside the club, the Wild Orchid, some eighty minutes later. Luck had been with them. For once there were no pileups, no traffic snarls to tie up all the lanes and bring traffic down to a maddening trickle. Instead, traffic had chugged along at the speed limit, which by most standards was still slow.

They'd made the trip in fifty minutes. The other thirty minutes had been spent trying to find some place to park that wasn't located in the next state. The lots filled up quickly on a Friday evening.

Brad frowned at the implications that working in a place this size had. How much business could it take in on any given night? It seemed fairly packed, but that could be because this was a brand-new show and curiosity had a power all its own.

"What could they be paying him?"

She prayed he wouldn't ask Jim that. Having silence between them was preferable to angry words and hurt feelings.

"The money's not the point," she reminded him.

Not in the real world, he thought. "Try telling that to a landlord when the rent's due."

"That's why he has a family to fall back on—" she emphasized.

He'd always believed in calling them the way he saw them. "And mooch from."

That wasn't the word she would have used, but this was not the time to get into any kind of discussion, no matter how innocent it began.

"Nobody ever started out at the top except for God." She looked at him over her shoulder. "Not even you. Jim's good, Brad. Give him a chance to prove himself and make something of his talent."

Brad made a noncommittal sound just before she grabbed onto his hand harder and dragged him over to the side.

"We have a table," she declared like Columbus's lookout when he first sighted land in the New World.

"Good, now let's get a drink."

Brad looked around to see if there was a waiter or waitress around to help him reach his goal. His patients were all covered for the night, which meant that for once, he had the freedom to have more than one drink.

He had a feeling he was going to need that freedom.

CHAPTER 40

The Scotch and soda Brad ordered had just arrived when the first show began. A middle-aged man, sporting a bad haircut and a rumpled sweatshirt and neon-purple pants, mumbled a string of mostly unintelligible words into a microphone. This prompted more noise in response, and suddenly, as the announcer backed away, the spotlight on the makeshift, boxlike stage widened, illuminating the presence of five people around a drum set and a keyboard.

Four males and a leggy blonde. It was a toss-up whether her hair or stiletto heels were longer than her outfit.

Brad took a long sip of his drink as the chords were being struck, hoping it would fortify him. He felt Stacey grab his hand.

"That's him. That's Jim," she whispered excitedly.

"I know which one Jim is," he told her. "It's hasn't been that long."

The droll comment had no effect. Her eyes were riveted to the stage. To her son, the performer.

"What do they call themselves?" he asked, strictly to be polite.

Stacey kept her eyes on the stage. "They don't have a name right now. Jim says they can't make a decision."

Sounded about par for the course, he thought, banking down his frustration. Brad took another sip and braced himself for what he felt was the ordeal ahead.

Music dueled with noise for mastery of the small interior of the club. The battle was intense, but short. Music won. The noise that surrounded the musicians slowly began to quiet down as people started to listen to the band with no name.

The leggy blonde's voice all but shook the walls as she belted out the song. Brad realized that the lyrics were vaguely recognizable. Like an old standard that had been given a shot of adrenaline and altered.

Not half bad.

Stacey slanted a glance toward her husband. Facing the stage, his profile was to her. With limited lighting, and most of that being cast on the band, she couldn't make out his expression. It didn't appear entirely rigid, as when they discussed Jim, coming in from opposite sides within the same conversation.

She took it to be a good sign.

But within moments, she found herself at the end of her patience and unable to deal with her curiosity any longer. Why wasn't he saying something?

"Well?" she pressed. The single word, though demanding, was swallowed up by the music. Leaning forward, she placed her hand on Brad's wrist to get his attention. When he turned his head in her direction, she repeated with even more emphasis, "Well?"

Brad had a face that poker players dreamed of owning and dreaded facing. It helped him in his line of work. Stacey found it maddening.

He lifted a shoulder casually, then let it drop. He had been raised to restrain his feelings, his emotions. "Better than well," he allowed.

The music faded into the background. Everything else stopped as she stared at him, her eyes widening. "Are you actually saying you liked it?"

Brad took another sip. Already, he was backing away so as not to face his emotions. For the most part, it kept him safe. "*Like* is a strong word."

In what world? she wondered. "*Like* is a lukewarm word," Stacey countered with feeling. "*Love* is a strong word."

A waitress walked by, bumping up against Brad as she carried a tray of beer bottles and glasses to another table. He frowned as he leaned forward, but the frown had nothing to do with the subject matter and who he was talking to.

"Yeah, well, maybe I like it," he said, trying to keep his voice noncommittal. He saw the trace of disappointment in her eyes. Maybe it was time to stop playing games. To stop protecting himself. All he'd succeeded in doing over the years was to isolate himself from everyone who should have mattered. Who *did* matter. "It's better than I thought it would be."

Having come this far—and it was farther than she'd thought she'd get—Stacey decided to go for broke. "And Jim?"

That took more Scotch and soda. Fortified, he nodded. "Him, too."

Triumph was heady, her head all but spinning. She smiled broadly at him. "More words," she encouraged. When he began to open his mouth, she stopped him, placing her fingers to his lips. "Not to me. To him when he comes over."

Brad merely shrugged again as the band launched into another number. His ice clinked in the chunky glass as he set it down to listen.

There were five in all. Five numbers, four of which turned out to be vaguely familiar to him, the way the first one had been. The audience, to Brad's surprise, seemed responsive as well.

The closing number was an original that showcased the blonde's powerful voice while not allowing it to overshadow the versatility of the band.

Stacey was clapping so hard, her hands moving so fast, Brad thought she was in danger of taking off through sheer wind velocity.

She leaned into him, raising her voice almost to a shout. The applause around them was deafening. "How d'you like that?"

"Not bad." He was completely taken by surprise when Stacey doubled up her fist and punched him in the arm. But he knew what she was saying in less-than-delicate terms. She wanted more out of him. "Good, actually," he told her. When she continued glaring at him, he added, "All right, very good. Surprisingly good."

Satisfied, Stacey nodded. She was beaming so hard, she could have served as an auxiliary spotlight. "Jim wrote that," she informed him proudly.

It seemed to be the night for surprises. "He writes music?"

"He's very talented, your son," she stated, trying to seem

matter-of-fact when all of her insides were elated and jumping up and down. "He just needs to hear his father say that."

Okay, maybe this was a little more than he'd bargained for. There was still an awkwardness between him and his son that had to be surmounted before any back-clapping took place. "You say it enough for both of us."

Stacey remained firm as she shook her head. "Not the same thing."

It was to him. Except, maybe better. After all, he and Stacey were a team, a set. A united front when it came to the kids. Or at least they used to be, he remembered. Someone had changed all the ground rules on him when he wasn't looking.

He looked down at his glass. There was nothing left except melting ice cubes. When he looked up again, he saw that Jim was making his way to their table.

Stacey was smiling broadly. Twice during the performance, he noticed that she'd managed to catch Jim's eye. He didn't have to ask to know that his wife was so proud of Jim that she could burst.

He supposed, if someone held his feet to the fire, he'd have to admit that he felt a smattering of pride right now.

The chair scraped along the bare floor as Stacey rose to her feet, throwing her arms around Jim. For once, he didn't flinch or pull back.

Maybe the kid *was* growing up, Brad thought. *About time.*

"You were wonderful," Stacey cried with enthusiasm. "They were all wonderful," she added, then declared with the certainty of a proud mother who had always had faith in her prodigal son, "but you were the most wonderful one of them all."

"So I guess you liked it?" Jim deadpanned. The facade lasted less than ten seconds. He was too happy, too excited. Too pumped up by the applause to maintain any sort of pretense or attempt at nonchalance. He turned toward his father, more than a little surprised to see him there. He decided to go for broke. "Dad?"

For a moment, Brad said nothing, seeking shelter in the din that had amped up again. And then he nodded. "Your mother tells me that *like* is a weak word. There's nothing weak about your playing. It's excellent. So was the last song."

That caught Jim completely off guard. His father rarely, if ever, gave compliments.

"You really think so?" Enthusiasm gushed from every pore. "I wrote it."

Brad nodded. "Your mother mentioned something about that." The words were coming a little easier, although by no means flowing. "I didn't realize you had that much talent. But then, I guess maybe I was always too busy to listen."

Because his father was assuming the blame, Jim felt magnanimous. He wouldn't let his father shoulder it.

Jim was smiling that shy smile she remembered so well from his childhood and shrugged. The shrug, she thought, was pure Brad.

"That's okay. You're a doctor. People depend on you. You've got more important things to do than to listen to my music."

Stacey, all Stacey, Brad thought. He caught himself searching for parts of himself within this human being they had created together.

"There's nothing more important than family," Brad told him, then realized with a start that he was all but channeling his wife, echoing something she'd told him a hundred times or more.

He glanced toward her and nodded, before getting back to the fledgling conversation he and his son were nursing along. It was possibly the first one in years that hadn't been started with recriminations being fired from one or the other side.

"Can you stay awhile?" Jim asked, looking first at her, then at Brad. Stacey felt her heart warming all over again. "We don't go on again until ten, but Julie promised to stop by with her new guy—"

"Who is it this week?" Stacey asked. "Did she tell you?" She'd found herself being partial to the tall medical student who had helped her buy her gym equipment.

Jim thought for a moment, trying to remember. "Sven something."

Stacey's eyes widened. *Well, what d'you know?* It was still Sven. Maybe her daughter was finally settling down a little. She had witnessed one miracle tonight. Why not two?

"Sure, we can stay," Brad answered. And then he looked at her and asked, "Is that okay with you?"

As if he had to ask. "That's more than okay with me," she assured him.

A host of enthusiastic words bubbled up within her, but she banked them down and just sat back. Content to listen to the two men in her life talk to each other.

Stacey reflected how far her life had come these past few months. A few months ago, everything was in a state of disrepair. Her house, her marriage, her life. Adequate, but not quite what she wanted. And becoming less so with each passing day.

And now, her house was almost finished. Almost entirely brand-new to the passing eye. Oh, there were still a few things to take care of and it wouldn't be perfect when it was done. Nothing ever was. All that meant was that there was room for improvement and possible modifications down the line.

A little like her marriage, she thought with a smile. Marriage was a living, breathing thing that needed upkeep, needed work almost daily. Over the years, it had grown stale and dark. Now it felt as if they had opened up the windows again, let the air in. And with the air, the sunshine. And a new wave of love.

For a woman who had just survived renovations to her house and seen the same process applied to her marriage, she felt incredibly empowered. And happy.

The change wasn't lost on her men.

"You look very content with yourself tonight," Brad observed.

"Oh, I am. I am." Stacey placed one hand over Brad's and one over Jim's, just as she saw Julie heading their way. Towering over her daughter was possibly her future son-in-law.

A girl could dream.

That's not "All there is," Peggy, Stacey thought. *There's always a hell of a lot more.*

* * * * *

*Be sure to read Marie Ferrarella's next romance
from Silhouette Special Edition,*
THE PRODIGAL M.D. RETURNS,
available August 2006.

Life.
It could happen to her!

Never Happened just about sums up
Alexis Jackson's life. Independent and
successful, Alexis has concentrated on
building her own business, leaving no
time for love. Now at forty, Alexis
discovers that she still has a few things
to learn about life—that the life unlived
is the one that "Never happened"
and it's her time to make a change....

Never Happened
by Debra Webb

Available July 2006
TheNextNovel.com

HN49

Just let it shine, it's payback time!

When a surprise inheritance brings
an unlikely pair together, the fortune
in sparkling jewelery could give
each woman what she desires most.
But the real treasure is the friendship
that forms when they discover that
all that glitters isn't gold.

Sparkle

by
Jennifer Greene

HN50 Available July 2006
TheNextNovel.com

They were twin sisters with nothing in common…

Until they teamed up on a cross-country
adventure to find their younger sibling.
And ended up figuring out that, despite
buried secrets and wrong turns, all roads
lead back to family.

Sisters

by Nancy Robards Thompson

REQUEST YOUR FREE BOOKS!

2 FREE NOVELS TO INTRODUCE YOU TO OUR BRAND-NEW LINE!

There's the life you planned. And there's what comes next.

YES! Please send me 2 FREE Harlequin® NEXT™ novels and my FREE mystery gift. After receiving them, if I don't wish to receive any more books, I can return the shipping statement marked "cancel." If I don't cancel, I will receive 3 brand-new novels every month and be billed just $3.99 per book in the U.S., or $4.74 per book in Canada, plus 25¢ shipping and handling per book plus applicable taxes, if any*. That's a savings of over 20% off the cover price! I understand that accepting the 2 free books and gift places me under no obligation to buy any books. I can always return a shipment and cancel at any time. Even if I never buy another book from Harlequin, the two free books and gift are mine to keep forever.

156 HDN D74G   356 HDN D74S

Name	(PLEASE PRINT)	
Address		Apt. #
City	State/Prov.	Zip/Postal Code

Signature (if under 18, a parent or guardian must sign)

Order online at www.TryNEXTNovels.com

Or mail to the Harlequin Reader Service®:

IN U.S.A.	IN CANADA
3010 Walden Ave.	P.O. Box 609
P.O. Box 1867	Fort Erie, Ontario
Buffalo, NY 14240-1867	L2A 5X3

Not valid to current Harlequin NEXT subscribers.

**Want to try two free books from another line?
Call 1-800-873-8635 or visit www.morefreebooks.com**

* Terms and prices subject to change without notice. NY residents add applicable sales tax. Canadian residents will be charged applicable provincial taxes and GST. This offer is limited to one order per household. All orders subject to approval. Credit or debit balances in a customer's account(s) may be offset by any other outstanding balance owed by or to the customer.

NEXT05

Sometimes you're up...
sometimes you're down.
Good friends always help
each other deal with it.

Mood Swing

by Jane Graves

A story about three women who discover
they have one thing in common—they've
reached the breaking point.

HN51 Available July 2006
TheNextNovel.com